THE MINE

Arnab Ray

hachette
INDIA

First published in 2012 by Westland
This paperback edition published in 2024 by Hachette India
(Registered name: Hachette Book Publishing India Pvt. Ltd)
An Hachette UK company
www.hachetteindia.com
1

ISBN 978-93-5731-933-1

For sale in the Indian Subcontinent only.

Hachette Book Publishing India Pvt. Ltd
4th & 5th Floors, Corporate Centre,
Plot No. 94, Sector 44, Gurugram 122003, India

Typeset in Adobe Garamond Pro 11.2/15
by InoSoft Systems, Noida

FSC
www.fsc.org
MIX
Paper | Supporting responsible forestry
FSC® C010615

Printed and bound in India
by Thomson Press India Ltd.

THE MINE

Arnab Ray, better known as Greatbong, is one of India's most widely read bloggers (http://greatbong.net). He is also the author of six books. Two of his books have been made into web series on major OTT platforms: *Sultan of Delhi* in Hindi on Disney+ Hotstar and *Mahabharata Murders* in Bengali on Hoichoi. A PhD in Computer Science from State University of New York at Stony Brook, and an alumnus of Jadavpur University, Kolkata, he is currently based in Los Angeles. Arnab Ray has a running column in the *Times of India* and can be found on X (formerly Twitter) at @greatbong.

Critical praise for *The Mine*

Arnab Ray's *The Mine* is a diabolically smart thriller.

CNN IBN

Thrilling, scary, magical.

Pritish Nandy

Darkness, fear, death and gore, *The Mine* has all the elements of a jolly horror jaunt. And the twist in the end is worth the read.

The Telegraph

A dark, disturbing tale of horror... it's bleak and it's unputdownable.

The Pioneer

Where the book scores is in the clever twists and turns the story takes and the way disjointed pieces come together. The end especially is a tour de force of masterful plotting.

DNA

Bloody, claustrophobic, and gripping from the first page to the last, *The Mine* has all of the pulpy feel of films like *The Descent* and *The Hills Have Eyes* with gruesome details layered at every turn. Clever plot twists keep the story chugging along through the individualized hellscapes of the mine that will leave the reader feeling just as paranoid as the characters trapped underground.

James S. Murray, *Tor.com*

To my parents

Preface to the 2024 edition of *The Mine*

Once upon a time, publishers would organize launch events in different cities for a new book within one or two months of its publication. At these events, the author would read a few pages from their book, answer questions from the audience, and sit to sign individual copies for those who wanted them. This was the best part of the writing experience; you got to meet your readers, you felt important, and you sold a few books (not enough, apparently, which is why these do not happen anymore).

At one of the book events for *The Mine*, and this was in 2012, a stranger held a copy with the first page open for my signature and then said, 'I read this, and all I can say is that I would hesitate to be in a room with you.'

While no author likes to be personally judged for the content of their work, I could not but take this as a compliment. *The Mine* is that sort of a book. It is a journey into the deepest corners of our mind (it's not a coincidence that the words sound similar: mine and mind), what is it that truly makes us evil, and how we cope with our own evil, whether it be through burying it away by denial, living with it through guilt, or revelling in it for we know that it is that which truly makes us who we are.

The Mine is unapologetically disquieting; the camera of the story does not look away, and in the description of the savagery, both physical and emotional, no punches are pulled. Almost all the incidents in the book that you might find gratuitous or gruesome are based on things that happened, with names, places, and times taken out. I say this because even though it is fiction, *The Mine* remains firmly anchored to the evil that people do to each other. In real. And if that terrifies you, it should.

The idea for *The Mine* came to me on a long bus journey of eight hours, in an age before cell phones distracted us away from thinking for long periods. The ending was what first came to me, more precisely, the structure of the ending (I am deliberately being vague for those who have yet to read the book), and then the rest of the story came to me by following that strand back, creating the principal dramatic conflict, and then coming to the beginning, and this started a pattern to my thinking for every book that I was to write after: get the end right, work back to the start. *Yatrik*, *Sultan of Delhi*, *The Mahabharata Murders*, and now *Shakchunni*, follow the exact same creative process.

Because it is, to me, all about landing the ending. This is true, especially for horror in the written form. Unlike cinema, you cannot play with darkness, sound, silence, and music. You cannot use creepy visuals; you cannot put in jump scares. So, the best you can do is to leave the reader disturbed, intensely disturbed, like wanting to look over your shoulder but being afraid of what you will find. Whether *The Mine* leaves you with that feeling, I do not know (I hope it does), but it's what it did to that stranger I met at my book event. And over the years, to many others.

And with that, welcome to the world of *The Mine*. The greatest evil lies deep inside.

Prologue

Mother had always warned him of the dark.

What she had forgotten was to tell him about the light.

There was something about the light in this place that never ceased to unnerve Asgar. It illuminated every recess of his mind, some of which he had realized in the course of his life, are better kept in shadow.

The summer sun too was unforgiving in its stark relentlessness. But at least it was real. The industrial light here was not. It could not be. Because Asgar was deep inside the earth, in a place where not even nature could enter unless it came with a company badge.

Perhaps it was not so much the brightness that made him uneasy, but the icy blue detachment of the ambient light, whose cold touch felt like that of a wet cotton shirt on a blustery, winter evening.

He had felt this way only in one other place before. The morgue.

Battered, mangled what-had-once-drawn-breath lying still on cold slabs of aluminium. Hushed whispers of the living trying to make sense of the dead. The stench of formaldehyde, grief and despair.

For the past day or so, Asgar had been unable to shake off the feeling that he was back in a house of corpses. It was irrational, he reasoned, this fear, even more so after all the real horrors he had seen in his fifty-two years in the world above.

He tried to stop thinking.

Turning his attention back to the control panel, Asgar glanced across at the dials as they glowed and flickered in a steady rhythm of their own. He could not slack off, he told himself. All alone in Level 3 Sector 5, a football-field-sized room with two-storey-high ceilings, he was conscious of the cameras that watched his every movement, and of the automated loggers recording each action at the console.

Right now, one of the sensors showed a reading that was 'off' the charts. That meant only one thing – one of the moving parts in Purifying Chamber 6 had come off, with the sensors picking up the resultant vibration. This necessitated, according to Standard Operation Procedure, a shutdown of Chamber 6 and an immediate manual inspection.

Shit. All such fuck-ups just had to happen on his shift.

He looked at the waveform intently. Then he flipped a switch, the one that the engineers called the 'Ear', its purpose being to 'listen-in' to the area where an anomaly has been detected.

'Help... Please... no!'

Asgar jerked back as if he had touched a hot stove.

What in the name of heaven was that?

His rational mind knew it was impossible. Yet there was no denying he had heard it. A voice, choked with tears, coming out from Chamber 6.

Asgar stood still. A bead of sweat dripped down his forehead and rested precariously on his brow. Building up in his bowels was a sudden pressure, a reaction to intense fear that had embarrassed him since early childhood.

Of course, he must be hearing things. The room was yanking the strings of his mind. The doctor-lady, that know-it-all with the pierced nose, would possibly look at him now and say, 'It is the forced isolation from your wife and daughter that is affecting you psychologically.'

The thing was that he knew the doctor was wrong. He was really happy to be away from his wife. Fat, complaining and moody – she had ceased to be of any interest to him years ago; just another creaking machine with interminable periods of bilious downtime that he was duty-bound to monitor. Making conversation according to the Standard Operating Procedures that marriage prescribed and conducting periodic 'Are you doing all right?' status updates, was all that was left of that miserable social compact. With the isolation and communication blackout that working in this mine had forced on him by contract, he was free of this distasteful duty for many months now, and for that he was most thankful.

Sexual tension? No, not even that. He had been a bad boy. As usual. A week ago, he had met Tanya in one of the rec-rooms. Tanya from the medical division. Twenty-two years old. The face of an angel. The body of a model. The mind of a whore. The energy of a tightly wound spring. Their sex had been animalistic, devoid of love, tenderness and the sappy strawberry-coloured mush that decades of reading romance novels had brainwashed women into believing was reality. Tanya, refreshingly, did not suffer from such delusions. Unlike his wife, she had never complained or cried. 'Is that the worst you can do?' she had taunted Asgar, throwing her head back mockingly, every time he thought he had crossed her boundaries.

Yes, it had been marvellous. And best of all, she had hardly seen the worst of him.

Yet.

The blood rush triggered by memories of Tanya subsided quickly as he unsuccessfully tried to clear his mind of what he had just heard. Had someone actually cried out for help? Impossible. There was no one here.

Only one way of knowing for sure. He flipped the switch again. 'I want to go home... please, let me go home...'

Asgar's blue shirt, framed by the large red and black company logo, now clung to his back, drenched with warm sweat. Was it happening to him? Like it had to the rest? No. He would not allow it.

'Get a grip on yourself, you old geezer. It's all in your mind.'

The panel now showed a yellow warning blip on Chamber 6. Action had to be taken immediately or a report of negligence would automatically be filed against him. That he could not allow, considering the amount of money at stake.

Closing his eyes, he paused for a few seconds, time enough for his beating heart to slow down. Practised fingers flying over the panel, he initiated a power-down. The hatch was now unlocked for a manual inspection. Grabbing his instruments, he descended the stairs that ran from the monitoring station into the machinery area. Chamber 6 was halfway down the massive hallway. He walked slowly towards it, fighting the strong urge to turn back.

Asgar was now at the service entrance to the offending chamber, a hatch large enough for a full-sized man to crawl through. He turned the lever. The door opened noiselessly. His face was illuminated by the red emergency light from inside, the one that came on whenever manual inspection mode was initiated. Only one thing left to do. Get into the machine.

And then on a sudden impulse he paused. Raising his head, he took a long look at everything around him. The high ceiling. The room. The unobtrusive cameras that he knew were there. The high-powered industrial lamps washing everything with their unearthly, soulless rays.

He sighed. At least the red emergency light inside would not be so cold. At least now, there would be some darkness.

Tanya sat in Rec Room 2 with a beer in front of her. Having just got out from the infirmary where she worked as a nurse, she had had barely enough time to take a quick shower, put on a bit of makeup and change into clothes that she could only describe as half-decent. Only a few more months, and then she would have the money to buy the kind of threads she wanted. No more hand-me-downs from her elder sisters and no more tremulous-with-tears 'We don't have money' excuses from her moronic lame-ass father, who carried the fact that he had no money to get his daughters married around like some bizarre badge of honour.

For now, however, the tight white shirt and the knee-length skirt would have to do. Not that she needed anything more to turn necks here. After all, this was a mining colony teeming with hormonally ionized men, separated from their families for months. Their standards were pretty low.

Sipping her drink, she noted, with more than a bit of amused arrogance, how most of these men hanging about Rec Room 2 had been eyeing her. That young kid from engineering, pretending to enquire about her increased workload at sick bay, but talking to her tits, that louse pretending to read a book, peering over it at every opportunity, the myriad men passing her to get coffee, trying to glance down her shirt-front as they walked by.

'Men,' she thought contemptuously. 'They think with their cocks. And fuck with their brains.'

Asgar had been different. For one, he was in a very senior position at the Mine, which meant of course that he jingled like a piggy bank. Even better, he seemed to know his way around a woman's body, unlike most guys her age who fumbled with a bra clasp as if it was a live bomb they were disarming. He was also married. Perfect.

She had also liked his style. Direct, confident and sure of what he wanted and how to get it, his eyes had been firmly fixed on hers as he talked. Within ten minutes of the conversation, he had calmly made it clear he was not interested in her brain. A few months ago, a guy had told her 'You complete me' and she had laughed in his face before walking away. This man knew better. Best of all, he did not once pull the 'My wife does not love me. Can I get a sympathy screw?' trick that married men try without fail to get girls into the sack, a trick that Tanya felt not only betrayed tremendous dishonesty but also a spectacular lack of imagination.

Tanya knew that most women would be put off by this 'coming straight to the point' but she noted, with some pride, that she was not most women.

They had gone straight to her room. Buttons flew. Fabric ripped. Skin was broken. Asgar was the rough kind, making no apologies for not being caring and tender. Exactly as she liked. He had tied her to the bed and rammed into her, with no more regard than a child would give to a rag doll.

What had really driven Tanya over the edge had been this supreme confidence in his prowess and technique. She had not let on how much she had lost herself in the intensity of her own submission. Instead, she had teased Asgar for his 'non-performance' hoping that his hurt masculinity would further stoke the fire that raged inside.

It had the desired effect. Asgar had hinted that he wanted to take her in one of the machinery rooms. It would be one heck of a 'show', in front of the cameras, the type that at least the guys in security would not forget in a hurry. Even thinking of it made Tanya cross her legs, bite her lips and turn red near her ears.

Suddenly her personal communicator beeped. Every employee had these devices to communicate among themselves, their only source of sanity since any form of contact with the world outside was rendered impossible.

There was a short text message. *Meet me in Level 3 Sector 5. Now.*

Tanya smiled. The urgency of the 'Now' seemed to scream out from the digital display. Oh my god! No kidding. He actually wants to do it in front of the cameras. Her knees wobbled for a second with insane lust. She left her unfinished beer on the table and nearly ran out. Elevator 2 was nearby. Inside the elevator were two men from the Security Division who, true to form, eyed her when they thought she was not looking. Tanya glanced at them with amusement.

Today is your lucky day, boys. You just might get to see the show of your life.

Tanya held the wall of the elevator to calm herself. The door slid open. Sliding her access card, she stepped inside the Machine Room. Asgar must be upstairs.

Climbing up, she found him not there. She looked once again at her communicator. Yes, this was where he had asked her to be. No mistake about that. It was also highly irregular for a control console to be left unmanned. She looked around with more than a bit of impatience. No one.

Damn. This message must be some hours old then. Such things happened with these bloody comm. devices.

Still, Tanya descended the stairs. Was Asgar lurking behind one of the machines as part of some kinky cat-and-mouse game?

Yes, that was it.

She smiled to herself, her breath progressively coming faster and shorter. All right. Two can play this.

Scream bitch. That is what he had said again and again while pounding her.

Now let's see who cries for mercy, you horny bastard.

Tanya moved her fingers to her shirt, removing it with a practised flourish. Yes, the cameras would see this but she didn't care. Asgar was testing her limits, just as he had done in bed. And she was damned if she was going to blink. She walked through the passageway between two machines. Her hand moved to the side of her skirt.

It slid noiselessly off.

Tanya felt proud. Proud of her body. Her youth. Her power.

She spread her hands wide and then, as if to challenge the heavens, looked up.

There, right above, halfway to the ceiling, balanced between two gigantic rotors, framed perfectly by one of the floodlights, was Asgar.

Even from there, he was still making direct eye contact with Tanya. Just like the day they had first met.

Except today those eyes were unblinkingly dead. Stone cold dead. She kept looking, rooted to the spot.

Asgar had been broken; arms twisted as if caught in the blades of a gigantic blender, neck snapped forward like a dried twig.

Tanya opened her mouth to scream. No sound came. The communicator she had been holding clattered to the ground. The screen flickered to life. A new message came up.

Scream. Bitch.

THE BEGINNING

A breeze as relaxingly cold as melting peppermint on water rustles the leaves, leaving not a blot of dark cloud in the sky. A golden winter afternoon, the kind no one wants to see end.

He stands outside the gates of St. Agnes Convent School. A smile, even brighter than the day, lights up his face.

Happiness. Pure happiness.

He imagines her delighted laughter, pealing through his entire being like an angel's song.

Perhaps she will be slightly angry at her dad, sulk a while, cross her arms and look away. But nothing that a hug, a few boxes of Lindt and a promise of not going away without telling her ever again cannot handle.

There goes the bell, followed by a few seconds of silence, the calm before the storm. And then an avalanche of joyous teenage girls, squealing, laughing and yelling. School is over. Winter vacation.

There she is, bursting out through the gate. The centre of his existence – Reshmi, her pale brown hair flowing in the wind, eyes sparkling like a brook in the rays of the sun. The prettiest girl in the whole wide world.

He starts walking towards her. Reshmi's gaze catches his. She raises her hands in excited recognition and starts skipping forward, pushing past the ocean of girls, her hands outstretched. He quickens.

Reshmi does the same. The fast pace becomes a full-tilt run, as he propels himself through the light air. One second more of separation seems intolerable.

And then he comes to a screeching stop, his heels digging into the gravel.

The smile vanishes. This cannot be real. No. It is not.

That is because Reshmi had been lost to him, many years ago, on a day like this.

So, who is that girl?

A creation of his feverish mind.

There is also no sun. No breeze. No happiness.

Just the painful consciousness of being trapped inside one's own dream. All alone.

Samar woke up with a start, clutching at the sheets. Sitting ramrod straight on the bed, he looked around, disoriented and distraught.

Where am I?

Then in a few seconds he remembered. Reshmi. Reshmi was gone. He, however, was still here. Sinking back into the pillow, Samar felt the stickiness of his sweat-drenched neck, cold and clammy in the air-conditioned room.

'It's all right. Just a dream,' a voice said very slowly, stopping at every syllable. It was his younger brother Sambit, standing in the doorway to the darkened bedroom, stooped slightly forward with concern.

'Did I scream out again?'

'No, you did not, Dada.' Sambit turned his head slowly to one side. 'You stopped screaming years ago.'

'Then why are you in my room?'

Samar immediately regretted the sharp sting of the words. He just did not like to be seen in such a weakened state, least of all by Sambit.

'There is a gentleman downstairs to see you. I told him that you were sleeping. He said he knew. He has been waiting for several hours... so I thought I would come to your room...' Sambit's voice fell away, afraid he had once again done something wrong.

'Someone who wants to meet me at this time of the night. What is he – crazy?'

Blinking like a frightened hare, Sambit mumbled, 'It is eleven in the morning... I... it is...'

Samar sat up, now fully awake. It did not come as a surprise that he had once again lost track of time. Those infernal blue pills. They had once been knights in sugarcoated armour, driving away the dark monsters that crowded his fitful dreams, whispering unspeakable possibilities, berating him for not trying hard enough, laughing at his impotence.

Now he missed those nightmares. That was because their place had been taken by something even worse – a state of almost perpetual hypnagogia in which Samar wandered the twilight zone between wakefulness and stupor. The wounds of the mind were never allowed to heal but were slit open every sleep-cycle by the serrated edge of false hope, only to be cauterized, with no opportunity given for the pus to drain out, by yet another wave of happy pills.

It was not just the medication though that had warped his sense of time. The fact that sunlight had been a stranger in the house also did not help. After Reshmi's disappearance, one of the many ways in which Samar had barricaded the outside world had been by keeping the curtains in his room drawn tight. His proffered excuse was that the light hurt his eyes. The real reason was that every time his fingers lingered on the heavy curtains, one of the many remnants in this house from British days, he half-expected Reshmi to jump out from one of her favourite hiding places.

And finally to complete the dissonance from the world of the living, there was the silence, smeared like treacle, slowing the passage of time to a tortured crawl. Once upon a time, even a sliver of peace and quiet would have been unthinkable in the 'Bose Palace', called so by people because of its size and its hundred-and-fifty-year-old heritage of pomp and splendour. From the crack of dawn, there used to be servants hurrying about. The thunderous bellow of his father, business magnate Pratap Rai Bose, would echo throughout the house. Anita, frail as a winter cloud, would sing whenever the fancy took her... which was often. Over everything, there would be Reshmi – throwing tantrums, laughing, creating the most monstrous din everywhere. Even Pratap Rai Bose, famous for his old-world temper, would not say anything to his only granddaughter. This of course meant that Reshmi ruled Bose Palace, in sight, sound and spirit.

Now things were different. Reshmi was gone. Pratap Rai Bose had become a picture on the wall, his stern face staring into the void that was his legacy. All that was left of Anita were her serene paintings of moonlit evenings and white flowers, rattling in the occasional draught that sneaked in through the window frame. The servants had been let go except some voiceless part-timers who mostly kept to themselves.

Of course, there was Sambit, Samar's younger brother. And even he was never 'fully there', having been rendered half-witted, or as the doctors preferred to call it, 'intellectually inept', by a brain seizure decades ago.

'What does he want to meet me for?' asked Samar, snapping out of his thoughts.

'He knocked. I let him in. He would not tell me, Dada,' Sambit said. 'Nobody tells me anything.' He added, the hurt in his voice barely concealed.

Samar held his head in his hands, rubbing away the sleep. 'Give me some time to get ready. And next time please do not open the door for strangers.'

Nodding in silent assent, Sambit slunk slowly away.

Fifteen minutes later, Samar descended the spiral staircase to the living room, wrapping around the housecoat that had once belonged to his father. He hoped this would not be some moron with a hard-luck story asking for money, labouring under the misapprehension that he was as sappily sentimental as his father, despite the tough-as-nails exterior, had been.

One look at the visitor however was enough to convince Samar to whatever his motive might be; it was not money. That jet black, old-fashioned suit he was wearing would in itself be worth a small fortune. The white silk shirt was not too shabby either. With a shining bald pate and exquisitely sharp eyebrows colour-coordinated with the suit, he looked like someone who had stepped out from a nineteenth-century British novel.

The man stood up as Samar entered and extended his hand. 'Good morning, Mr Bose. I hope you had a pleasant night's sleep.' The strength of the grip belied his age, which Samar had guessed was in the sixties. For some reason, the smile of politeness that accompanies a handshake lingered a little longer than was normal.

'I am sorry to keep you waiting, Mr...' Samar detached his hand from the hold.

The stranger gave him a beady reptilian stare. 'Please call me Arnold Paul.'

'Ok, Mr Paul. To what do I owe the pleasure of this company?' The brusqueness in Samar's voice betrayed no such pleasure.

Arnold Paul adjusted the lapel of his coat and sank back into the couch, making himself thoroughly at home. 'We would like to retain your services for a small job.'

'You must have me confused with someone else. I do not offer any kind of services nor do I perform jobs.'

Arnold Paul sat quietly, looking straight at Samar. 'Seeing that there is an ashtray here, would you mind if I smoke?'

The man was getting ready to dig in for a long siege. He had obviously anticipated this reaction.

'No, I don't, Mr Paul. But I think we are done here.' Samar made a move to get up.

Arnold Paul's thin emaciated fingers held the cigarette quietly. He looked downwards at the gently glowing circle from which thin tendrils of smoke snaked out. 'You are the Government of India's point person for industrial security systems and electronic surveillance.' Paul looked up again. 'Or perhaps I should say *were*. For the last seven years you have been a private operator providing your consultancy services to iron ore mines in the Ukraine and oil refineries in Iran. No, I won't go on making a list of all your projects. I am sure your employers would not want that or, for that matter, neither would you.'

Samar did not like getting caught in a lie, that too the first thing in the day. 'I can see you have done your research. Anyhow I am sure you already know this, but I will still tell you if only because I like wasting my time.' Samar paused to sneer, 'I never took jobs from random people waltzing into my living room, even during my greediest days. Second, and this is perhaps the most relevant to our discussion: I do not work anymore. Good day.'

Once again Arnold Paul ignored the brush-off. He remained seated. 'I will give you the first point. This is irregular... yes... my arrival like this straight at your doorstep without a reference. I do, however, happen to know that you still work. About eight months ago, you did a highly classified job for the Indian government in Pakistan. Too bad Operation Zeus got compromised.'

Operation Zeus had been a rotten idea from the start. He had taken the job despite his better judgment, purely on the basis of an assurance given by one of the most powerful men in the government that the police would reopen Reshmi's case and put their best men on it. 'Better to put your trust in a cross-eyed, toothless whore than in the government,' his old boss, Sunderan, used to tell him. In his eagerness to find the truth about Reshmi's disappearance, Samar had forgotten that bit of sane advice. It did not take him long to regret this lapse. Zeus had leaked like a ninety-year-old with a poor bladder, two operatives had wound up with bullets in their brains and the promise made to him was quietly forgotten.

'We can keep on playing this parlour game. You make a little disclosure about me. I sit and think, "Wow, how come he knows even this?" You feel delight in your little achievement. It's a nice diversion, I accept. But the thing is, I am too old and too goddamn tired for such games. So, if you would not mind...' Samar gave a mock bow of surrender, his hand now pointing straight to the door.

Arnold Paul leaned forward. Perhaps he had got the message. But no. 'Four hundred thousand dollars for two days of work. All paid upfront. I know the very best do not come cheap, but I am sure you will accept that this is more than a fair amount.'

'Indeed, very generous. But I do not need money. My brother and I are well looked after.'

Arnold Paul looked pensive. 'I understand you personally do not need the money. But the Pratap Rai Memorial School does. Am I correct?'

The Pratap Rai Memorial School was one of its kind; a school for rehabilitating the victims of trafficking. Sambit had suggested it be named after Reshmi. Samar could not bring himself to attach the word 'memorial' after Reshmi's name. Doing so would be the ultimate surrender for a father's heart, that bloody mass of muscle that refuses to give up, pounding crimson hope through the veins long after the brain has accepted the futility of it all. So he had named it after their father.

The original plans had been to convert most of Bose Palace into a hostel and add another wing for the school. But that was where the problems started. The Bose fortune had been largely exhausted hiring the best private dicks in the country and greasing the worst public dicks of justice. All in the hope that Reshmi would be found. All for nothing.

A large corporate house, for which Samar had once done a job, had kindly come forward as a sponsor for the wing. It was only too late that he realized that it was a scam, as heroic as punching a three-year-old in the nose – the kind that accountants and managers congratulated themselves on pulling off successfully. Not that he understood it fully, but it was some complicated accounting sleight-of-hand consisting of handing over a huge cheque in front of flashing cameras, moving money off balance sheets as expense, cashing in on the tax break, and then quietly begging off later, citing adverse market conditions.

All construction had come to a halt and the project had become yet another good intention, fallen by the wayside, to add to what Samar felt had been a lifetime of missed opportunities and sorry choices. Quite by chance, a line had just been thrown at him. Four hundred thousand dollars was a lot of money. He was damned if he was going to walk away from this.

'What's the job? And where would I have to go?'

Arnold took a deep puff, blowing smoke out of his thin dry lips with the air of a cock that just won the fight. 'Aah. At last. Interest. Very good. There are of course a few pre-conditions.'

'The trap at the end of the cheese you mean? But of course.'

'Nothing that you have not worked with before. Just absolute secrecy.'

'Will I be told anything about the job now? Or am I supposed to go in blind?'

Arnold shook his head slowly. 'Very few people, outside those that are there, are aware of the existence of this project. This is why I am not at liberty to say anything about my client or the nature of your duties. All I can say is that this mission is right in your domain of expertise. Otherwise, we would not have been spending this amount of money. Now if you choose to sign the contract we will have to leave immediately. Time is something we do not have a lot of.'

A few pieces of paper and a silver pen had materialized on the glass table. Samar leafed through the contract. The standard boilerplate with no-disclosure, no-liability and we-will-deny-having-employed-your-services line items he had seen numerous times before.

'Two things you cannot bring with you. Communicating devices – basically anything that transmits a signal. And, of course, no weapons.'

Samar scratched his name in, without a murmur of protest. Arnold Paul's teeth, like small kernels of white corn, flashed quietly. 'Excellent. Mr Bose. Excellent. You will not regret this. Trust me.'

For some reason, Samar was sure he could not.

He was never much good at packing, hurling whatever clothes he could get hold of in the general direction of the handbag. If only Anita had been here. Samar looked up at the picture of her on the wall, taken many years ago on a holiday in South Africa. Somehow he felt, she was looking back at him, nodding sadly at the way he struggled with the zip. So many years of living out of a briefcase and still he had not learnt.

I never will, Anita.

The only thing he made it a point to take was Reshmi's small, multi-coloured teddy bear, her favourite stuffed toy, the one she kept around her even after she was a teenager. It had since then become a constant presence in Samar's suitcase everywhere he went. Once upon a time, he kept it around so that he would press it into her arms, the day she came back. Once all the doors of hope had slammed shut and Samar, in anger at the world, had closed the curtains of his life, he had still kept it at the head of his bed, if for nothing else but as a remembrance of happier days.

Positioned on the side table, looking back at him morosely, was the bottle of blue pills. Should I bring them along? The decision was surprisingly swift. No, he would not. This journey had to be alone. The nightmares could join him if they wanted to.

Sambit was standing right near the door, neither inside the room nor out, noiselessly watching Samar's adventures in packing. Samar remembered the way he had lost his temper earlier in the morning. No wonder Sambit was keeping his distance. Walking up to him, Samar held him gently by the shoulder. 'I will be gone three days at the most. Salim-chacha will be in every day. If you have any trouble, any at all, you call Dr Gafoor. Understand?'

Sambit nodded, not making eye contact.

He is angry at me, thought Samar. He does not like it when I leave. 'Do you want me to make arrangements for you to go to Dr Gafoor's home for a few days?'

Dr Gafoor ran a sanatorium. Samar had wanted to get Sambit admitted there after the servants had been let go. Only then, he felt, would he get the proper attention he needed. But Sambit would have none of it, weeping and flying into a frightful fit whenever the possibility was mentioned. Dr Gafoor also was of the opinion that Sambit would stay more rested and peaceful with his elder brother around. But now with him going away, Samar wondered if it would be a better idea to have Sambit under supervision.

Sambit vigorously shook his head from side to side, a dribble of spit snaking down the side of his mouth. 'No, no, no. I have a lot of work. The roses need tending. The weeds have grown wild this year...'

Samar cut him off. The big garden in front of Bose Palace was Sambit's obsession. He would spend days on end quietly working in the flower beds, tapping on the soft earth with the hoe, caressing the petals with his fingers. According to Dr Gafoor, this was therapeutic for Sambit, as it gave his life purpose and direction. Samar did not want to transplant him from what he called his 'happy place'.

'Now, don't carry on, please. It was just a suggestion. Fine. Look after the garden. And take care of yourself.'

Sambit fell silent. Samar walked down the stairs to where Arnold Paul stood, following his descent with his eyes.

'I am ready.'

They walked out through the main door and onto the gravel path that cut through the garden towards the road. A black Mercedes stood parked on the corner.

The lawns stretched luxuriantly on either side. All this tragedy and the grass had still remained as calmly green as it always had been, almost as if Nature did not care for anything other than its own beauty.

But he cared. And as long as he did, they would always be here. Anita on a wicker chair, her legs stretched out in front, humming contentedly to herself. Father, out in the sun reading the newspaper, grumbling over the fate of the world. Reshmi hopping around on one leg like an innocent sparrow. Sambit hunched over with a small spade in hand, watching his niece with kind indulgent eyes, asking her gently not to trample the flowers if she came too close.

'One for sorrow, two for joy... repeat after me no, uncle?' she would plead. 'I... cannot remember... the words.' Sambit would slap his head, a smile stretching from one ear to another. And Reshmi would laugh 'I will teach you, uncle. I will.'

Memories. The more beautiful they are, the deeper they cut.

'Coming, Mr Bose?' Arnold Paul had stepped ahead and was standing, holding the car door open. There was no mistaking the hurried impatience.

Just then, Samar felt a strong grip on his upper arm, tugging him back with some force.

It was Sambit, his head turned slightly to the side, voice gurgling with a sudden transport of emotion. 'Remember... remember to forget.'

Sambit sometimes said things that made no sense, especially when he was sad. Through long experience, Samar had learnt that it was best to ignore him then. He gently detached himself from the grip, smiled and patted Sambit on his head.

The sky was daubed with wet shades of grey. It seemed to swell, like it does before it starts weeping.

'Go in, Sambit. There is rain in the air. Don't catch something now.' Sambit did not move.

Samar knew it was better not to insist. The last thing he needed before he left was a temper tantrum. Getting into the car, he waved. Sambit rocked on his ankles to and fro, raising his hand slowly in reply.

It had been almost thirty years ago, on a cloudy day, just like this, that he and dad had left Sambit. A very different Sambit. He had been a precocious ten-year-old with a prodigious ability to master any musical instrument almost instantly.

They had gone to Mussoorie for the summer holidays. Dad, Sambit and him. The weather had been horrible; a holocaust of rain ruining the week. The day before they were to leave, the deluge had stopped. Sambit was running a slight fever. But Samar, all of twelve, had insisted that they drive to the blue mountains. Going back to Calcutta without seeing them would be a tragic waste. Dad thought it would be best to leave Sambit behind in the hotel room. He had stood just like this, at the gates, waving them away. When they came back eight hours later, Sambit was lying on the balcony, wracked by brain seizures, shaking uncontrollably, eyes turned to the back of his head, his favourite mouth organ clutched tightly in his hand. By the time they reached a hospital, something terrible had come to pass.

What they had thought was a 'little cold' had been the onset of a rare form of fever, one that had wracked his brain with seizures and left behind a mass of tangled nerves where there was once a healthy child. Sambit never made music again.

As the car rolled out, Samar looked back out of the window to see Sambit standing like a silent sentinel on the steps, framed against dark grey storm clouds, the grief of having been left behind still carved on his face, eyes following the car as far as he could. Pretending to clean his face with his forearm, Samar wiped away the tear swelling at the corner of his eye.

It had been three hours since they had left Kolkata. In that time, Samar had not learnt much, either about where they were taking him or why. The only thing he knew, with absolute certainty, was that he intensely disliked Arnold Paul.

Usually, people needed to open their mouths to get on his nerves. Arnold Paul's unique ability seemed to be that he could do so through silence. On the way to the private hangar at Netaji Subhash Chandra Airport, Samar had tried to learn something about his assignment. Nothing much, just the basics. Arnold Paul had shaken his head slowly, as if Samar was a kid asking for too much chocolate. 'Sorry, Mr Bose. I am not authorized to say that at present,' he had said with an air of condescension. After three attempts, Samar had stopped asking questions, seething in anger.

He had hoped to cool down once he boarded the chartered jet. There also he had no luck. He was positioned bang opposite Arnold Paul, unable to avoid the piercing gaze and the trace of a smile that hung precariously from his lips. It was evident that he was enjoying Samar's discomfiture, mocking him with a silent 'Wouldn't you just love to know?'

Samar was not willing to give him the pleasure of acting officious again. This was why he did not say anything when he looked out of the window and saw, to his surprise, vast expanses of sand. Nor did he utter a word when the pilot announced 'Please fasten your seatbelts. We are making our descent.'

It was Arnold Paul who finally broke the uncomfortable silence. 'We are here. The Thar Desert in Rajasthan. Not what you expected, I presume?'

Samar looked back at him, 'Sorry, Mr Paul. I am not authorized to say that at present.'

The old man broke into a wide smile, baring his spotlessly white teeth. 'Very droll. Very droll,' he said raising his finger in front of his nose and waving it to and fro.

As the plane bore down towards the desert, a momentary spasm tightened Samar's stomach. Had he been brought to this desolateness to be executed and buried silently? No one works for the government's top-secret espionage division without making a few powerful enemies. But then, he reasoned, they could have just as well abducted him from home, without paying the four hundred thousand dollars to the Swiss bank account he still maintained from his spying days. He had personally confirmed the transaction had taken place before leaving Kolkata. No, they definitely needed his services. For the moment.

The landing was not smooth. The plane careened from one side to another, shaking, coughing and sputtering, ultimately coming to a screeching stop on a sandy tarmac. Samar tried to get up. The seat belts, which he now noticed were not standard issue, suddenly snapped into position – locked.

'Standard security protocol, Mr Bose. Please remain seated till the door is opened.'

Lahore. They had been compromised. A swift blow to the back of his head and hours later, he had found himself with hands and feet tied to a chair in a dark warehouse. All the memories came streaming back and, involuntarily, he gave a forward thrust. His stomach dug into the hard leather. It did not give.

'Good thing you didn't let me bring my weapon. Or else you would have regretted this.'

'Well at least one of us has been wise,' Arnold Paul sniggered.

Five more minutes of intense staring at Paul and then two burly men in military fatigues entered with Uzis slung across their shoulders.

Arnold Paul was all better now. 'No need to get alarmed. A bag search and then a pat-down. Nothing you would not have to do if you were getting on an international flight.'

The seat belt lock was disengaged with a gentle click. 'This is just to make sure you did not bring communication devices or firearms. Please stand up and do not approach your luggage in the meanwhile.'

Samar sprang to his feet aggressively. One of the guards stood behind him and started patting him down while another held his hands stretched out to the side.

'Oh damn! I was hoping for a full-body cavity search.'

Arnold Paul directed the other security personnel to Samar's bag. 'I am afraid you are taking this very personally. In a while, you will yourself understand why we need to do all this.'

'Personally? Not at all. Not only do I enjoy being kept in the dark as to the nature of my mission, but I also immensely enjoy the feeling of another man's hand brushing my balls. For providing this type of pleasure to your men, I charge a bit more than what you are paying me.'

The second guard was rifling through his handbag with a practised hand, inspecting for false bottoms and linings. They brought out all his things, went through each item, then folded them neatly and put them back in the bag. The lid closed easily this time.

'Thanks, boys, for doing what my wife used to. Folding my clothes, giving me... mmm... well, never mind...'

The banter was deliberate. Samar was eyeing the reaction of the guards to his provocation. They did not look him in the eye even once, nor did his taunts have any effect on their faces or on their precisely clinical efficiency. No, these were not the 'security contractors' even the most paranoid typically hire. No ex-wrestlers. No ex-servicemen. No fired cops. These people were mercenaries, the best of the best. Samar guessed they were Bulgarian. He had seen their type a few times before and from what he knew about them, in addition to their deadly efficiency and total lack of any scruples, they were insanely expensive. And someone had enough money in hand to employ these people as guard dogs.

Whew. Maybe I got shafted on my four hundred thousand. Should have asked for more.

'He is clean,' said one of them in a thick Bulgarian accent. The others nodded.

'I apologize once again for the intrusion. This is solely for the protection of our commercial interests.'

Samar stepped out of the plane carrying his own case. The Bulgarian mercenaries shadowed him closely. Arnold Paul walked ahead with a mumbled 'It will take us ten minutes'.

Despite it being late afternoon, the sun here was still out in all its might, its molten yellow rays making the hot sand crackle. The incandescence seemed to burn through Samar's eyes, making him curl his head into his chest. Long periods of staying locked inside his bedroom surrounded by darkness, he realized, had made him highly sensitive to natural light, especially when it streamed down at him mercilessly. To compound his problems, a strong gust of wind blew specks of hard sand everywhere, grating Samar's face like small diamonds.

'A sandstorm seems to be in the air. We need not worry. We will be far away when it happens.'

Again, bait to get me to ask a question. Samar did not rise to it.

They rounded a dune. Right in front of them was a military bunker. It was surrounded by a barbed-wire fence with one gate. Samar's practised eye picked out the surveillance cameras mounted on structures that had been made to look like cell-phone towers. What caught him by surprise was the presence of mounted turrets, grainy pictures of which he had seen uploaded in one of the underground sites he loved frequenting, the ones that prided themselves on leaking classified documents.

If he was not wrong, this was a deployment of what he knew to be an experimental technology being developed at the US Department of Defense – Killzone, a fully-automated, multiple-sensor-driven targeting system which could detect something as small as a rat within the assigned zone and take it out with clinical precision, without any form of human intervention.

The gate through the barbed wire was open. As they entered the bunker, all four of them, a dull chill ran down his spine. Industrial air conditioners were turned up to the maximum inside. The momentary tremble must be his body reacting to stepping from the heat outside into this refrigerator of a place, he reasoned.

Inside the structure, half-submerged in the ground was a well-lit circular metallic enclosure with its door already open. It was quite large in size, easily able to accommodate fifteen people at a time. Samar guessed that it was an elevator.

'Our installation is entirely underground. This bunk hides the lift from prying eyes. We have three other such lifts, one of them for cargo. These are our only entrances.'

Now Arnold Paul was volunteering information. Some new mind game no doubt. Samar had no clue as to what it might be. But a syllable never escaped this person's lips which did not carry the stench of a larger private design.

'After you, sir.' Arnold Paul stood aside and, with a theatrical flourish, stretched out both his hands as the party filed into the cylindrical lift. When he spoke, his voice echoed inside the metallic walls, imbuing hollow impersonality to the upbeat greeting.

'On behalf of my employers, let me welcome you to the place we call simply, the Mine.'

Samar trembled once again. *Damn, it's cold in here. Will get used to it. I guess.*

As the door to the elevator slid noiselessly shut, Samar turned around. A final flash of yellow-gold streamed in. Then the outside was gone. *Perhaps I should have kept my curtains open all these years. So much sunshine has slipped through my fingers.*

A huge circular table, gleaming black like polished onyx.

Five strangers hunched around it.

Searching glances of cluelessness. Stifled silence.

Samar felt like it was the first day of college all over again, that same air of expectant awkwardness. Not all of them were strangers to each other though, he realized; clumped as they were into small groups of two and three, separated by empty chairs.

He leaned back on his chair sinking into the plush leather, looking at the gigantic company logo right in front of him. Two concentric circles, the outer one thick, bold and pitch black and the inner one thin and crimson stared back at him like a bloodshot eye.

How long had he been in the Mine? Seven hours? Eight? Did it really matter inside the earth where the great timekeeper of the sky had been rendered irrelevant? What did matter was that he had slept the soundest he had in months. No dreams, no blue pills and no tortured walk on the shaded path of hypnotic wakefulness.

The beeping on the communication device that had been handed to him had woken him up. A message, typically as cryptic as possible, from Arnold Paul had instructed him to get ready for a meeting with the chief operational officer of the facility at the conference room on Level 5. There had been no need to find the place. Two discreetly armed, stone-faced mercenaries had escorted him noiselessly.

'Hello. My name is Karan Singh Rathore...' So tall was the owner of the hand that he had to crane only slightly forward to shake Samar's hand, even though he was seated a chair away. The voice brought back pleasant memories of dear old Father Braganza from high school. A deep, gravelly baritone; old-fashioned bifocals; large swathes of grey through a head still full of hair; a firm grasp; and most tellingly, a gentle smile that made one feel immediately at ease.

'Never trust a weeping whore or a laughing pimp,' his old boss at Special Operations, Sunderan, used to tell him. To that circle of mistrust, Samar had added men who made a good first impression. He gingerly shook the proffered hand and was about to return the introduction when the door slid open.

Samar gasped noiselessly. Her bronze skin glistened in the bluish light, her piercing eyes seemed to be making eye-contact with everyone in the room at once and her hair cascaded like a waterfall of impenetrable darkness. The lady that had just walked in radiated an aura of arrogant power. The boss. There was no mistaking that.

She took her position at the head of the table, adjusted her crisp business suit and spoke. Brisk and to-the-point. Having apologized for keeping them waiting, she introduced herself as Lilith Adams, the chief operational officer of what she described as a 'consortium of investors with interests in mining, energy and infrastructure'.

In other words, thought Samar wryly, shady investors who wanted to keep their identities secret. Well, they had put up an insane amount of money to run an operation of this size. But who was he to complain? They had paid him well. Their desire for secrecy was well-deserved.

She then looked around the room and asked the assembled to introduce themselves before she made her presentation.

Samar grimaced. The round table, the sombre group of individuals, the 'introductions' all reminded him of the grief therapy sessions Dr Gafoor had coaxed him to attend a year ago. He had dropped out after two sittings, unable to take any more of the gaggle of grief-hobbyists around the table wallowing in the perverse pleasure of spreading their misery to others.

The elderly gentleman that had shook his hand, Karan Singh Rathore, Fellow of Royal College of Medicine, was the director of Pujara Centre of Communicable Diseases.

A big shot. And a doctor. Doctors. He never liked their lot much. Death's little courier boys. That's what they are. What was the man's name? Dr Chatterjee. Or was it Bhattacharjee? Who cares? All that mattered was that practised tone of empathy and the rehearsed shake of head. 'We tried everything. But it was too late. I am sorry.'

'No, you are not sorry. It's not your wife who lies dead on that bed there. The only thing that would make you sorry would be if you didn't get paid. But you will get my money. 'Because doctors collect either way – on life and on death. So bloody stop pretending you care, you fat ass.'

He had wanted to say that. But he could not. Mumbling something that sounded like a 'Thanks', he had slid into the hospital room for one last look at Anita. Blue and white. The colour of the room. The colour of death. There his wife lay like a shattered porcelain vase, serenely beautiful till the end. Her frail heart had not been able to take Reshmi's disappearance.

'Where do flowers go when they wither?' Anita had asked him once. Well, now she knows. She is with them, after all. The tears had flooded down as he had sat there for hours, holding her limp wrist.

I will find our baby. Somehow. Some day.

But for now, a job had to be done. Only then would he go home. Samar turned his attention to the matter at hand. The lady sitting next to the doctor was now introducing herself. She too was a doctor, but of the PhD type – Dr Anjali Menon, till recently the assistant director of the Archaeological Society of India.

Then Samar saw her. He wondered for a second how he had not noticed her before. Maybe because he was not expecting such a child to be down here in the Mine. Maybe because the girl's head barely came up to the table. Maybe because she was in a wheelchair. But once he did, his heart missed a beat. The same hair, the same prominent nose. Reshmi.

Dr Anjali introduced the little girl as her daughter, Anya. He decided he would avoid looking in that direction if possible.

The next in line had a boyish face which Samar figured some women might find attractive. Exquisitely set hair, carefully maintained stubble, an expensive suit, not a fold or thread out of place. Samar recognized the type – dandy. Or what was the term they used nowadays? Metrosexual. Akshay More, PhD in forensic toxicology. What? He was an assistant professor at Princeton University? Samar shook his head in gentle disbelief. *Looks more like a slick advertising executive.*

The young lady right next to him, with over-sharp features and a rather permanent frown, was Dr Preeti Singh, a clinical psychologist with a focus on 'deviant behaviour and mass psychosis'.

What a weird cast of characters.

Never comfortable with attention, Samar felt the familiar knotting in his abdomen as the eyes of the room alighted squarely on him. He introduced himself as an expert on security surveillance systems, with experience in security audits of industrial installations. Should he mention his intelligence background? After a second's deliberation, Samar decided he would. It was never good to be excessively modest about one's qualifications in front of strangers, especially those who are not shy about theirs.

Lilith Adams now took charge. 'I understand you all are extremely eager to know why you have been asked to come here at such a short notice. So, I will get straight to the point. This facility, as its name, the Mine, suggests so obviously, is a mine. But we don't just dig things out of the ground here. We also process them and make a product. So, think of it as a mine and a factory, all rolled into one.

What we mine here is something rather extraordinary. I won't get into the exact scientific details. Strictly need-to-know... hope you understand.' The accompanying smile was hardly genuine. 'But for the sake of some clarity, let me just say that what we dig for is a very special kind of crystal, the most potent source of energy perhaps in the whole universe. Think of each minute crystal as a storehouse of enormous quantities of pure, raw power. As an example, I have been told that the breaking down of one properly processed crystal would keep Mumbai moving for three months.'

Hushed silence in the room. Samar detected a somewhat incredulous light sneer from Dr More.

Lilith Adams stood up from the chair and took a few paces back, standing right below the company logo. 'No exaggeration, but the world's energy crisis will soon be a thing of the past. Two things however are holding us up – first, we have still not perfected the technology of processing the crystals and second, we have yet to get governments to buy into this new source of energy.'

As she paced up and down, her words took speed, like a train gathering momentum as it rolls out of the station. 'There are billions of dollars riding on the success of this project. As that should make obvious, there are powerful agents who would like to steal our intellectual property and sabotage our manufacturing. That is why we have taken enormous precautions.'

She cleared her throat and looked around the room. 'No operational details are to be revealed to the public until we have a handle on the industrial production of the crystals and the policies behind distribution. I hope this explains why we do not allow cell phones or internet connections at this facility. Employees here are contract-bound not to have any kind of connection with the outside world. In other words, they cannot leave till the project is over.'

Preeti opened her mouth to say something and then kept quiet. Karan Rathore looked down at his nails, studying them intently.

'Some time ago, we were able to locate a sizeable deposit of the crystals here in this part of Rajasthan. Since then we have worked real hard to build this pilot installation and start mining as fast as we can. Our project has been successful in that we have managed to construct something as massive as this in absolute secrecy.'

'I am sorry for interrupting, madam.' It was Akshay More, the dandy, rolling the word 'madam' with barely concealed sarcasm. 'You are telling us to believe, among other impossible things like magic crystals, that you in Rajasthan managed to build an installation of this size so hush-hush that no one knows a thing. You seriously expect us to believe that? In this country, no one can so much as sneeze without the TV channels putting their fingers up your nose.'

Lilith Adams simply cocked her eyebrow. 'Most people seem to think so.'

Samar looked down his nose at this overdressed young man, remembering something he had read a long time ago. *The fool is he who thinks he knows everything, the wise is he who knows he knows nothing.*

Akshay beat a retreat. 'Maybe I have been away from the country for too long.'

Preeti Singh now decided to speak, having been struggling to stay silent for a while now. 'While walking to this conference room, I saw two women in uniform. The Mines Act of 1952 specifically prohibits women working underground in a mine. I presume you also didn't apply for a mining permit because that would put the details of your operation in the public domain. My main concern is that, if we choose to associate ourselves with whatever you have planned for us, we will be participating in something that is patently illegal.'

Lilith Adams' impassive exterior changed not a bit, not even at the sharp inflection of Preeti's voice at the end. 'The mining that takes place at the bottom floor does not employ women. Women are only employed in the processing part of the facility in engineering and in the medical division. Now, to your other concern. Since you say if we *choose to associate*, let me remind you of one thing. You have already associated with us by signing the contract and taking payment. Considering the mode of delivery of the said sum of money, Dr Singh, I presume you won't be declaring it to the government either.'

Aah so the stern young lady has kept the transaction off the books. Like, I presume, every one of us here. As old Sunderan would have said, 'Not even the biggest fart can smell his own fumes.' Samar curled his tongue to the side, suppressing the smile.

Lilith Adams moved away a curl of hair from her forehead with a flick of a forefinger, as if dismissing Preeti's impertinence from her presence. 'Now, coming to why we brought you here. All work was going smoothly and on schedule till two days ago. That day, around 1 p.m., Squad Delta working in Sector 2 of the active area hit something on the ground. It seemed to be the dome of some buried structure, apparently a small shrine or dwelling of some sort. Well, we would have broken the dome and that would have been that ...'

Samar glanced sideways at the archaeologist lady. The mention of bulldozing a buried shrine seemed to have initiated no hand-wringing from her. She kept staring fixedly without any change in expression.

The boss went on. '... within an hour of the discovery, one of the junior superintendents got his hand stuck in a piece of equipment. It was the first time in months of operation that we had such a serious mishap. A minor fall or a broken ankle, yes – but definitely not someone losing his right hand. We stopped the digging for that day in light of the incident. During dinner, the chief of Squad Delta, who had been leading the dig that day, tried to injure himself.'

Karan Rathore coughed gently, 'Excuse me, but what does *tried to injure himself* mean in this context?'

Lilith Adams paused a moment, struggling evidently for words, whether out of concern for Anya or the need to underplay the situation, Samar could not decide. 'He took a knife and tried to cut his own throat. The people sitting with him were alert, or else he would possibly have succeeded.'

Adams went on, after once again taking a few seconds for breath. 'The next day, several of the people from Squad Delta reported severe mental disturbances. News spreads in a closed space like this and before long, the miners were refusing to work anywhere near Sector 2. Things took a further turn for the worse when one of the drill machines near the structure broke, again without any apparent reason. Then at around three in the afternoon, one of the engineers who had happened to be in Sector 2 the day the structure was uncovered was found dead. He had... well... we never quite figured out how or why... he had entered into heavy machinery without properly shutting it down. As if that was not enough, the lady who had stumbled onto the dead body went into severe shock.

'Since that time, the miners have stopped working. They say that the place is cursed.' Lilith Adams let off a dismissive sneer. 'We approached their representative and impressed on him the need to not let a series of accidents, no matter how unfortunate, stop the project. As part of the negotiations, we agreed to stop mining till a committee of external experts investigated the recent events. That committee, ladies and gentlemen, is you.'

Preeti Singh had once again, been trying to say something for some time, but just didn't seem to be able to time the start of her sentence in the midst of the flow of words.

'Dr Preeti Singh will look at the psychiatric condition of the workers, while Dr Rathore observes their general health. Mr Bose will review the security of the installation and investigate the possibility of sabotage in the recent incidents. Dr More's brief is to study whether gases that have hallucinatory effects are being emitted from the dig-site and to suggest countermeasures, while Dr Menon's is to see if the structure, in total or in part, can be relocated. We do not want to disrespect the sentiments of the miners, if it can be avoided. At the end of forty-eight hours, we shall re-convene here in the presence of a worker's representative and, based on your recommendations, we will make a decision on the future of this project.'

Lilith Adams looked around the room, expecting questions. Now Preeti Singh could speak. 'Considering that the total isolation of your workforce is essential for the secrecy of your operation, what is the procedure followed when one of them falls sick or gets seriously injured, like just happened here, and needs urgent care outside? What happens if someone just wants to... you know... get up and leave?'

Lilith Adams answered – a chilly blast from an open refrigerator door. 'Our medical facilities here are more than sufficient for dealing with most emergencies. In case one of our workers needs medical treatment not possible here, we have arrangements to transport him to a medical facility till he recovers. Even there, we have ways to make sure that he will not be able to communicate with anyone. As to people wanting to resign and leave, they just cannot. That is their contract. That is why these people were paid a lot. A lot.'

Preeti Singh interrupted, one eyebrow arched up. 'So, in essence, you are saying that you have bought their freedom. Does that not sound a bit like slavery?'

Lilith's tone was razor burn on a cold morning. 'In slavery, people do not have a choice. The employees here had one. They chose to put a price tag on their freedom, in the same way people put one on their brains.'

Once again, she smiled to break the tension. 'Also, it is not as if we have bought them forever. Just a few months more, and they will be free to go and tell the world all about what they did here. By that time, we would have gone public with this technology so it will not matter.'

Samar spoke up for the first time. Something had been bothering him, more than the rather extraordinary problem he had been given to solve. 'I understand that the workers signed away their freedoms. But what about us? I know we signed non-disclosure agreements but what prevents us, given that there is a lot of money here, from talking to your competitors? The way I see it, it would be in your best interests to keep us here for the duration of the project, with some help, of course, from your Bulgarian bouncers.'

A murmur of disquiet went round the table.

'Let me try to answer your concerns, Mr Bose. You must understand that the decision to have you all here was not part of our plan. It is quite a disaster for us in fact. But there is no other option for us, given the stubborn insistence of the miner's representatives for an external review of the facilities. We have no intention to keep you here for more than two days. That's a firm assurance.

'But as you may well have figured, we have ways of safeguarding our secrets. Unlike the large number of permanent staff here, you are just five people. It will be easier for us to keep a watch on your activities once you leave here. I won't lie. You will be under surveillance. And yes, I know that is not legal, like a *whole lot of* other things. However, we will do whatever is needed to protect our investment. If we detect any intent, and

I *mean* intent, to violate the non-disclosure agreement, we will not hesitate to take preemptive countermeasures.'

Lilith Adams' eyes glowed like burning embers that had just been stoked. Samar had been chased by crazed killers in Rwanda running after him with machetes and had bullets whiz pass his head during a drive-by shooting in Vladivostok. He had the eyes, ears and the nose for danger. He sensed it here, in Lilith Adams. Money, power and a lot to lose. You do not mess around with such people. Somehow, he felt the others had also cottoned on to that.

It was Karan Rathore's smooth voice that now soothed the air rubbed raw. 'Ms Adams, it is unfortunate that our meeting has gotten off on the wrong foot. It is possibly our fault.' He looked around the table, searching for expressions of support. 'Perhaps it's just the whole suddenness of being called here that has made us unduly on edge. Or perhaps it is this level of secrecy that we men of science are not used to.'

'Or maybe it is just the curse of that thing down there,' sneered Akshay. 'Whatever it may be, we may have come across as combative. I can assure you that we will do our best to solve your problem.' A silence marked the truce.

Karan continued being agreeable, expressing an interest in his work that no one else seemed to be exhibiting, 'Can you please give us details of the accidents that have happened here at the facility?'

'All medical records are with Dr Anaida Gupta, down in the medical centre, where the three patients are. They are being looked after in facilities comparable to anywhere in India and you can of course check that out yourself. Our personnel records will be made available to you. Medical histories, resumes, the results of their physicals. Everything.

'All we want at the end of forty-eight hours is to know whether you feel it is safe to continue mining. And once that is done, you can go home. Trust me. You will all go home.'

Karan Singh Rathore now stood up, his massive frame looming over the assembled company, casting a shadow of authority. He started making teams, drawing up a schedule, setting terms of reference on how they would finally come to a decision.

Samar looked appreciatively at Rathore. *He is definitely maneuvering himself to be the leader of the group. Go for it, old boy.*

'Yes, chop-chop everyone. Start earning your pay,' snorted Akshay, disagreeably, just as Karan finished. Samar rolled his eyes. *In every team, there is always one guy who is trouble.*

Akshay's obnoxiousness continued. 'I was told the equipment I had asked for would be here when we started working. Well, since I don't think you guys go outside much, I am afraid to ask. Is it here?'

This time Lilith Adams smiled the kind of smile the teacher gives a petulant student. 'It is already here. Our research lab and its staff are also available anytime you wish.'

Samar felt the need to show that he too was with the programme. 'I assume you have surveillance tapes of these incidents? If you do, will we get to see them?'

'The security room houses all the tapes. We have nothing to hide here, Mr Bose. This is not Sierra Leone.'

Samar looked up at Lilith Adams. She was looking straight at him, her eyes shining with a colour of light not present in the room. Their gazes locked for a second. She broke it instantly and started talking about other things.

This is not Sierra Leone.

In the very few hours that it had taken from the representative's demand for an outside team to Arnold Paul coming to his house, this lady had got hold of the kind of information that Samar had thought would have taken the most well-equipped intelligence agencies years to acquire, things that had been long buried in his past. And now she was sending him a message.

She knows.

Dr Anaida Gupta surveyed the two external experts with more than a bit of suspicion. As if working overtime with three medical crises on her hand at the same time was not enough, now there were two 'experts' here to second-guess her decisions.

It's all eyewash. They are here to go through their motions. I am here to go through mine.

Dr Singh looked okay enough. She was her age, early to mid-thirties. Looked like someone she could work with. And oh boy, would she kill for that figure, reed thin and yet curved perfectly, like glass blown by an artist. Perfect shoulder-length hair and glowing skin, this lady has aristocracy written all over her.

Dr Rathore she was not so sure about. In her experience, it had always been the directors of institutes and those with similar appellations who caused a problem. No one got into management without poking their noses and tongues into the affairs and orifices of others. To top it off, this man was old, the kind whose only contribution to any discussion was complaining.

When had he last written for a journal or done something of any use to mankind? Possibly before I was born.

Anaida remembered how she had been passed over two years ago at Medville for the post of division head. If only she had been better with her people skills, her mentor, who also used to wear a black blazer like this Dr Rathore, had told her. Rubbish. What he had merely meant was that she should have tongue-polished his walking stick if she had wanted to advance. The three of them were seated in her office, which she always noted was about a tenth the size of what she would have had, had she been today the division head at Medville. But she was making in a month what she had made in a year at that place, and, even better, she was not reporting to anyone. That, however, had just changed.

Karan gave a hospitable warm smile, the kind that melts ice-cream. 'Just wanted to make sure at the start, Dr Gupta, that we are not here to look over your shoulder or comment on the quality of the care. We don't want to be treading on your toes.'

Just great. That usually means he intends to do exactly that.

'Of course, I understand. I would not mind some expert advice here, considering the craziness of the last few days.'

Take that for people skills.

'Only here to help. Nothing more.'

Oh God, the fossil is trying to be friendly.

Anaida Gupta looked down to the gadget she held in her hand. 'Getting down to business. I have just authorized your communication devices to download the medical records of all the personnel here. Not that you are going to find anything much there. Most of them are in the best of health. I did all the health pre-screenings about a year ago and we had pretty strict criteria on whom to take. I did not do pre-screenings for the security division, which is about twelve people. They came from outside. I don't have their medical records either.'

'Was a psychological profile done for all the employees as part of the pre-screening?'

It was the lady whom Anaida had thought would be easier to deal with who had asked the question. The tone of her voice had an unmistakable 'I am sure you were not qualified to do that' sourness, something that Anaida did not much care for. Just like the shrink to have an attitude about real doctors.

Adjusting the stethoscope around her neck, almost as if asserting her authority, Anaida spoke, 'No, Dr Singh. You will just have to ask the authorities why they did not insist on it. Perhaps it was considered to be a useless cost... since there aren't really many qualified people in mental health.'

Anaida regretted the last sentence just as it had left her mouth. Yes, her people skills did need work.

She briefed them about the patients housed in the Medical Bay – Abdul Saeed, Tanya Chowbey and Jaal. Dr Rathore buried himself in his communication device. 'Just had a look at the records of your patients and also of the deceased. Absolutely perfect all of them. The only thing is Asgar might perhaps have been pre-diabetic. Too late for him, I'm afraid. Can we first look at Abdul Saeed, the junior superintendent? I presume he is in the medical area next door.'

'Yes, he is. It might sound weird when I say I am not so worried about a man who lost his hand two days ago, than I am about the other two people currently in the medical area. Could you please look at them first?'

Karan started to walk out. But Preeti had not moved. 'Dr Gupta, is there something wrong?'

Anaida Gupta turned around. 'Excuse me?'

'Your hand... Are you all right?'

Holding her wrist, Anaida asked, 'Oh the shaking you mean?' Seeking to brush it off with a nonchalant smile, she said, 'Must be too much caffeine.'

'That shaking looks like something a bit more serious than too much coffee. You sure you are fine?'

'Well, it's been a bit hectic around here. That's true.'

The next question that Preeti asked took Anaida by surprise. 'So, what do you think is responsible for all these accidents?'

She smiled sweetly. 'I am not paid to find out what is responsible. Just paid to give the patients the best quality care I can provide.'

Preeti would not let the matter drop so easy. 'I understand. But surely, besides being a doctor, you are also a person. And people have opinions.'

Anaida shrugged, 'Right now I am here as a professional. Not as a person.

So, what I think is irrelevant.'

Preeti narrowed her eyes to a slit. 'Whatever you tell us will be in confidence.'

Yeah, 'in confidence,' right. Cameras everywhere and bugs kept god knows where. Plus, even if Big Brother was not watching, fat chance I'm going to put my faith in these people not to rat me out. Too much money in this for me.

Anaida tapped her clipboard on the table and put on her best official voice. 'As a scientist, I of course would not deduce any correlation between the discovery of an ancient structure and the accidents that have happened. The only scientific explanation I can think of is that hallucinogenic materials are present near the ancient structure.'

Anaida looked towards where she knew the camera was. Preeti was standing with her hands crossed, looking intently at Anaida. 'Do you think this place is cursed?'

Anaida now understood what was going on. This lady was putting her on the couch, checking out whether she had lost *her* marbles also. *The nerve.*

'Let's not burden Dr Gupta with questions she cannot answer,' Karan said gravely.

Preeti gave Karan Rathore the glance she reserved for people who purposefully bumped into her from behind. This old man, she figured, obviously had a problem with qualified women. He had not even thought twice before butting into her line of questioning.

Probably not used to women being anything better than nurses.

Karan now made a definite move towards the door. 'Maybe we can start with Tanya Chowbey?'

Anaida gave a tired smile.

'There isn't much you can get out of her, I'm afraid. I know this is not really a medical diagnosis, but the best I can say is that she is a hollow shell of a human being.'

The words struck Preeti like an arrow to the heart. For a second, she shuddered.

Med Room 3 was very different from what Dr Rathore had thought it would be. When Lilith Adams had said that they were providing the best facilities the country had to offer, he was expecting it to be the kind of hyperbole that heads of corporations frequently use when talking about employee welfare. 'We are all a family', 'We take care of each other', and all that fuzzy-speak that has become so much part of our daily dose of bullshit that people just shut their brains to it.

Here, however, she was not exaggerating. The machinery that was in each of the rooms here was state-of-the-art as far as emergency room technology and trauma care went. But it was grossly inadequate for the case at hand.

Tanya Chowbey had once been a pretty woman. Now she was a ghost, lying straight on the white hospital bed, even whiter than the spotless sheets. Her expressionless, vacant eyes, framed by pitch dark circles, stared at a fixed spot at the ceiling.

From the half-open lips, it seemed as if she had been about to say something when a great weight had been forced down her throat. She shook slightly, like a stuttering gramophone head, as if still struggling to get the words out.

'She has refused to eat. Hence the IV,' Anaida said as an explanation, pointing to the plastic tubes.

Karan asked, 'Has she said anything?'

'No. Not a single word. Ever since they found her there...'

Preeti held Tanya's right wrist, shaking her head disapprovingly. 'Deep psychological trauma. As a qualified psychiatrist, I must recommend she be sent to a fully equipped mental facility. She risks irreversible loss to her mental health every second she is kept here without treatment.'

Anaida rolled her eyes.

Dr Singh really likes making her recommendations 'as a qualified psychiatrist'. She is almost afraid that no one takes her seriously otherwise.

Karan felt the need once again to step in. 'Could you please tell us how this happened?'

Anaida looked nervously around once more. 'Well, she and Asgar, the engineer who was found dead stuck in the machinery, were as far as I have been told engaged in some sort of... well how should I put this... sex game.'

'Sex game in a Machine Room?' asked Preeti, the disgust barely concealed.

Karan once again studied Preeti. For a psychiatrist she did get shocked easily.

Anaida was now visibly embarrassed. 'I don't know everything; not in my professional capacity that is.' She looked down at the floor. 'Tanya was one of the nurses here and she had been having a fling with this man, Asgar. This she told me herself. You see, Tanya was the last one who could stay silent.'

She stopped. Considering what had happened to Tanya, the last line sounded insensitive. 'I didn't mean it that way of course. I just meant she was pretty open about herself.

'I think she had gone downstairs for some kind of meeting with the man. No one really knows what happened there. She was discovered looking up at the corpse. The shock of that sight I suppose has been too much for her to bear.'

Preeti's voice, once again, hit a rather high and accusatory note. 'At the cost of repeating myself, I have to recommend urgent psychiatric care and that too as soon as possible. You cannot very well leave her here for the duration of her contract.'

Anaida thought it better once again to stay silent.

'I don't think you are quite getting the gravity of this situation. Look, she cannot even talk. So, you needn't worry about her revealing the details of your operation and...'

Karan interrupted, 'It is okay. I shall speak with Ms Adams...'

Preeti had had enough. 'Dr Rathore, do we have a problem working together? Because whenever I open my mouth, you seem to butt in. Is it because I am young? Or is it because I am a woman?'

Karan kept his cool, almost as if he had been expecting this outburst for the last few minutes. With an agreeable smile masking his emotions, he said, 'Let me assure you that I respect you professionally. But the thing is, you are asking questions which Dr Gupta either cannot answer or does not have the authority to reply to.'

Anaida looked fearfully up at where she thought the cameras were.

Karan continued, 'As it is, we are kind of looking over her shoulder, and I would feel, if I were in her shoes, resentful of our presence. She has been doing a great job under the circumstances and subjecting her to questions that are not hers to answer merely creates more stress.'

Preeti closed her eyes and took a deep breath. *Control yourself. Now. Do not lose it here.*

Karan pointed to the exit. 'Now, if we could go and meet Jaal. There is nothing much more to do here. Right, Dr Singh?'

Preeti walked ahead, neither responding to the question, nor making eye contact with either of the two. Anaida looked at Rathore and mouthed silently: 'Thank you.' Rathore nodded his head in acknowledgement.

Anjali and Akshay stood together in the lift as it sped down to Level 1, the place where the structure was. Anjali shuffled from one foot to the other, periodically looking up at the fluorescent light above, if only to avoid having to make eye contact with Akshay More.

They had been joined by a man from the engineering division. In an orange jumpsuit and unruly hair, he looked more a boy than a man. Could not be more than twenty. He had given Akshay the equipment he had asked for, with an awed smile and a hushed 'Sir, are you from Princeton?' In response, he had got a rude grunt and an angry scowl from Akshay. No 'thank you' for the equipment. Not even a polite smile.

From the way he strutted about with his chest thrust out in front of him to the way he looked down at the world arrogantly from his beak, Akshay More was a prick, in every sense of the term. Anjali had no doubts about that. A decade ago, if someone had been as openly rude as Akshay More had been to this junior miner, she would have sheared his feathers off before he could get another squeak out. But now she had changed. Changed a lot.

She tried to compensate for Akshay's brusqueness by being polite to the young kid. 'So, what's your name?' she asked as they stepped out of the lift.

'Zak, assistant research scientist in the materials lab,' he said with an eager smile. Had he ever combed that hair, wondered Anjali, looking at the untidy mop.

'So, how long have you been here?'

'Oh, ever since the project began.'

'Must be a long time. Don't you find it difficult staying like this, totally cut off from the world?'

'Me? The world outside is way too crazy. Don't you think so? Like you are walking down the road, three people come over to you and run a knife through your eye. For what? No other reason than the joy of taking away something that you will never get back. Miss that? No, madam.'

'But people do have families outside, right? Wife? Children? Don't they miss them?'

Zak moved his right palm over his head, smoothing the hair down. 'From what I have seen, many people actually like it this way. They say it's the money. But I think different. Money is just an excuse. Most of them are too afraid to say or even accept to themselves how glad they feel to be away from those they claim to love.'

Akshay, who had been walking behind Zak, broke his silence. 'This guy here is a cynic. How refreshing.'

'Well, sir, we do miss our family from time to time. But this is not as bad as you might think it to be. Life here has a pattern. There is also the daily motivation – of hitting your earning targets. Together they do a pretty good job of keeping you... well, I wouldn't say "happy" but definitely... well, I guess I don't know what to call it.'

Akshay touched Zak's forearm, a gesture of chumminess as genuine that of an insurance salesman's. 'Come on, don't lie. You guys do get messages to your family outside, don't you? There must be some underground operation here that our Lilith madam does not know about.'

Zak was heartwarmingly sincere. 'No, sir. It is just not possible. There are no towers anywhere and the hatches to the top are always monitored. Plus, we wouldn't risk it. Too much money to lose if you do not play by the rules.'

Anjali admired Zak's professionalism. His voice betrayed not a bit of discourtesy towards Akshay, despite the rather intrusive probing. They walked a while quietly down a long passage.

'So, what do you think of what's been happening for the past two days?' Akshay asked, with a conspiratorially dramatic lowering of voice.

Zak's face darkened a shade. 'I wouldn't know sir. I was not in the group. But yes, nobody in that team has had it easy ever since. I'm sure you know all about it. Cannot tell you anything more, I'm afraid.'

They were now in front of a gigantic metal hatch. Zak seemed slightly relieved that the conversation had ended. 'From here, we enter Active Area 2, where the digging is actually going on. Outside the door, you are technically outside the installation. We won't have temperature control. It might get slightly warm.' He smiled, enjoying some private joke. 'You will be entering one of the tunnels that we have dug just a few minutes after you pass the door. The path will be illuminated... so no need to carry lights. But you do have to wear these gas masks.'

Anjali asked, 'Weren't the miners wearing gas masks when the structure was exposed? If they were, why are we looking at poisonous gases as a cause?'

Akshay looked at the gas mask in his hand. 'These are pretty sad. For an operation that's supposedly spending so much money, these seem more like Halloween masks than serious mining equipment. By the way, I wouldn't be just looking for gases but also for bacteria. There are life-forms, nasty ones at that, which are found to live in suspended animation for thousands of years deep inside the earth. Then you shift stuff about and they come back like a bad dream. I just hope the lab upstairs will be able to do the cultures I need. Ah, well, if they can't... it won't be my problem then.'

Zak put on his mask. So did the other two. They stepped out.

Anjali was instantly enveloped by a burst of intense heat. Red mine-safe lights were periodically visible, arranged like floor-lights in an aeroplane, imbuing the whole cave with a crimson otherworldly hue. Striated red and black shadows reminded her of the company logo.

She missed the cold clamminess inside. It was better than this dry, claustrophobic heat.

Anjali was no stranger to digs or to extreme temperatures, having worked painstakingly in the heart of insanely hot Madhya Pradesh. She had never felt this breathless though, almost as if she were wrapped in seven blankets and tied up. Perhaps it was the knowledge of the thousands of tonnes of rock looming over her head, silently threatening to bury her, that made her gasp desperately for air. Then she thought about the flimsy gas mask and the possibility of dangerous particles. Immediately regretting the deep breaths she had taken, Anjali stood, trying to collect herself.

Zak spoke. His voice had changed, no longer as cheerily wholesome as before. 'Madam, I am sure you feel it. I noticed how you stopped.' He was speaking deliberately slow, almost as if he wanted to let every word sink in.

'No, it's just, I feel...'

'There is no need to go inside the cave.'

Anjali could not believe she heard right. 'Excuse me?'

'Madam, there are no cameras or bugs outside. They won't know anything. Just stay here awhile, then go back and tell them some bullshit. Not that they plan to listen to anything you have to say.'

Akshay asked, 'So you think I should screw your boss? As I said, this man is a cynic.'

Zak came closer. 'I know they are paying you a lot. Money to them is not a problem. However here is my question – how much do you value your soul?'

He pointed to the cave. His eyes, revealed by the transparent slit of the mask that allowed him to see, glowed with an aura of hysteria, reflecting the redness of the cave in front. 'The rock-teeth above, the red tongue, the darkness that frames it, the heat coming out from the throat – tell me sir, does that not remind you of a mouth?' Zak croaked, 'Inside is the heart of the devil. Go back.'

Akshay's cockiness seemed to have disappeared for a second, but he remained as sarcastic as before. 'The only way I am going to lie to your boss is if the devil pays me more. I am for sale, but only to the highest bidder.'

Zak shook his head. 'I see. Mockery. What we do not understand, we make fun of. The way of the world, sadly.'

'Dr Menon, our friend seems to have watched a few too many horror movies in his time and is a first-class philosopher to boot. Deadly combination, I say.' Akshay guffawed loudly expecting to hear a confirming snigger from Anjali.

To his surprise, Anjali stayed silent, staring at the red light. 'Let's go in', she said, almost with an air of resignation, before she started walking towards the abyss.

Akshay followed. His sneering laugh died away in the darkness.

The room was submerged in total blackness, save for a solitary halogen light suspended from above. Bathed in streams of whitish-blue lay a middle- aged muscular man secured to a bed, his skin tinged bloodlessly marble, his gleaming eyes following the new arrivals like a panther waiting to spring.

Anaida moved slightly closer to the bed, as gingerly as if approaching a wild animal in a paper cage. Preeti had been keenly observing Anaida's hands. The trembling had definitely become more pronounced.

'Hello, Jaal. Management has sent two experts from outside – Dr Preeti Singh and Dr Karan Rathore. They are here to help you.'

Jaal studied the new arrivals, struggling against the heavy restraints, trying to twist his body from one side to the other.

Preeti looked down at the man. Her mind rewound many years back to her childhood. Grandfather had brought a stray pup for her to play with. Toby, she had called him. Some of her most pleasant childhood memories were with Toby, running through the park each chasing the other, snuggling together under the mild winter sun, rolling his floppy ears in her fingers till he whimpered in pleasure, Toby's wet black nose rubbing against hers.

They would hide in the closet, clutching each other in fear as her parents fought, cringing every time a plate clanged to the ground or a vase was smashed against the wall. Then father left for good. Mother began to leave in the evenings and come back late at night with strange men, too busy to tell her a bedtime story.

Toby never left her. Always a hand away, curling himself into a ball right next to her feet, his head would rest peacefully on her toes, the only comfort a little girl needed.

Then one day, Toby changed. Grandfather had tied him to the wall, and he had lain there, struggling to break free of the leash, baring his fangs and barking. Preeti remembered the crazed eyes, unfeeling and cold. She had gone to pet him. He had snarled violently, almost trying to bite off her hand. Grandfather had dragged him away. She had gone up to her room, trying to blot out the sounds of Toby's nails scratching the floor and of his violent barking echoing through the house. She had buried her head in her pillow and cried.

She knew she was now truly all alone, her only friend gone. And worst of all, she would never know why he hated her.

Jaal had the same crazed look in his eyes. From somewhere far away, she heard once again the scratching of sharp nails, reverberating through the years of pain.

She shuddered. Putting on her best detached psychiatrist voice, she said, 'Hello, Jaal. How are we doing today?'

Karan stepped back, letting Preeti take control.

Jaal stopped struggling. He looked straight up at the ceiling, not making eye-contact with Preeti. 'Wrong question.'

'Excuse me?'

'You heard what I said... slut... wrong question.'

Preeti was taken back. Yet she tried to keep that from showing. 'So, what is the right question then?'

'It should be "How are you doing today?" Not we.'

Preeti was used to her patients being aggressive. 'I get your point. My mistake. How are you today?'

Jaal cackled, the blue veins in his neck bulging out angrily against his pale skin. 'I was doing bad till you two came. Now, I feel great.'

'So now, let us go over the events of the past two days, shall we?'

Jaal was in no mood to answer the question. 'You know why I feel great?'

'No, you tell me.'

''Cause I see in front of me two dead fucks. You do know, don't you, that we are all going to die inside here,' Jaal laughed aloud. A howling kind of laugh.

'Why do you feel we are all going to die here?' Preeti adjusted the slender metal rim of her glasses.

'Because I was there. I touched it. I saw what is inside that place. There is only death. Revenge. Pain.'

Jaal tossed his head from side to side, his body stretching hard against the restraints. His eyes popped open. A wave of some sort of energy went through him, his knees, waist and chest spasming one after another. The viciously aggressive man had suddenly changed instantly into a shrivelling mess.

'Help me. Save me. Please. I beg of you. They are coming for me. Please.'

Jaal lunged forward, his legs jackhammering against the bed. Preeti moved back two steps at the suddenness of the movement. Anaida was approaching with a syringe. Karan caught her by the arm and gestured for her to stand back. His gentle voice broke through the tension. 'We can only help you if you listen to what we say. First, just tell us what happened when the structure was discovered. You were there, right? You were the leader of the team.'

Jaal sank back to his bed. Closing his eyes for a second, he clenched his fists trying to bring a level of self-control. 'We had fallen slightly behind schedule. Since they link our pay to it, we were working double hard. One of the rock-faces had been really stubborn. Full power had been given to the drills. It fell... but after a lot of effort.' He moaned. 'I wish it hadn't.' Jaal seemed to have forgotten what he was saying, looking straight into the halogen lights. For a minute, he stayed silent. Then he was back. 'But right behind the rock was something we had not expected to find.'

Karan asked, 'The shrine?'

'I don't know what it is. It is not like any shrine I have seen. Perhaps you have seen one where there are carvings of big-tittied sluts being impaled on gigantic cocks but I haven't.'

Preeti cringed at the language, the flushed face betraying her intense distaste.

'What surprised me most of all was that our instruments had never detected this structure before. As a matter of fact, I was calibrating my machines when we heard a scream. That was when we saw old Abdul had got his hand stuck in one of the hand-drills. You do know that the way those things are built, it is almost impossible for this to happen accidentally – the drill cannot start when it is open.'

'Accidents are just like that. Accidents,' said Preeti.

'No, they aren't. Why is it easier to believe that a machine, designed not to operate when it is open, will accidentally start on its own, than it is to believe it was caused by that hideous building? Why is it easier to believe that everything works in the universe as a happy consequence of randomness than it is to believe that someone makes it go that way? People like you who disbelieve are motherfucking idiots. You will die. The world will be better off for it.' The aggressive Jaal was back. Advanced schizophrenia, thought Preeti.

Karan's voice lost none of its calmness. 'Okay, Jaal. I understand I am stupid. But what happened then? Why did you try to kill yourself?'

'Because I had seen what lay beyond the dome. There are shadows there, live shadows, shadows of people you know, shadows of the things you did. Angry shadows. That rock was what lay between us and those shadows. I broke the rock. I let the shadow in.'

Preeti looked at Karan. 'Classic case of delusional paranoia brought upon by the interpretation of an accident as some kind of act of God... I will be back to take a better look.' Preeti turned around, as if to leave.

Karan stepped out of the darkness and stepped closer to Jaal's bed, into the circle of light. 'So during dinner, who tried to kill you? The shadows?'

Preeti looked up at Karan. *So, he wants to indulge in this man's fantasies. That kind of therapy approach almost always ended up going in circles, in her experience.*

'No, no. I am too smart for them. You see, the shadows – they don't want to just kill you. They want to see you dance. They want to see you wag your tail.' Jaal shook his finger to show the action of a tail wagging. 'Once they have amused themselves by seeing how far you are prepared to lower yourself in order to stay alive, then they kill you. And they laugh. Ohhh, that laughter...' Jaal shook his head violently again trying to beat his chest with his head.

'But you see, sir, I tried to deprive them of the pleasure. I tried to win. But I couldn't...' He started to weep inconsolably.

Anaida looked at Karan again. Karan nodded his head. The sedative was still not needed. 'So, tell me more about these shadows. Whose shadows did you see? Do you know any of them?'

Jaal fell silent. He was still crying, his chest shaking with the intensity of his sobs.

Preeti sided up to Karan. She whispered loudly, 'Where are we going with this? Asking him to explain his delusions will only make him conjure up more fantastical things to justify the original delusions. This does not work, Dr Rathore.'

Karan ignored Preeti totally, his eyes fixed upon Jaal who had calmed down somewhat. 'It was many years ago. I was nineteen then. Or was it eighteen? Don't remember very well. One night, Uncle came to our place. He was not really our uncle, we just called him that because he would give us kids some money for our fun and games. He would provide protection from the cops whenever they hauled us to the lockup. In return, we would do small jobs for him, like pasting his posters, getting people to vote for him, knocking the teeth out of his opponent's supporters – you know small things...'

Karan was now in command. 'What kind of fun and games are we talking about?'

'Oh, nothing much. Just some drinking and dancing, maybe smoking some stuff...'

'I get it. So, what did Uncle do at your place?'

'He talked with a lot of passion about how our gods, our very way of life was under threat. I had never seen him like that ever before. He was normally a very peaceful guy. Uncle gave all of us something or the other. Me – I got a sword. It was one fine piece of metal. With that in hand, we set out into the night.'

Karan's voice was hypnotic. 'How did you feel?'

'I felt great. No more doing small muscle jobs for a few rupees or a bottle of cheap liquor. Now I was in God's army on my way to do His work. You would not know how it feels... old man... working for a cause greater than one's own hunger and thirst.'

Karan concurred. 'Yes. I have no idea. So, what happened then?'

'The first house we stopped, we attacked from all sides. The people inside had been forewarned. They had barricaded themselves. But we were prepared too. LPG cylinders were brought in a truck. We lit them up and threw those burning motherfuckers right into the house. Oh, those poor bastards. They had no chance. They came running out right into our midst.'

White froth was now running down the front of his lips. He licked it away with a slurping sound. 'Some of us had dragged their women out. It didn't really matter what age they were, I guess. All of them could be fucked. And they were. Their screams. You should have heard them scream, echoing through the night. You could even hear it above the bursting cylinders and the general din. It was that loud.'

Karan caught Preeti's reflection in a small mirror on the wall. She was quivering with rage. Karan quietly stood between her and Jaal. 'And did you also enjoy the women, Jaal?'

'No, no, not me. I don't use God's work as an excuse to wet my wood.'

He looked sideways leeringly at Anaida and then went back to looking at the ceiling, desperately trying to keep the storm inside him. 'I had been given a sword and was damned if I was not going to use it. An old man leapt out of a burning room through the window, right in front of me. I caught him by his hands. He kept saying – "No, no, son, have mercy on me. I am like your grandfather".' Jaal trembled his voice, obscenely mimicking the old man. 'I said nothing. I just gripped my sword and swung it as hard as I could. The swoosh through the air was beautiful, like a perfectly timed six.' Jaal's eyes lit up. 'Something hit the ground with a dull thud. It was as if a jackfruit had dropped from a tree. Before I could move, it splattered all over me, like a tubewell bursting on a hot day. Warm blood, glorious blood gushed out.'

Karan probed further. 'So that felt good?'

'Like you would not believe. I was God. Life and death. Both in these hands. Do you think being God feels good?'

Karan thought for a second. 'Yes, I think it does.'

'I just went swinging the sword at every bastard who came in my path. Sometimes for variation, I would plunge it into a stomach. Sometimes I would do it from the back.'

'You didn't feel at the time that this was wrong, I suppose?'

'No, of course not. Everybody was doing it. Not just that, they were putting on a show. Some of them were putting tires on people right on the street and setting them ablaze. Some others were making them get in lines and bashing their heads in with lead pipes. Necessity is the mother of invention, they say. Cruelty is the father. I say that.' Jaal went through a weak tremor. 'I was at least being merciful dispatching the vermin quickly. If what I was doing was so wrong then why was God letting it happen?'

'You still didn't tell us why you tried to cut your throat during dinner. What you just told us was that you have killed many people.'

'Old man, do you have a whore charging you by the minute waiting in your room? What's your hurry? I am coming to it.'

'Sorry, Jaal. Do continue.'

'After that, me and three others took a jeep and went to a place Uncle had told us we would not be expected. We were not. It was a small house. I didn't know it at that time, but these people were sitting on a plot of land which the local building promoters wanted vacated. What I did know was what Uncle had told us – that they hated people who believed in our God.'

'The family had no idea what hit them. They were sitting for their evening meal. There was a mother, one daughter and three sons. The people with me dragged the daughter outside, kicking and screaming. Put her in the jeep. Fuck, she looked sweet. Tits like lemons.' Jaal paused. A minute. Then another. Preeti came forward to say something, Karan motioned her away.

'The mother held her three sons to her chest. None of them were more than ten. She was swearing at us first and then started pleading. What a hoarse, ugly voice she had. I pulled one out from her grasp and finished him off with one blow. One fucking savage blow. The second one took three. There was a lot of fight in him. The little fucker just would not die quietly.'

Preeti whispered, 'Why are you letting him continue this sickness?'

Karan sat in rapt attention. He did not reply. 'By that time, I was in full rage. The mother was just sitting in the corner wailing. I took her third son from her and held him by the arm. Then pulled her up by her hair and made her sit at the table. Asked the bitch if she was hungry. She kept bawling and beating her chest. I took her eldest son's severed head, put it on her plate, and told her if she wanted her last son to live, she should finish her meal by mixing it with his blood. That sure caught her attention.'

Preeti left the room. She had had enough. Jaal continued unabated. 'What was amazing was that she didn't protest. She actually stopped crying. And then started eating. To be honest, I don't remember much except her eyes. She kept looking at me, her finger pushing the rice into her mouth now soaked with her son's blood.'

'What happened to her and the last son?'

'I killed them too.'

'Then what?'

'Nothing. Nothing happened. Some boys got arrested and were released in a few days. The cops never came for me. Uncle became a minister a year later. I got a really good job, thanks to his recommendation. Everything was fine.'

Jaal once again gave a savage lunge at his restraints and lay still once again, tears running down his pockmarked cheeks. 'Everything was fine till the night that thing came out. I was sitting to eat when my food... I am not making this up, sir... my food turned red. And then reflected in the steel tray I saw those eyes. No mistake. Those eyes. The eyes of the mother. The three kids. The old man. They were surrounding me. And then a number of people I could not even make out. It was a dark night and I had not seen their faces. But I knew who they were. I stood up and threw away the plate.

'And then I heard a voice. It was the mother's.'

'What did she say?'

'She said: *Why*? That's all she said. It was then I knew it. They were here. All of them. To ask me *Why*? Kill me they will. That they are going to do as sure as I have a dick. But not before I answer that question. *Why*? I am not a brave man, sir. I took the knife and tried to punish myself, slit my neck the same way I had slit theirs. I figured if I did that to myself, then perhaps they would go away. Perhaps they would find their peace. But they just laughed. All of them in unison. Ever since that, they have been here. Everywhere. In the room. Outside. Inside. Looking.'

Preeti was standing outside gesturing at Karan to come out. Karan got up from his stool. 'So why did you do it, Jaal? Why?'

'That's what I am truly afraid of. I just don't know. I really don't know.' He started weeping again.

Karan shook his head sadly and strode out quickly without once looking back.

And there it was. A semi-quadrant of a dome peeking out of the ground, just where the drill machine had knocked out a gigantic chunk of the cave. Most of the structure still remained embedded in the rockbed, unseen to the eye. But even the little that was revealed was enough for alarm bells to go off in Anjali's mind.

This is all wrong. All totally wrong.

First of all, it was buried way too deep. She did not know of any ancient structure from recorded human history found so far below the ground's surface. Second, as far as she knew, there were no records of any civilization this old in this area. Though she would need radiocarbon dating to determine the age, her gut feeling told her that this would predate the earliest discovered structures in India – Mohenjo-daro and Harappa. And yet, its construction and the texture of the rock, glistening and smooth, reflecting the red light, nothing like she had ever seen before in monuments of comparable antiquity.

In normal circumstances, a discovery like this, one that rewrote accepted knowledge, would have made Anjali ecstatic. It would definitely make her career, a career that Dr Pande and his acolytes had tried, with varying degrees of success, to suffocate.

But this was too beyond the pale to be not treated with scepticism. Hoaxes were not unheard of in archaeology. Ancient statues sometimes appear out of nowhere and within a month, tourism booms as a happy consequence. Professors, three months before they come up for tenure, magically discover ancient artefacts. Here, however, things were different. There was no motive of economic or academic gain. If anything, the discovery of this structure had been of immense inconvenience to the mine-owner. Plus, getting something of this size immersed in solid rock seemed to be quite impossible indeed. No, this was as real as real could be. That bothered Anjali even more.

Some sick mind or a number of them had come up with the panels on the dome wall. To call them revolting would be an understatement.

It was not the nude female figurines that made Anjali's stomach churn. Nude sculptures of women on the walls of temples in India were not uncommon, emblematic as they were of ancient India's veneration of the sexual act as a religious experience.

Here, though, it was different. The nude women on the walls were not having sex. No. They were being tortured, maimed and brutalized in the most gruesomely imaginative ways possible. The effect was accentuated by the fact that the figures had been carved into the dark rock expertly, making them tremendously life-like. It almost looked like these were real people who, while writhing in immense agony, had been frozen into the rock in a state of eternal torture. Not just frozen, but also shrunk to a quarter of their sizes, as a final indignity. Anjali shivered, despite the heat.

'Snuff.' Akshay More's voice made her turn towards him. 'Snuff is a kind of erotica,' he continued. 'Too hardcore for women I suppose. It involves the mutilation and torture of females.'

Anjali focused her attention back to the frescoes. Akshay continued unabated. 'There is this whole underground movie thing where they kidnap women, torture and cut them up on film and then sell the tapes to those who go for these kinds of things. I saw it once in a movie, forget which... it had that guy from...'

'*8mm*. Nicolas Cage and Joaquin Phoenix. Directed by Joel Schumacher. Yes, I know what snuff is.'

Anjali gave Akshay a long and hard look through her mask. *Too hardcore for women. This man is possibly a bigger idiot than I thought.* Her voice betrayed nothing of what she felt.

'Snuff isn't something that's very new. Torture of women for sexual gratification has a long history stretching back to Roman times. Caligula is of course the name that first comes to mind. But he was not the only one. And not even the worst. Like him there were many emperors and nobles who, growing up on a diet of debauchery, had their fancies turned towards the more extreme, once they found that ordinary sexual activities had lost their ability to arouse. Turkish Sultans were known to cut off the breasts of women and drown them in the Bosporus for nothing other than the kick they got out of it. It is just that I have never seen such explicit sculptures anywhere in the world, and certainly not in India.'

Akshay was setting up his instruments and collecting readings. But it was obvious that he was less drawn to that task than he was to the carvings. 'I do not know whether it is so much violence towards women or violence in general that people find so attractive,' he mumbled absentmindedly.

Anjali stretched out her right hand to touch one of the gruesome panels. She was expecting the cold hardness of unfeeling rock. Instead she felt throbbing heat, almost as if she had touched living flesh. Pulling her hand back, she looked to see if Akshay had noticed her reaction. He had not. He was going on.

'I remember, once, many years ago, a thief had been caught in our neighborhood. He had been tied to the lamppost and people were raining blows on him. His head had been split open, and the wretch was crying for mercy. Yet they went on targeting exactly the spot where he was bleeding like a pig. The people who were doing this were not crazy kings who have had too much fun for their own good. They included the aunty who would call us to her house and give laddoos, the uncle who would play cricket with us and a kid who was barely a few years older than me. Even my dad, who was not a violent man at all, stood around, cheering the crowd on. I remember what he was saying "The police will only let the bastard go. Teach him a lesson he will not forget." I also did not feel at all bad for the man at the time. I was only twelve then. Was it the violence or the helplessness of the thief that was goading the crowd on? Or a sense of perverted justice? I have no idea.'

Akshay fell quiet, lost in his own thoughts. Then he spoke again. 'So, Zak was right. The heart of the devil – is that what this is?'

'Whether this is the heart of the devil or whether the person who made this has the heart of the devil I do not know. What I am pretty sure of is that this structure is immensely old. Other than that, I am pretty clueless.'

'Demon worship...'

'Demon worship in India? Unlikely. We have never really had a concept of absolute evil in our culture – even mythic villains like Ravana and Dushashana are nothing but flawed characters, wronged by circumstances or by their own failings. But definitely not pitch black.'

Anjali craned her neck closer to the rock, taking care not to make physical contact with it. What had looked like random marks in the rock, a sequence of arbitrary lines and dots, seemed to have a pattern to them. The pattern of a script. If she was not mistaken, there were captions to the panels, written in the Palaeo-Hebrew alphabet.

It was wrong. All wrong. All wrong.

Anjali needed to share this, even with the stranger who was with her. 'This is the weirdest thing I've seen today. And I have seen a few.'

Akshay moved in closer. 'What?'

Anjali pointed to a panel. 'These panels have captions in Old Hebrew, a nearly extinct language.'

'Old Hebrew? Isn't that from the Middle East? Ancient Jews and stuff? What's that doing in Rajasthan?'

'Yes, I know. Quite bizarre.'

'Can you decipher what it says?'

Akshay looked up. The panel above was gruesome in the extreme. It was a carving of a naked woman impaled on a tapering pillar. It did not need much imagination to realize that the pillar represented a phallus. The woman's breasts were tilted up at an insane angle. Her eyes were closed and her mouth open, the lips twisted to the side as if in the middle of an earth-shattering shriek. Whether it was in monstrous agony, or in rage, or in pleasure, he could not decide. It was obviously the intent of the sculptor to leave all possibilities open.

Perhaps the artist meant to say that they were essentially the same.

Anjali broke the silence. Her voice echoed in the cave. 'Those that are in passion shall be overwhelmed.'

Akshay looked at Anjali with a start. 'Excuse me?'

'That is what I think this one says.'

They now moved to the adjoining panel. In it there was a topless woman sitting at what looked like a judge's podium. Her breasts were being held up by the table and she had a hammer in her hand. Her face, like all the others', was also twisted in a scream. But it was clear that this was not a scream of pain, but of anger. Right behind her was a gigantic hammer, poised to drop on the woman.

Anjali kept looking intently at the script, struggling with the translation. 'Those that judge shall be judged.'

The next one had a woman on all fours, her behind raised obscenely. The artist seemed to have taken a perverted delight in carving her bottom, thought Akshay, in the same way that teenage boys delight in bathroom art, making exaggerated sexual caricatures of lady teachers and female classmates. Her legs and arms were tied to horses who were galloping away, pulling her limbs apart from their sockets. Despite that, there was an expression of bliss on her face, as if she was welcoming her fate.

Anjali spoke, her voice strangely calm and unemotional, like a doctor delivering a verdict on a patient. 'Those that ravish shall be ravaged.'

A woman stood in the next panel, straight and proud. Her head was tilted towards the sky her hands outstretched. Her tongue was out, forked and elongated in a lascivious way as if she was fellating an invisible object. Behind the figure was a gigantic snake which had wrapped itself round the woman's nether regions. It was mimicking her expression, its tongue also vulgarly stretched out, about to enter the woman's ear.

'Those that poison shall be poisoned,' Anjali sighed.

The next was slightly different. For once the woman was not nude. And that was her punishment. She was wrapped from head to toe in a cocoon that was attached to a pole. The only things that could be seen were her eyes and lips.

'Fuck, man. Her lips are stitched together. And there are needles through her lids, just to keep her eyes open. What in the name of…?'

Akshay left the question hanging.

Anjali merely said, 'Those that watch shall be made to watch'.

Finally, they arrived at the last panel that could be made out, the others having been worn away by age. It was very different from the others. Here, the woman was clothed, in a long flowing gown. Not just that, but of all the carvings on the dome her garment was the only thing that was coloured, in a perfect white.

Anjali said, 'That paint is made from grinding white rock. Very interesting, but once again makes no sense. But at least that is very typical to Rajasthan.' Their attention went back to the figure. The lady not only had the privilege of being covered but also seemed unfettered by any contraption of torture. She was serene and composed. Surrounding her, however, were three black shadows, keeping their distance, maintaining a perimeter.

Anjali knitted her brow. 'Very, very strange. This one actually has nothing written under it.'

Akshay looked up at the panel. The lady in the flowing white robe struck a chord somewhere deep inside. It reminded him of something. Or someone. His eyes stayed on her for such a long time that Anjali noticed too. Akshay realized he was being watched. He quickly collected himself.

'Whew. Quite a freak show here.'

'To that I will agree.' Anjali stepped back. Right at the centre of the structure was a scribble in a straight line. She squinted her eyes. There was another message, one that she had not seen before. 'We were in your past. Your futures will be with us.'

Anjali exclaimed aloud, 'So very interesting. An actual *memento mori*.'

'Mmm, what does that mean? You have lost me again.'

Anjali loved lecturing, especially to oversmart young men who thought they knew everything.

'A *memento mori* is Latin for *remember you will die*. It is artwork that exists to remind people of their mortality and of the wages of sin. The most famous *memento mori* remains a set of controversial paintings by Nicolas Poussin depicting two pastoral scenes of matchless beauty. In it there is a phrase *Et in Arcadia ego* which is Latin for *I exist even in heaven.* This is interpreted, among other things, as a reminder that death or evil is present in the most beautiful of places. Other famous *memento mori* are Michael Wolgemut's *Dance of Death* or *Danse Macabre*, a disturbing work of art that is still not a patch on this nasty thing we see in front of us.'

'You are quite knowledgeable...'

Anjali felt the familiar tightening at the base of the back of her neck and the telltale clenching of the shoulder. It was not the first time she had been at the receiving end of this kind of male condescension. As one of her friends used to say 'A pretty woman is by default dumb. And you are prettier than most.' Many years ago, she would have shown this twerp his place. It wouldn't have been pretty.

But now she just let it pass. *I am different now. Or at least I hope I am.* 'Wow. What excitement this will create in a conference of bone-collectors.'

'That it will.'

'Good for you. Your career is made. Bad for that lady though. You are not going to let them blow this away.'

Anjali stayed silent.

'They cannot move this to another place, I am guessing?' Anjali nodded her head. 'Obviously. It's too deep in the rock.' 'But it's quite... I don't know... evil, isn't it?

Anjali stood still, her eyes scanning over the carvings. 'As an archaeologist, I am trained not to judge. I am trained to be objective and rational. Most importantly, I am trained to preserve...'

Not that I would say this aloud, Dr More, but despite my training, despite my better judgement and despite my desire for fame, I sincerely hope that they raze this thing to the ground.

'So, are you always this big a prick or have I just caught you on an off-day?'

Eleven years had passed since Akshay had last seen her. Yet the haughty lift of the eyebrow, the slight flaring of the nostril, her supreme faith in the effect she had on men and the bludgeon of a tongue had remained the same. Preeti Singh. Like the touch of ice-cold ice cream on an exposed cavity, she still sent a tingling sensation down his nerves, a raw throbbing pain that was addictive in its hold, compelling him to reach out for another scoop, knowing fully well that things would just get worse.

They had gone to college together in Pune. But that was in name only, their worlds being light years apart and not just because he was in chemistry and she in psychology.

She: the most popular girl in college, eliciting aaahs and oohs as she would get down from her chauffeur-driven Mercedes, her heels scrunching the gravel in hurried self-consciousness, scarf flying in the wind, not pausing even once to look to her side. He: the geek in a well-worn cotton shirt with the President's scholarship, his beat-up secondhand bicycle propped up against a tree trunk, watching from afar.

She went to Paris for her summer holidays. He took the local train back to his one-room tenement in Mumbai.

She would hang out after classes at Elixir, Pune's hottest and hippest watering hole, shooting tequila with Vicky and their gang.

While at the same time, he would be spending his evenings lying. Lying to fathers whose sons he taught basic chemistry: 'Ravi will pass this year. Guaranteed.' Lying to fat kids struggling to get a 36 waist up above their knees: 'Trust me, sir. I have been a salesman at Fashion House for some time now. These trousers fit you excellently.' Lying to his mother: 'Don't worry about me. Encash that money order as soon as you can. I have more than enough to take care of myself.' Lying on his bed in the hostel, stomach balanced on a pillow, devouring books on advanced chemistry and biology borrowed from the library.

Their paths had crossed once. It had been the annual prize distribution ceremony. She had been voted Miss Sandham College or something as grandly silly as that. He had done something comparatively insignificant like winning the President's Gold Medal. They had sat on the stage next to each other. He had fumbled and bumbled on about himself and she had politely smiled back.

Today, when she had walked into the conference room, and once again into his life, he had felt that old familiar breathlessness again. This time, however, he had been much more confident. A PhD from MIT and a faculty appointment at Princeton gives you the strength to look Preeti Singh in the eye. The Harrods suit and the Cartier watch also don't hurt. Their hands had shaken each other's. She had taken the seat next to him.

They were equals now.

Preeti of course could not 'place him'. That Akshay had not found surprising. He would not remember himself either, to quote Kevin Spacey from *American Beauty*.

And now a few hours later, they were sitting in Preeti Singh's quarters having a mealtime conversation about good old times. Well not really a conversation, more a one-way monologue from

Akshay. Anyone who had gone to Sandham College knew these stories – the professor who once came to class naked, the female teacher who turned out to be a man, the guard who tried to commit suicide by eating mud.

Not Preeti, she had no idea. Again not surprising, considering that she rarely hung around after class with anyone. The waiting Mercedes would whisk her away before anyone could ask her out for coffee. But today, she appeared interested, smiling mildly from time to time, the 'What next?'-s and 'I never knew'-s providing enough encouragement for Akshay to go on and on.

Then suddenly in the middle of the conversation, this rather blunt accusation had been hurled at him, like an uppercut to his jaw, in the 'devil-may-care' style that Preeti Singh was famous for. After all, it was she who had made college lore by asking a senior professor, 'Sir, do you have a problem talking to my face?' in front of the entire class.

'Emm, excuse me?' Akshay More's carefully cultivated American accent slipped away for a second.

'You were being quite an asshole back there in the conference room.'

'I was?'

'So, is this how you usually are?'

Akshay's first reaction was to say, 'You weren't too polite yourself in the conference room.' But he bit his tongue. After all he could not afford to be as honest as Preeti Singh. God had not been so kind to him.

'I guess I agree with the old doctor, with what he said before. The stress of not knowing why we had been brought here got me a bit testy. All of us have our different defence systems. I guess being an asshole is mine.'

Preeti nodded her head. 'You seem almost a different person now. Nice and warm.'

Akshay did not know what to say. He looked down at his plate hoping the answer would manifest itself there. Preeti meanwhile kept scooping the corn into her mouth. For a slim girl, she did have a ravenous appetite.

Suddenly, out of the blue, she said, 'I came here for the money. I need it.'

'You need money? Wait, that was supposed to be my line!'

It should actually have been. An assistant professor's salary and the occasional consulting gig for pharmaceutical companies paid well. More than well. But they did not fully cover his forays into New York's exclusive circles.

The black-tie charity dinners, the weekends in the Hamptons and the thousand-dollar champagne bottles had bled his wallet dry. Even if he could somehow knock that habit of living large, there were the payments on the house. He had been suckered into buying a cool million-dollar property near Princeton at the height of the housing bubble. Now that the market had tanked, he was finding it impossible to get rid of.

Preeti wiped the corner of her mouth with a napkin. Akshay did the same, once he realized a scrap of vegetable was hanging from the exact same spot on his own lips.

'Yes, yes, I know. How come the Mercedes-riding rich bitch needs the money? That's the question, isn't it?'

Akshay stayed silent.

'Well, the great car and the trips to Milan and Monaco that got me the rich bitch tag in college were all on Ma's money. Not on Dad's.' She grinned self-consciously. 'Actually, I should be careful when using the singular Dad. I have had many dads – three by best count. Ma was the use-and-throw type. Or that's what she thought. It was she who actually got used and thrown away. The last one, he used to be our manager, also cleaned out our accounts for good measure.'

'Sorry. Had no idea. So that's why you suddenly left college.'

A hard smile crept across Preeti's face. She put the bowl to the side and leaned forward. 'Aaah. But that was not the reason I left college. The bankruptcy happened a few years later. You do know why I left, don't you?'

'Well, I mean. People did say things. But they were just that. Things.'

'What kind of things?'

'Not important. As I said, people talk.'

'No, no, honestly. What did you hear? Come on. I know what kind of things were discussed by the guys at the college canteen and below the tree.'

Akshay hesitated, trying to find the appropriate words. 'The rumour was that you got knocked up by Vicky.'

Preeti slurped a spoonful, looking at Akshay intently. 'Uh huh.' She shook her head as if expecting something more.

Akshay thought it best not to say anything. For a few seconds that stretched like hours, they sat in silence.

'I was raped.' The bowl made a large clank on the table as she put it down.

Akshay tried to say something. Preeti raised a finger asking him to not interrupt. 'Hold the "I am sorry" or "I understand the pain". I have come to terms with it now.'

'I... I... don't know what to say. I had no idea.'

'I am surprised you don't know. I was sure somehow the scandal would have got out, despite Ma's best attempts.'

'No. It didn't. If it had, you are right, I would have known.'

'Vicky. The bastard. Got me drugged and then had his way.'

'I thought you were...'

'Doing it with him?' Preeti flipped an eyebrow up. 'No, we were not. He had asked me for sex several times before, but I had refused. A little old-fashioned I suppose. So, he decided to take matters into his hands… the bastard, the little motherfucking bastard.'

'But this never went to court. Right? Else we definitely would have heard.' Akshay could still barely conceal his surprise.

'Of course, it didn't. Family honour and all. Ma, very typically, tried her best to hush it up.'

'You let her?'

'I fought with Ma. A lot. I wanted the fuckface to hang. But he had drugged me so deep I couldn't act as my own witness. Quite an artist our friend, he did not so much as leave any physical evidence of his act. Lawyers said we didn't have a case. And Vicky's lawyers would be far better they figured, his dad being a big-shot diamond merchant and all that... so going against them with what we had would have been suicide.'

A quiet fire glowed in her eyes. 'At least I got my own back on Ma.' She lifted her left hand to show her fingers. There was no ring. 'And never will. Swore off men from that day on.'

She brushed away the hair that had fallen across her forehead. 'There is a reason I am saying this to you. In case you think this dinner-time conversation and all the discussion of good old days may lead to some action... it's obviously not going to.'

Akshay recoiled, 'No, no, nothing like that. Please... I had no...'

'Well, it's only natural to expect that things go somewhere. Just did not want to lead you on. I have been called a cock-tease before. I don't much like it.'

Whether Preeti was being honest or simply showing that she had lost none of the 'I am better than you' arrogance, he could not decide. Akshay urgently felt the need to change the topic of conversation.

'So how did you find Dr Anjali Menon?' asked Preeti.

'Mm... well... where did that question come from?'

'Well, since you weren't being able to change the topic, I had to.' She said with a wry smirk.

'Ah, yes. Very knowledgeable lady...' Akshay did not know what to say. 'I guess... She is okay...'

'Okay... just? I thought you would be more taken with her.' Akshay was curious as to the direction this conversation was taking.

'Such a man's woman, isn't she? You know, keeps eyes demurely downwards, back arched, musical voice, beautiful skin, hair cascading down shoulder-length, all the perfect curves in the perfect places...'

Akshay found the cattiness quite amusing. 'Well, she should not have brought her daughter along. No place for a small paraplegic kid.'

Something flashed in Preeti's eyes, like the twirling edge of a sword. 'I don't think she had any idea of where she was going. Neither of us did.' Shaking her index finger, she said. 'And I like that she brought the girl along – tigress-like possessiveness over one's cubs. Way better than some mothers I know who would just as well stuff their daughters far away from sight.'

'So how was the doctor?' Akshay asked, trying to steer the conversation away yet again, noting the rising emotion in her voice.

'Old stick-in-the-mud. Knows his stuff perhaps but has a problem working with women. Moron.' The anger had not gone away, just found a different target. Now she lowered her voice. 'I find the spook interesting though.'

'Samar, you mean?'

'Yes. In the conference room, his eyes were going all around the table, measuring us up. Something about him that does not quite add up...'

Preeti seemed to suddenly lose herself in thought. Akshay concentrated on finishing his dinner. Suddenly she reached out and grabbed him by his hand. The action took him by surprise, as if cubes of ice had been slipped into his shirt. 'Whoa. That is one ugly scar. How did you get it?' she said, looking down at a massive red angry gash that ran from Akshay's wrist up to his elbow.

Akshay's heart was beating fast. Preeti's skin felt like warm velvet. 'Oh, I thought this was common knowledge at Sandham College. Perhaps not.'

'No, I don't know. What happened?'

'In my first year, I got a little careless in lab. I was conducting what our old Professor Banerjee called *unauthorized experimentation*, trying something I had read in a book, without, of course, quite understanding the basic principles. I ended up setting the lab on fire. Barely escaped being kicked out, my good grades and puppy-dog face possibly helped me there.' He rubbed a finger down the length of the scar, almost contemplatively. 'A small memento of my foolishness. Lucky it was just the hand and nowhere else.'

Preeti seemed concerned. 'Does it hurt? Even now?'

'Off and on. Yeah.' Akshay did not tell her how the damaged nerve cells still sent false signals to the pain receptors, and how many nights he had stayed awake, feeling as if on fire. That would expose him too much to the last person to whom he wanted to be exposed to.

Preeti was still holding his hand, her fingers running gently over his scar, almost involuntarily. 'Some wounds don't heal. Do they?'

Akshay squirmed involuntarily. Realizing suddenly the intimacy of her gesture, Preeti let go and jerked back, almost as if recoiling at this moment of vulnerability. Her face hardened, the mask of haughtiness pulled back in a flash.

Akshay sat still, the steady rumbling in his chest bringing back 9 o'clocks from eleven years ago, waiting for a high heel to step out through an open car door. 'Perhaps they do heal. But only... but only if we allow them to.'

Rec Room 2 was always crowded. Cheap liquor, half-decent music, boisterous conversation and the odd knockout like Tanya – it had essentially everything that one could ask for at the end of a hard day's shift. Now however, it stood morosely empty, like a stadium after a home game defeat. The management had stopped all alcohol; the last thing they needed was drunken disorderliness in a place where even the sober hallucinated.

As he entered Rec Room 2, Samar felt a constriction of his heart. There was no reason for the unease, he had told himself. Far from being reassuring, that seemed to bother him even more.

The first time he had felt this bristling on the back of his neck was when the lift had descended into the Mine. He had dismissed it as the natural anxiety of entering a closed place, deep in the earth, with no idea of what was expected of him. Over the past thirty-six hours the feeling of disquiet had only intensified. The butterflies that had taken permanent residence in his stomach seemed to have dull blades on their wings, scraping his insides with each flutter. It seemed that the fear of the miners had spread like a poisonous puddle all around, sneaking underneath even his mind's door.

One did not have to have a particularly developed sense of empathy to be able to feel the oily blackness of these dark waters. In the course of his security audit, everyone Samar had met had been petrified. To their credit, they did not speak of it. Yet there was no mistaking the way they would leave their sentences unfinished, as if they were too scared to finish them the way they had started it.

He dismissed the fear from his mind. Perhaps he was not so much scared as worried. Worried there was something he was missing. Everything in the facility had checked out fine. His only concern had been the tape of Asgar's final moments. He had watched it again and again, pausing each frame. The way Asgar stood still before descending into the hatch without turning the machine off, the way he looked into the camera – there was something about that which kept gnawing at Samar. Something... something... but what was it?

Samar was about to leave when he noticed that the room was not totally empty. In the corner, half in shadow, sat Karan Rathore. He was not alone. At the same table, Anjali Menon was working furiously on one of the laptops that she had been given, her gold earring sparkling in the half-light. Once Karan Rathore raised his hand in an acknowledgement of his presence, Samar had no choice but to walk over and join them. Not that he particularly wanted to. He was never the chatty type.

Samar pulled up a chair, the screeching sound of the leg scraping the floor echoing through the silent room. Anjali did not look up from her work, oblivious seemingly of his presence. Karan though smiled warmly.

'So, all finished with your inspection?'

'Yes.'

'Well... what's the verdict?'

'I think the documents that were given to us specifically forbade us from discussing our findings with each other till the final debriefing.' Samar regretted the cold sharpness with which that came out. This possibly innocent, well-meaning question deserved a more polite answer. But honestly, he was damned if he was going to get those that watched them angry.

The smile never left Karan's face. 'You are right. Sorry for asking.'

Samar gave a small apologetic cough. He now felt obliged to indulge in small talk. Karan Rathore seemed only too ready to oblige. Not so Anjali, who ignored the exchange, still staring fixedly at the screen and typing on the keyboard.

Karan seemed to notice where Samar was looking. 'Anjali took some pictures of the shrine downstairs for the presentation. And now she just cannot stop obsessing about them. I presume you have been there.'

'Yes, I have.'

'Quite... interesting don't you think?'

'Not really. I have seen bathroom art in high schools which is better. And scarier. Worthless crap if you ask me. What is interesting of course is how it seemingly has affected...'

'Worthless crap?' Anjali breathed heavily, her disgust hitting Samar flush on his face. She looked up from her screen. 'I suppose since history and art aren't really your areas of specialization, you can speak about them without violating your contract.' There was no mistaking the tightening of the shoulders and the harsh pursing of the lips. Anjali Menon was done here. With a shrug, she closed the device sharply and stood up. 'Need to check up on Anya. Will finish this from my room.'

'So, you won't be back before the debriefing?'

'I do not think so.'

She twirled gracefully and left without so much as an acknowledgement for Samar, the brisk pitter-patter of the heels on the smooth floor leaving one in no doubt that she had not been particularly charmed by the company.

Karan smiled wryly. 'You must excuse her. She is a bit touchy about history. And art.' Then as almost an afterthought, he added, 'Plus she has not been the same for many years, after her husband Nikhil's death.'

'You've known her for a while it seems.'

'Oh yes, I knew her husband very well. He used to work in my lab.' Karan propped his chin on his crossed index fingers, looking up at the ceiling. 'You could say Nikhil was my favourite student. So young, so many possibilities, his death such a great loss to the world of science. Nikhil had walked in while a burglary was in progress at his apartment. The lowlife possibly panicked when caught and... oh my god, it was horrible. So needless, so...' He took off his glasses and started polishing them with a handkerchief. 'After this happened, she changed... how much you cannot imagine. Such a happy child she had been before that...'

'I understand...' Samar wondered why the old man was letting it all out. Maybe he needs to justify her rudeness. Maybe he just needed to talk. Old men usually do.

'People say God is merciful. That He is kind. But not to all. Not to all.'

Samar did not reply. Not that he believed in God, but he did not for a second doubt that the world was a heartlessly unfair place. He had seen too much of it to pretend otherwise.

'It would have been one thing if Anya had been born like this. At least we could say – this is how He made her.' Karan pointed upwards. 'But Anya had once been a healthy child, just perfect. He took it away, in front of us all, to make us all suffer, to make us all regret. The cruellest thing in the world, Mr Bose, is the world itself.'

'What happened to Anya?'

'Damned if we knew. This was a year after her father died. In May. Anjali had been at a conference and Anya was with her grandparents. She developed a sudden fever in the evening. By morning, full waist-down paralysis had set in. As if that was not strange enough, the part of the brain that deals with speech also inexplicably shut down.'

'And nothing could be done?'

'No. I took her everywhere, showed her to the best doctors. Nothing they could do. Nothing I could do.' The wrinkles around his eyes twitched.

Samar thought about Sambit. It had been much the same with him. He remembered what Dad had told Ma after he had brought Sambit back from the hospital. Ma had dropped to her knees, banging her head on the railing in anger. Dad had just run his hands through her hair, letting her vent, physically not restraining her in any way. 'It was his fate, Karuna. His fate failed him. Not us.'

'Anjali blamed herself. I have told her many times. I have told her many times that even if she had been there with her, nothing would have changed. But a mother's heart...'

A father's heart too... a father's heart too. Samar knew how sharp a knife regret was. Not a day had passed when he had not held himself responsible for what happened to Reshmi. If only he had been there that day, if only he had not left, if only he had given more attention.

'That's why she always takes Anya wherever she goes... Not that she could have known beforehand, but Anjali should not have brought her here. There's something not right...'

'So, the shrine downstairs bothers you, does it? Like it does the miners?' Samar was intrigued.

Karan got up from the chair, his imposing frame looming like a dark cloud. Leaning slightly forward, the light slanting off his silver-framed spectacles, he said in a soft, almost hypnotically polite voice.

'A shrine is just a pile of stones. And a mine... just a hole in the ground. No, it's not the place that bothers me. It's the people. Always the people. Because true evil', he said tapping the left side of his chest gently, 'the greatest evil... lies deep inside.'

When did I get this old?

An unkempt shrub of white-and-black that passed for a beard, harsh lines radiating out from the corners of his eyes like dry rivers – Samar could barely recognize the man reflected back from the gleaming polished tabletop. There was a time when he used to have a stylish French cut, heavy-framed black glasses and carefully symmetric sideburns – the 'queer poet look' Sunderan and the other burly moustachioed men at Special Operations used to make fun of. Didn't matter what they said of course. He didn't have to sleep with them. What did matter was Anita. He remembered her singing *'Kya karoon Ram, mujhe buddha mil gaya,'* every line framed by her lightly ringing laughter, when she had discovered the first strand of grey on his head. Now, as he ran his fingers through his scalp, there was more white than black there, growing wild like angry weeds. Anita would be dismayed to see how much he had let himself go.

Samar was tired. That could be expected, given that he had been awake for the past thirty-six hours. But it was not the draining tiredness of the kind that he had become used to feeling back home, even when he had been lying in bed almost the whole day. This was like the exhaustion after the end of an exam: the head is woolly, the eyes burn but yet you feel strangely invigorated, looking forward to the vacation.

There would be no vacation for Samar though, nothing even closely resembling any kind of relief. But after many years, he felt he had something that he wanted to do, now that the Pratap Rai Memorial School would be a reality. But first there were other things to be done. The blue pills would be flushed down the toilet; the past few days he had managed just fine without them. He would go out in the sun more often, maybe even do some gardening with Sambit.

Now, if he could only get through the final debriefing session. At the moment, time seemed to be circling around, like water struggling to go down a clogged drain. Dr Anjali Menon was droning on about the structure downstairs, using slides projected on the big screens.

Lilith Adams, he was sure, was not interested in this academic dawdling. The worker's representative, a sloppy overweight pig of a man, sitting next to her with an angry scowl on his face, periodically cracking his knuckles out of nervous agitation, would care even less. They just wanted to know her verdict. Nothing else. Yet Anjali kept going at it, as if she was in front of her class.

Blotting out Anjali's monotone, Samar looked inwards, a technique cultivated from sitting for years in long lectures from ministers and undersecretaries. For some time, there had been something that had been poking at him, like a sharp point of wood below the mattress, ever since he had seen the tape of Asgar's last moments. Yet he had been unable to put his finger on it, tossing and turning over and over again. He flicked through the memory of the past few hours. There was something he needed to follow up on. A question he needed to ask. A place he needed to look at.

No, nothing. Too tired to focus. I am sure it's nothing important.

'Now my recommendations.' Anjali Menon's voice brought Samar back from his thoughts. Finally.

It was another five minutes before Anjali Menon wound her way to a conclusion at last. The structure, despite being almost impossible to place on a timeline, was still one of considerable historic significance. According to the laws of the land, this had to be referred to the Archaeological Survey of India. Relocation was impossible both physically as well as legally. So, her recommendation was an immediate stop-work at the site and a notification to the authorities.

Samar noted the way the blue-uniformed brute's mouth opened in a half-smile, flashing a rather ominous canine. What caught his attention more was the expression on the face of Lilith Adams or more precisely, the lack of any. She sat looking vacantly at the wall, almost as if her soul had floated out of her body.

Cannot blame her. This was boring.

The next person under the spotlight was Dr Akshay More. He pulled up a number of slides. These were so bizarrely technical that Samar felt sure the intent of the presentation was just to overwhelm the audience with the weight of his scientific knowledge, a series of 'Ha, I am smarter than you because you have not the foggiest idea of what I am talking about' sucker punches, which went well with his arrogantly superior demeanour.

The doors of Samar's mind were again closing. An image lay hidden in the shadows. It was important, this much he knew. Like an old tune that refuses to come to the lips, it kept gnawing away.

'I would say, without reservations, that this place is safe from any kind of hallucinogenic organic or inorganic material.' Akshay paused, closed the presentation device and said, 'Not that anything I said made any sense to you all. Now here is what is you paid me for. My recommendation is: Mine on, Ms Adams. Mine on. Make yourself rich. And us too. As for you Mr-Union-Leader-Whose-Name-I-Have-Forgotten, I leave my supporting documentation here for your review.'

The equalizer had come in. It was one-one.

Dr Preeti Singh shot up to attention. Samar felt, looking at the way the presentations had been going around the table in seating order, he should have been next. But Preeti was already loading her slides, without even a look around the table. Karan Rathore tried to say something, looked once at Samar apologetically and then fell silent.

It did not take a prophet to know which way her recommendation was going to come down. Each of her slides was filled with snippets from the interviews she had conducted. They read like extracts from a lurid horror novel. Foetuses being wrenched out from unwilling stomachs. Rivers of blood. Children being sacrificed. And these were the milder ones.

Preeti cautioned against dismissing these testimonials as the ramblings of people with bad dreams. People don't usually have such lucid and internally logical nightmares. They also don't dream when they are awake. Even if they did, there was no way so many people could be having such disturbing waking visions at the same time, unless a root common cause could be assumed.

The worker's representative butted in for the first time. 'What root cause do you think that is? It's that thing, isn't it?'

'I have no scientific basis on which to propose any cause. All I am saying with confidence is that these nightmares are not independent events, there is some single circumstance or event giving rise to all of them.'

What they had on their hands, according to Preeti, was perhaps the most severe case of mass dementia documented in a closed community that she knew of. These people had to be moved out. Now. The conclusion of her presentation was unambiguously dire. Violence could start any moment if mining was allowed to continue.

The hulk in the blue miner's suit was nodding happily. Lilith Adams remained stone-faced.

Samar cleared his throat. The ball was now at his feet. Unlike the others who had a presentation with them, Samar had a report. It was based on a template for inspections that he had used in the past. He ran over the checklist quickly, looking at the PhDs with a pointed *This is the way it is done.* His conclusion had been simple and definite. The installation was secure and no attempts at sabotage had been detected. He didn't need to look at the representative to know he was scowling.

Two-two and it was all up to Dr Rathore.

Karan had neither a report nor a presentation. All he had was height, presence and the weight of his voice. He started with a note of appreciation for Dr Singh and her efforts. He then summarized the examinations he had conducted. There was nothing physically wrong with those who had been at the dig site. No medical evidence of a contagion has been found. However, he did feel that psychologically the workers were not equipped to continue. Given that his terms of reference were simply physiological, that aspect would not influence his recommendation.

Preeti Singh threw up her hand in disgust and looked round the table. 'That's a cop-out, if I ever saw one. Terms of reference?

What kind of slimy legal claptrap is that? You know very well these people are in no mental state to continue, which is all that is important.'

The rich gravelly voice betrayed not a trace of defensiveness. 'What I know is irrelevant. I had been given a frame of reference, that being strictly physiological. You have already given your verdict on the mental state of the employees. Including that in my assessment would be double-counting an opinion. My finding stands. I have not found anything that requires a stop-work.'

Preeti said something in response. The brutish worker's representative voice bellowed like an angry foghorn, defeat not sitting well with him. Lilith Adams' triumphantly crisp voice cut through the noise. Everyone now seemed to be speaking all at once. Samar heard none of it. All that came to his ears was the rapid thump-a-thump of his own heart. His tiredness was gone. He was very much awake.

This was because the thing that had been teasing him for some time now had just come floating out of the dusty dark attic of forgetfulness. It stood under the arc lights of his mind, its intensity flooding his senses.

The late afternoon rays of the sun, long and lazy, had vanished behind the clouds. A winter evening had descended quickly, the fastest thing that happens in Kolkata where, in general, the world spins slow. Reshmi was standing on the path from the door to the gate. Normally there would be Laxman sitting there with his rusty old firearm. But he had gone back to his village and his replacement had vanished, like he did every evening.

'Go back into the house. It's getting late.' Samar had gently admonished Reshmi. The replacement needed to be spoken to firmly, he had thought. Running errands for the neighbors for extra cash had to stop if he wanted to keep working here.

'But Dad, you just came back two days ago. You can't leave now.' She had stood arms crossed, tears streaming down her cheeks. Anita was in the hospital again and Reshmi was worried.

He had wanted to take a few months off to deal with Anita's illness. The communication had come in from Sunderan an hour ago. The mole inside the Prime Minister's Office had turned up dead in a garbage dump fifty kilometres outside New Delhi. All leaves were cancelled, the team needed to reassemble in the capital within twelve hours.

He'd known it would take at least a month before this crisis would be sorted out. He couldn't tell Reshmi that. Much easier to lie. After all, lying convincingly was what he had been trained for. Even if he hadn't, little daughters always trust their daddies. Always.

'I will be back tomorrow morning before you wake up. I promise, darling. Now get inside.'

Reshmi had stood still, weeping silently.

'Now.' Samar had repeated the last word with more emphasis. He had then kissed her forehead, hurried to the car, got behind the wheel and driven away. That had been the last time he had seen Reshmi. The last time he had truly been him.

Since then, Samar had replayed those last few seconds a million times, in dreams and in wakefulness. He had never forgiven himself for being so preoccupied that he did not look back even once to check whether Reshmi had actually walked back into the house. Even more, he had not forgiven himself for heartlessly wiping Reshmi's tears and leaving.

But what had escaped every guilt-soaked re-living had been something else. There had been a person standing near the gate, a person he had never seen before, a person who did not belong to the area. Their gazes had met for a second and then he had dismissed the presence from his mind. This was Kolkata after all and seeing strangers on the sidewalk outside your home in the late afternoon was not something that was worth remembering.

That memory of that silent shadow had, all of a sudden, come rushing back, whistling through the tunnel of time. But why now? What had triggered it? It was the answer to that question which had sent the blood racing through Samar's entire body.

That face. He had seen it again. Very recently.

In the last thirty-six hours. Here. In the Mine.

Samar tried to calm the storm raging inside him. All he could be sure of was that that man was here. Who it was still escaped him, a burning void in his mind.

A gentle hand tapped Samar's shoulder. It was Dr Karan Rathore. 'Not paying attention in class I see.' He wagged his finger engagingly. 'Naughty, naughty.'

'Yes, I suppose it has been a very exhausting few hours.'

'That I will agree it was. Exhausting and stressful.'

Samar got up. 'So school is over then.'

Karan's hand still pressed on his shoulder. 'Not quite.' Was there something wrong?

'Nothing to be alarmed about.' There was a faint reproach in Karan's voice. 'You were totally out of it, weren't you?'

Samar felt sheepish. It did not look good for a two hundred thousand dollars a day consultant to space out during a briefing. As a matter of fact, it was very unprofessional.

Karan filled him in on what he had missed. There had been an agitated verbal cross-fire in which evidently everyone except

Samar had pitched in. From what Samar gathered, Preeti had been outraged, the focus of her anger being equally divided between Lilith and Karan.

Lilith Adams had announced that she was calling an all-hands-to-deck meeting down at the dig site. The decision to restart the dig would be conveyed immediately to the workers. Since all employees would be down on the first floor, the six of them had been requested to stay here in the third-floor conference room till security could come up and escort them outside.

'Yeah, I suppose they are afraid we will steal their silverware. Pity, 'cause I was planning to take my soap and towel.' Akshay said, obviously not too happy at having to wait. 'Ringside view, people. This is all the entertainment we are going to get before we leave.' He pointed to the TV screen on the wall.

Lilith Adams was walking into the large room which opened out into the dig site, the place where the miners changed into their masks. Two Bulgarian guards stood to her side.

The bluish feed, transmitted from a single security camera mounted on the wall some distance above where Lilith stood, was shakily grainy. Even then, one could clearly make out her face and that of the security guards at her side. Through the chatter of the assembled miners flowing up crystal clear via the sound system, tension and anxiety diffused into the conference room, two floors above, like the heat from a distant forest fire.

Preeti shook her head in disbelief. 'This is crazy. I, for the life of me, cannot believe they are going to start drilling right away.'

Anjali had her hand on Anya's wheelchair. 'Honestly, did you think it would be any different? You think with so much money at stake, anyone cares for what we have to say?'

'Yes, of course. This thing was fixed from the start.' Preeti was looking straight at Karan, her lips curled in anger.

'I was not the only person here who could not find anything conclusive. So please stop presuming that I am part of some conspiracy.' Karan looked away to the screen, avoiding Preeti's attempt to stare him down.

Lilith Adams began speaking. She had just gotten one sentence into her speech when a male voice came clear through the PA system. 'I do not want to die here.'

Another voice, more aggressive than the first one: 'Open the gates, whore. I am not going to die here.'

Preeti buried her head in her hands. 'I knew this was going to happen.' Anjali had recognized the boyish, throaty voice. 'That's Zak, isn't it?'

Akshay nodded his head. 'Not quite as polite any more is he? This is the kind of radical change in character you were talking about, Preeti?'

Preeti did not reply.

The security guard behind Lilith made a sudden movement. She kept calm though, and continued summarizing what had just transpired in the meeting. There was yet another interruption. Another voice cut through the airwaves, even more enraged than Zak's. 'This was all a set-up. We don't care a fuck for what those people say.'

'Let's knock down the gates.'

The security guard had unholstered his weapon.

A violent chorus drowned out Lilith's voice. One could make out just one word amidst the din, being repeated again and again.

Kill. Kill. Kill.

The cocky smile had vanished from Akshay's face. 'Fuck, man. They are going to be coming for us now. We need to leave the place.'

Samar agreed. Many years ago, he had been in a diamond mine in Sierra Leone on his first private assignment as a security consultant. There he had seen a miner's mutiny. It had not been pretty.

All of a sudden, Lilith Adams raised her hand showing everyone what she was clutching in her palm. The violent murmurs died down for a moment. 'This is a remote detonator. I had our security staff rig up mining explosives round the shrine. Since none of you agree to drill, I am going to blow this up with my own hand, just to show all of you there is no curse here. Nothing to be afraid of.'

'Did I not tell you how fixed this was? They had been planning to blow up the thing all the time.' Preeti got up in anger, kicked the chair and started moving towards the door.

Lilith's voice was now totally drowned out by the noise. Two of the guards shouldered towards the front, ready with their guns cocked. The camera picked up backs of heads advancing menacingly closer to where the woman stood, like ants crowding around a lump of sugar. *They are going to begin shooting.* Samar knew it now. There was no turning back.

Then it happened. The PA system boomed with the sound of an explosion. The camera trembled. A cloud of smoke and debris curled up from where the chief operations officer of the Mine had just been standing.

Samar felt the blow of a hammer at the base of his stomach. *The bomb had not gone off near the shrine. It had detonated right where all the people were.*

A projectile, thrown up by the impact of the blast, hit the camera with a savage force.

Preeti gasped out loud. Dashed against the camera screen was the lifeless head of Lilith Adams, snapped clean off her body.

Her eyes were fixed straight at those in the room. A smile was pasted on her face, macabre in its incongruity with the violence of her death. Her black hair, radiating outwards, remained stuck momentarily to the glass, framed like a spider in the middle of a web, before it dropped away. Blue static crackled.

The pure pain of those down below shot up through the ground, paralysing those upstairs with its intensity. The earth shook with another, even more violent, explosion.

Then everything went dark.

THE MIDDLE

Samar looked up at the ceiling, his head throbbing with a dull, diffused pain. The light above him flickered and hummed, while in the background, a disembodied mechanical voice swept through the room: 'Aggressive security protocols engaged. System lockdown in progress.'

A familiar sensation of terror seeped through his being, like a blot of black ink on white parchment. He had allowed himself, once again, to become a victim of an accident.

The first time had been fifteen years ago. He was driving on National Highway One in the dead of night. Suddenly, a truck had leapt out at him from the side, its headlights blinding him momentarily. His Honda had floated up in the air, like a matador caught on the horns of a bull. As glass shattered, metal twisted and the world around him went into a tailspin, Samar had felt disassociated from it all, almost as if he was watching someone else in a movie. Recoiling in expectation of agony, he had been surprised by its total absence, swept as he was by a warm sensation, not unlike the buzz after a good shot of rum.

The pain came soon though, as inevitable as the sound of thunder after lightning. But the physical trauma was nothing compared to the mind-numbing sensation of guilt which gripped Samar, an all-consuming flood of self-reproach at having made an error in judgement.

Ever since that, he had avoided driving. Not that he would ever tell anybody, more so because he was after all somewhat of a spy, but every time he needed to make a lane change, his palms would get sweaty on the steering wheel, clutching it more tightly than was needed, obsessively looking over his shoulder at the passing line, endlessly dithering on when to make the move, reminded over and over again how he had never seen that truck coming. If he could have made that mistake once, he could make it again.

He never had though. Not on the road anyway.

For now, his mind raced over what had just happened, trying to take stock of the situation, breathing long and hard, trying to keep from hyperventilating. Lilith Adams was dead. Something terrible had happened down at the dig site. There had been two explosions. Possibly more. What had happened to the people downstairs? What about the people in the room? Were they dead too?

He felt sick. Very sick.

A small hand gripped his wrist firmly. It was Anya, sprawled stomach-down on the ground, right next to him. Her wheelchair was a foot or so away, tipped over to the side, its wheels still moving round and round.

Looking into her eyes, Samar could sense how scared she was. He tried to calm her down by saying 'It's all right.' But then he realized she had beaten him to it, consoling him wordlessly with the palm tightening reassuringly around his wrist.

Get a grip on yourself, Samar. Even a little girl can feel your fear.

'Oh my god, Anya, are you all right?' Anjali Menon had come crawling over to where Anya and Samar had fallen. Still on her knees, she lifted the frightened girl into one of her arms. Anya's head was still turned towards Samar, her gaze frozen on him.

Dusting himself off the ground, Samar tried to regain whatever was left of his composure. 'Are you okay?' he asked Anjali. She confirmed she was fine with a quick nod of her head, her full focus on Anya. Once convinced her daughter was unhurt, she clutched Anya tightly to herself, turning her face away from Samar, trying to control what obviously were tears. Whether they were of relief or of guilt, he could not quite figure out.

There was noise in the room now, of chairs moving and people struggling to their feet.

'No one hurt here?' Karan had come over to their side of the table, his voice deadly calm.

Akshay More was propped up against the wall, looking vacantly at the screen at the opposite end of the room, almost as if he expected to understand what had happened from just staring intently at it. There was now only static there, trembling pulses of black and white, mocking all attempts to make sense of that which had come to pass. 'What the fuck...' he mumbled to no one in particular.

Karan was moving purposefully through the room to a chair that had been thrown back away from the table. Preeti Singh was sitting there slumped forward; hands stretched stiffly to the side, her lustrous hair covering her face like a black curtain.

'Preeti...' Karan patted her on the back. There was no acknowledgement, either in voice or through movement.

Akshay's attention now fell on the hunched figure in the corner. Taking three long steps, he stood right next to Preeti's chair, concern writ large on his brow. 'Preeti... what...'

Anjali's eyes had bloomed large in fright, looking intently at where the two men stood around the silent girl.

Samar knew what she was thinking. He was thinking it too. Tanya. That girl in the room. She had also...

Then Preeti moved. It was very slight alteration in position, just a gentle tremble of her shoulders. Her head still nestled lifelessly on her chest, like a broken doll. The slight shaking of her shoulders soon became a rhythmic heaving. Preeti was wailing. Yet not a sound came from her lips, almost as if she was trapped in a transparent, soundproof room.

Akshay sank to his knees. Holding Preeti in a half-embrace, he whispered, 'It is okay. We just had an... accident. No need to...'

Preeti said nothing, still wracked by the intensity of her silent sobs.

Akshay moved her hair away, ostensibly to make eye-contact.

Whatever he was going to say, however, never left his lips. Brutal purple rings, ugly in their freshness, had appeared around her eyes, almost as if someone had punched her hard in the face. Tears kept streaming down her cheeks and yet she uttered not a word.

'How did this...' Akshay's sentence once again remained unfinished as, all of a sudden, the giant flat screen on the wall sprang back to life, the striated lines of black and white replaced by an oppressively tight, flickering close-up of a familiar face.

'If you are seeing me now, that means I am already dead.'

Lilith Adams leaned forward towards the camera, adjusting the shoulders of her black jacket, the radiance of her smile slicing out through the screen like a sharp blade.

'An apology from my side is in order. I have not been entirely honest about a number of things. Not that a few lies should bother this present lot, considering that all of you have led lives rich with deceit. But still.'

A muffled groan came from the room. Samar wanted to turn around, but he could not. The shock of the image on the screen had turned him to stone, like it had done to everyone else.

'This place is a mine. That part was true. What I did not tell you was what exactly it is a mine for. Here, ladies and gentlemen, we extract something very special, very valuable. An energy source that cannot be exhausted, one that generates itself as it is being produced, creating an endless cycle of more and more power. Here we mine fear.

'Fear, the most potent source of energy in the world. It keeps nations in motion, fuels the march of history and makes you, should you find yourself in a strange dark alley, walk faster than you have ever done before. Unbelievable, isn't it?

'For the past year or so, the miners have been our ore. Of course, they had no idea as to their real purpose. They were fed the same lies as you were, given specific duties and enough money not to ask too many questions. Unknown to them, we have been priming them for the past few months, in the way ore is pre-heated, tapping into their fright. For the real energy generation though, we needed a violent reaction. To set that in motion, a catalyst was required. The buried temple was that catalyst, releasing the collective fear as a volley of the purest dark energy. Magnificent. And very, very profitable.

'In any mining operation, there are different grades of ore. These people who we brought here were of the best kind, *the prime* I should say.'

Lilith Adams laughed shrilly, closing her eyes in delight. 'Criminals each and every one of them, yet they have never been caught by the law. Upright honest citizen is what the world knows them as. But they... they know different. Wracked by their consciences, they have spent their whole lives looking over their shoulders, fearful whether anyone has come to know of their secrets, fearful of having to answer for their sins.

'This is the very best raw material one can hope for, on the edge as they are. You just have to let their devils shake around a bit and boom! As we speak, those damned souls are boiling real slow in the throes of the worst kind of pain one can imagine, their last sweaty breaths, their final screams of agony as they get melted alive into rock, unleashing the most elemental form of fear. Priceless.'

The image on the screen flickered for a second before stabilizing once again. 'This of course brings us to this group: the so-called experts, smart people who had a choice in life and yet chose to be among *the guilty*. You are the prime of the prime, the most valuable ore.'

Lilith Adams chuckled. 'The good news is that you are alive. The bad news is that there is a reason for that.' An instant's pause.

'Each one of you has started on a journey, the countdown to whose end has already begun. There is something that your friend Dr Akshay More has forgotten to tell you, something that he found in the course of his snooping about in our labs – canisters of GX, which has certain interesting effects on human beings, primarily on their nervous systems. The details of this marvellous gas Dr More can enlighten you on, once I am done. The reason I bring this up is that GX has been let loose in the air conditioning vents. This means that time is one thing you do not have.

'Throughout your lives, you have avoided having to make restitution for your sins. Today however the shadows of the past will finally catch up.

'And as you walk this path, there will be fear. Oh yes. Trust me. There will be fear.'

Still, no one in the room spoke, all of them welded to their positions.

'I am sure you have seen those little contraptions where rodents run on wheels, their motion driving a small toy windmill. Welcome to that world of rats, my friends. Welcome.'

For the first time since she started speaking, the smile vanished from Lilith Adams' face, being replaced by an expression akin to sadness. 'I will make a promise. A promise that I intend to keep. I shall see you all again.

'On the other side.'

The television screen went dead.

The static on the screen crackled, like echoes of heartless laughter, devilish in its joy and avarice.

Preeti Singh leaned forward on the table, her head held in her hand, still silent. The others stared at each other, too stunned to speak.

Anjali was the first to break the spell. Kicking back the chair she was sitting on, she moved panther-like right up to where Akshay was standing. Gripping his collar hard, she forced his head back against the wall in one fluid move. Caught unawares, Akshay staggered back off-balance, his eyes flying open in surprise.

'Okay, asshole, why don't you start off by saying what exactly is going on here?'

Karan jumped into the melee, holding Anjali by her forearm, pulling her away. No match for Karan's strength, she lost her grip and stumbled back, hitting the side of the table.

'He knows everything. Look at that face.'

Akshay adjusted his collar trying to recapture some of his poise. 'I have no idea... trust me...' He looked towards Samar, expecting some kind of support. There was only a hard stare back.

Karan had released his grip on Anjali. She slid a few feet away, still fuming.

'Yeah? So why did she take your name? Only your name?'

'I... I... well...'

Anjali closed her eyes, her fists clenched. The effort she was making to control the volume of her voice was evident, too evident, thought Samar. Akshay had realized that too and had backed himself to a corner, putting as much distance between him and Anjali as he could.

'I don't know what secrets you are hiding or how you are involved with all this.' Her voice choked. 'But I have a little daughter who cannot move or speak. I don't know about us, but she definitely does not deserve to die. So, if there is anything you know that can help us, please...'

'None of us deserve to die here. None of us will,' said Samar with emphasis. 'But yes, Dr More does owe us an explanation. A bloody good one at that.'

'I am just as afraid as any of you. Trust me,' said Akshay, visibly wilting under the collective gaze of anger from the room. His voice had now become a high-pitched mousy whine.

This time it was Samar who moved right up to his face. 'We don't care whether you are scared or not. Start talking, else,' he clenched his fist, bringing it inches from Akshay's face, 'you are going to start hurting.'

Akshay cringed yet again. 'Okay, okay... just give me a second.' Akshay rubbed his neck where the collar had dug in from Anjali's sudden assault. Samar withdrew.

Karan said, 'Wait. Before we question him, what about those downstairs? Should we not go and try to... you know... help them?'

Akshay still had his hand on his neck. 'You heard the lady. They are all dead. Trust me, with what we are breathing in, we too will be very soon.'

Samar disagreed. 'We don't know if they are really dead. All we have to go on are her words. If by her own admission she has not been straight with us for so long, why do you think she is telling the truth now? That mining fear thing seemed pretty much bullshit to me...'

Anjali had moved away, close to Anya. Akshay stepped forward to the centre of the room. 'Don't tell me, we are going down *back there* to find out?'

Samar was already moving towards a corner of the room, near the door. 'Fortunately, there is a very simple way of finding out. Each floor has four security panels from which one can get an instant status report of the whole facility. We are in luck. There is one right in this room.'

Standing in front of a small square in the wall, his fingers pressed something. Immediately, a keypad spun out from inside the wall. Samar typed in the password and the keyboard slid to the side, revealing an extended panel in the wall. A small touch-screen terminal glowed greenish-blue.

Samar knew there was a question waiting for him, one whose presence he was sure of without turning his head.

Akshay asked it. 'My... isn't that interesting... someone else seems to know his way around.'

'Please, Dr More, this is not the time for...' Karan began, but Akshay would not be stopped.

'What about that password? Did you simply guess it? Or was that a master hack?'

'I did an extensive security audit of the facility, one that required me to know more than a bit of the systems here. They gave me a few passwords.'

'Very believable,' Akshay said smilingly. 'Almost as believable as the mining fear thing.'

Samar's expert fingers danced over the screen as a 3-D wire-frame model of the underground facility came up, overlaid with a heatmap and flashing security-alerts.

Oh my god.

Anjali's broken 'What do you see?' made Samar realize that he had spoken that out aloud.

'The bottom two floors show an ambient temperature reading of close to a hundred degree Celsius and rising. There are fires raging in many sectors down below, as these flashing red spots show.'

'So that means...' Karan left the sentence unsaid.

'Yes, that means they are all dead. No one can be alive in that temperature.'

Karan walked up to the panel, staring at the screen. '"Trapped downstairs, boiling real slow." Wasn't that what she had said?'

'How long till the fire reaches this floor?' asked Akshay, well aware that they were just one floor above it. He was scared once again, the aggressive cockiness of a few seconds ago gone.

Samar turned around and looked at him. 'That's the thing. This facility has secure blast doors that are designed to engage in an emergency. The blast doors have been activated at each level and all the elevators have been powered down, sealing the lower floors from the one above. That also means not a single miner would have been able to make it up.'

'But wait,' Anjali said, 'Doesn't that mean that we too are sealed behind a blast door from the level above us? We are trapped here, also, aren't we?' Her last few words almost died in her throat.

Samar felt it now too. Panic. What had started out like the slow tap-tap of a leaking faucet was now a gurgling flood, spreading rapidly throughout, drowning out all rational thought. For years, he had mulled over the possibility of death, but it always had been on his own terms. But not like this. Not by being buried alive.

Breathe Samar. Breathe. You have been in bad situations before and you have come out. The rush of oxygen helped to roll back the waves of fear, at least for the time being. They still remained though, like a mighty ocean fuming quietly behind a dam.

His mind focused on Karan's voice, marvelling at how totally free of emotion it still was. 'She talked about a journey.'

Samar asked, 'You seriously believe a word of what she said?'

'I don't know what to believe, Mr Bose. All I know is that people have died downstairs, and we are stuck.'

Samar pointed towards the panel. 'We have only seen what we are being shown.'

Akshay butted in sarcastically, 'Aaah. The reality of our world is limited by the perceptive power of our senses. How profound. Exactly the kind of horseshit I want to hear before I die.'

Samar continued. 'I meant to say that we do not know for sure if the people down there are dead or dying. Or whether Lilith Adams had her head cut off. All we know is that the terminal shows us a temperature and the screen a sequence of images. We have no way of knowing whether these two things actually happened, do we? For all I know, this could be a smoke-and-mirrors carnival trick. Lilith Adams could be watching us from the cameras up there at this very moment and everyone could be alive and having beer.'

'This is some kind of practical joke? You think someone spent billions of dollars here constructing a gigantic fun-house? Why in the world would anyone want to do that?' Akshay sighed in exasperation.

Before Samar could reply, Anjali interrupted. 'Before that, I still would like to know about the gas we are breathing here. Somehow, you never really answered that question.'

'It's just going to take a little time to explain, and I am not at my best when I have to keep constant watch over whether a crazy lady is going to jump me or a strange man is going to punch me in my face.'

'We have time. Time enough to know how long my daughter has.'

Akshay began, 'Around the 1970s, the CIA started working on a gaseous compound based on research done in Nazi Germany. It was codenamed GX, being fifth in the line of the G-series after GA, GB, GD and GF. The X after G was to distinguish it from its competitor, VX, commonly thought to be the most lethal nerve agent in existence. Trust me when I say that VX has got nothing on GX when it comes to causing nightmares. Anyhow, in the 1990s, the plug on chemical agent research was pulled by the US government, at least officially. But there were strong rumours that the research had just moved underground, funded by private capital.'

'When I said I had time, I did not mean time for a full-blown lecture. Just tell us the facts – what is GX going to do to us and how long do we have? That's all I want. My daughter...'

Karan touched Anjali on her shoulder. 'Please let Dr More finish. As it is, given that we are locked on this level, we are not going anywhere in a hurry.'

Akshay looked nervously at Anjali, but continued. 'Around four years ago, an ex-PhD student of mine showed up at my door, needing some advice. At the Virginia-based defence contractor where she was employed, they were working on a defence project where a neural agent was being tested on rats. Its purpose was to stimulate their neural pathways... oh geez, now this is becoming a lecture... mmm... tickle the nerves so that they can perform, for the want of better word, superhuman feats. Their goal was to create a substance that could be used as a boost for soldiers in battle situations – make them move faster, jump higher, lift heavier weights. Based on certain documents that had come into her possession, she had no doubt that the gas they were testing was essentially nothing other than the elusive GX, research into which had officially been discontinued.'

Samar interrupted. 'Pardon me, but how would inhaling a gas make people Superman?'

Anjali shook her head, 'I just cannot believe we are having a nice academic discussion here.'

'To answer your question,' continued Akshay, 'It is a scientific fact that human beings use a very small portion of their brain and overall, a tiny fraction of their... how shall I put it... neural bandwidth. From ancient Hindu yogis to Japanese martial arts experts, wise men have sought to harness the power of the inactive parts of their nervous system through intense physical activity, sensory deprivation and several other techniques. GX is unique in that it, theoretically at least, chemically simulates that experience of "enlightenment". As you know, and pardon my jargon, the nervous system is a complicated electrochemical system and what GX does, in layman's terms, is to crank up the power of the signals, in essence turning on the cells in the dormant parts of your brain.'

'But did you not say GX is a nerve gas? Those were weapons, right? What you say sounds like an acid trip at the worst,' Samar asked.

'I used the word theoretically. The thing is no one knows what exactly goes on in the brain, there is way too much variation in the human species to predict how an individual would react to GX. In practice, GX has always had the opposite effect to what I have just said. The whispers have always been that GX was tried on human subjects, without their knowledge. It was found to induce hallucinations and waking nightmares, agitate pain centres all over the body, sending false signals of agony to the brain, ultimately leading to paralysis, coma or, at the least, persistent maniacal behaviour. My student reported having seen rodents literally start eating themselves, after exposure to GX, you know, chewing through their tails.

'Yesterday, while analysing the samples from the dig-site, I chanced upon a storage area with cylinders of chemicals. They were being kept securely at extreme low temperatures in liquid nitrogen basins. I would not have thought twice about them, except that they were filed in the inventory control system as Agent H. This was exactly the name of the substance my student was working on. Agent H, GX... same thing.'

Anjali looked down, trying without much success to control her tears. They stood precariously on the side of her eyes before sliding down her cheeks.

'Coming back to your question, I do not know how much time we have. Once again, the effect of GX on human beings is unpredictable. No one knows how fast the blood absorbs it and how one will react to it. But yes, the odds of you being able to levitate like a fakir or lift five hundred pounds are minute, compared to the chances that you will, within a few hours, lose your mind.'

He paused for a while and then moved his glance to Preeti Singh. She was slumped over the table, asleep. Her eyes were fluttering rapidly, her head moving violently from side to side, as if she was in a dream from which she could not wake up. 'As you can see, for some of us at least, the effects have already started.'

'You knew that they had stockpiles of GX here. Yet during the final debriefing, you did not consider it something important enough to mention? Why?' Karan Rathore's voice remained as calm as ever, despite the pointed edge of the question.

'Using your own words, it was not part of the frame of reference. Remember, Doctor?'

To the side, Anjali Menon sat on the chair hugging her daughter, struggling to get control over herself. Karan's brow was still knitted, the gentle irritation still evident. 'No, it very well was part of the frame of reference. You heard Dr Singh's report. That Jaal, Tanya, Asgar and almost all the miners exhibited symptoms consistent with the inhaling of GX was something a smart man like you would definitely have deduced. Why did you not think it worth mentioning?'

Samar felt the need to mediate. There was always time to regret, always time to ask questions. He had learnt that the hard way. 'There is no sense in pointing fingers now. We need to stick together if we are going to get out of this.'

'Get out of this?' Akshay, with his hair disheveled was increasingly looking like a cornered terrier. 'We are trapped here till we start going mad... which part of that did you not understand?'

'Of all the cock-and-bull-stories I have heard in my lifetime, this energy production through fear takes the cake. I refuse to believe it.' Samar stood at the head of the table now, his knuckles balanced on the top, leaning forward. He needed to show he was in control, if only to convince himself of the fact.

'From what I have seen of this facility, it is less a mining facility and more a military installation. It has some of the latest surveillance and security systems installed. When I came in from the top, I saw some of the most secretive military technology at the entrance. As we heard from Dr More, they have stored an experimental nerve gas here. The security officer whom I talked to told me of the existence of state-of-the-art booby-traps planted all over that were to be triggered in case there were attempts to escape with company property.'

'Booby-traps! Brilliant. So that's what the "aggressive defence system engaged" message we heard means. Now we won't be able to even leave this room to pee. If we do, we pop like popcorn.' Akshay's fingers simulated an explosion.

'What I think has happened is that we have been dropped into the middle of a gigantic military experiment. They want to see how we, a group of intelligent human beings with multiple skills, would be able to negotiate a survival scenario against a set of security measures, under extreme stress and against a ticking clock.'

Karan thought out loud, 'The rodent on the wheel?' Samar looked at him. 'More precisely, rats in the maze.'

Anjali asked, 'So what you are saying is that nothing has happened downstairs?'

'I cannot say that for sure. Lilith Adams, I am sure, is very much alive. But as for the workers, I believe they too were part of the experiment, perhaps for the exposure to the GX over time. As Dr Rathore said, that would be the most likely explanation for their feeling of panic, their violent dreams, them trying to kill themselves...' Samar looked at Karan for affirmation.

Karan looked lost in thought. 'It could be... a reason.'

'I studied Asgar's final moments on the surveillance camera for two hours. There was something not right about it, but at the point I just could not put my finger on what exactly it was. The more I think about what I saw, I feel he was...'

Suddenly Samar's head spun. He was being sucked back through time, away from this place, like a house caught in the vortex of a tornado. There she was – Reshmi. It was that afternoon again, the day of their final parting, the darkness falling on Kolkata like a bucket of black paint. All these days when Samar had revisited that scene, he had seen the silent plea in those eyes, asking him not to go. But today there was something different. Her glance, this time, was turned toward the shadow at the gate and there was fear in them, definite fear.

Then he heard it, a clear musical voice that echoed with crystal-like clarity, almost as if she was reciting a line from a nursery rhyme.

Daddy... danger.

'Are you okay, Mr Bose?'

The shadows were closing on him fast, like the walls of a hungry Venus fly trap. He found himself trapped, slimed and squishy, buzzing his wings helplessly. Samar opened and closed his eyes rapidly. Again and again. No, he was not mistaken. The room somehow seemed smaller than he remembered it, and the faces of everyone larger.

What just happened? Was he losing it?

Karan seemed to understand what he was thinking. 'You fell back onto your seat. I was afraid we were losing you too.'

Samar stumbled unsteadily to his feet, embarrassed at being the centre of concern. 'Yes, yes of course. Now where was I? Oh, right. What I was saying is...' His legs trembled once again, and he flopped back into the chair.

Karan's hands tightened around him reassuringly. 'Relax, please... you look very sick ...'

Samar did not stop. He did not want to show his weakness any more than he already had. 'What I was saying...' the train of thought came back, 'is this experiment requires us to make it through the Mine. Locking us behind blast doors defeats its purpose. If they wanted to kill us, they could have done it many times before. No, the plan is to have us go through the obstacle course of booby-traps and to see how they work in a real-life situation.'

'So, you think there is a way out? If only to drive us into the path of their experiment?' asked Anjali.

'Sealed from the outside world. Limited avenues for entering and leaving. This place is built like a test range. Wait, let me draw a very rough schematic here.'

Samar took out a pen from his pocket and started scribbling in his notepad.

'Here we are. For the time we have been inside the Mine, we have been moving through the facility using these two lines of passenger elevators, which I have marked with the two big Xs. As far as I know, these have now been deactivated by the security protocols.

'With the elevators offline, the only way of going from one floor to another is through the blast doors. I have drawn each blast door as a black circle and numbered it, at approximately the positions I think they are. Each blast door is accessed by an inclined ramp. I have darkened those lines. Those ramps are normally used to wheel heavy machinery up and down. We will have to use these to get to the blast doors.

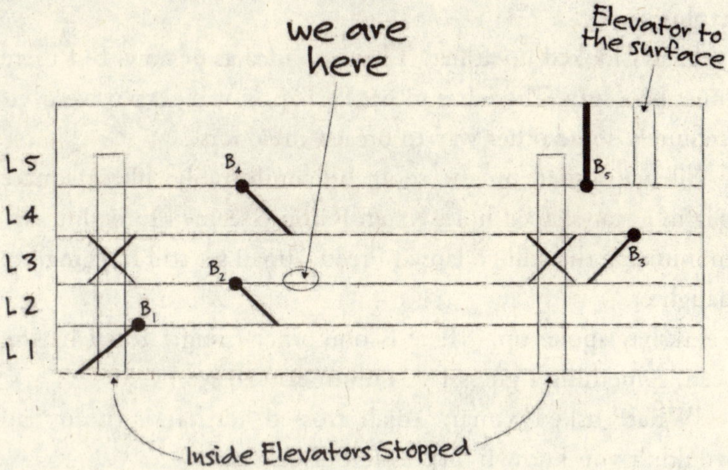

'You will see, however, that the elevators inside the facility run from Level 1 to Level 5. For reasons of security, there is a separate main elevator which goes to the surface from Level 5. The main elevator is secured from the facility by a blast door of its own, the B5 in the diagram. The bold perpendicular line there signifies that this is a totally contained part of the facility through which that blast door is the only way through.

'The good news is that Lilith Adams' room has the master override controls of the Mine. If we can reach Level 5, where her room is, then we can open the last blast door and activate the main elevator.

'The bad news is that in order to get to Level 5, we need to go through two blast doors B3 and B4. They do have their weak points, the locking mechanisms. When I say weak point, I still mean reinforced metal protecting the electronic circuits.

But then again, if we rig up small explosive devices, we could blast through the locks.'

Anjali scratched her forehead. 'But where would you get explosive devices?'

Samar looked up at her. 'I have no idea as of now. But there must be a way. There has to be. Perhaps not by explosives, but definitely some other way to breach the doors...'

Silence settled on the room, uncomfortably, like a square peg in a star-shaped hole. Karan Rathore seemed to be intently monitoring the still-collapsed Preeti. Anjali sat still hugging her daughter.

Akshay spoke up, 'There is one other thing I recall having seen, something I guess I was not meant to see.'

'What?' asked Samar. Anjali crossed her hands in an 'aah wouldn't you know it' expression of disgust.

Samar remembered what Lilith Adams had said. *Sneaking about in the lab.* Akshay More had definitely been snooping around, considering the number of things he had seen. However there was no time to confront him with it.

'Do you know what aqua regia is?' asked Akshay, his eyes still glowing with excitement.

Karan said, 'The king of acids. Isn't it?'

Akshay nodded. 'Nitric acid and hydrochloric acid in a three to one ratio. It can dissolve almost all metals. Now there are even more powerful corrosive agents like fluroantimonic acid, made up of equal parts of hydrogen fluoride and antimony pentafluoride. The principle between all these superacids is the same – take two acids and mix them when you want them to be used.

'Now in the lab that had stockpiles of GX, I found cylinders of a super-acid codenamed Agent Astra. It is about as powerful as fluroantimonic acid and works on the same principle. Again,

I never figured out how they managed to store the constituents of Agent Astra safely but evidently they have. Well, if we can get that onto the locking mechanism of the blast door, we could melt a sufficient area of it for us to go through...'

Akshay looked towards Samar for his reaction.

Samar brushed his index fingers on his lower lips, thinking. Thinking hard. He remained convinced that they had been left the tools for their salvation The real test was for them to figure out what those were and make their way to the light above, despite the inevitability of the pain and loss that lay on the way.

Kind of like life.

Making eye-contact with Akshay, Samar grunted in affirmation. 'We need to take a look.'

'It's on this floor, Lab Delta. A long way from here though.'

'So why don't you just go and get it? I thought you liked snooping around,' spat out Anjali.

'Not with the booby-traps out there. I like my head, thank you very much, and would like to keep it on my shoulders.'

'Fine then. Stay and lose your head here.' Anjali whispered under her breath. 'If you ever had one.'

Akshay shook his head angrily but held his tongue.

'Just tell me how that thing looks like and where the lab is. I will get it.' Anjali took a step towards Akshay.

Sending her outside alone would not do, thought Samar. Even if she somehow managed to survive whatever was out there, she would waste too much time finding whatever they needed. Akshay had to be the one to go. He was damned if he was going to let Akshay and Anjali be alone together. And he was double damned if he would let Akshay go unsupervised. The man did not seem to be the type that could be trusted.

Samar said, 'I think it's better if Dr Menon stays here with her daughter. I will go. I know a bit about booby-traps.' Samar held

Akshay firmly by his upper arm. 'Come on, let's get moving.'

'Brilliant! So, you as my babysitter are supposed to make me feel reassured...'

'No,' Samar breathed down heavy into Akshay's face, breaking into a wolflike parody of a smile. 'It should make you even more scared.'

Preeti Singh was in a deep trance. Her mind was floating away, like a plastic bag caught in a wild draught, to another place, another time.

Standing in the witness box, she dug her nails into the cold, dark-brown hardness of the wooden railing. The peeling plaster of the dusty court-house, the sweaty oppressiveness of the packed galleries, the creaking of the ancient fans and most of all the gazes of a hundred people, all silently gleeful at the spectacle, made her close her eyes, unable to take it all in.

'Dr Preeti Singh,' the defence lawyer, looking at her through his dirt-caked, thick bottle glasses, loved the sound of his voice. 'As the expert consulted by the prosecution, what is your opinion on the veracity of the victim's claims?'

It was the scandal of the year. Randeep Kalra, India's hottest young star and the heartthrob of millions, had come home drunk one night and proceeded to rape his domestic help. That was her story of course. He, on the other hand, protested absolute innocence. A setup, he claimed.

The matter was hardly open and shut. The girl had not reported the case for days, evidently out of fear. There were no witnesses and no physical evidence – her word against his. What did Randeep do to the girl? Was it sex or some other indignity too awful to be mentioned? What would be the fate of Randeep Kalra's forthcoming release, reportedly the most expensive movie ever made in India? Would he lose his endorsement contracts? What about his marriage to the daughter of a chief minister – how long would the wife 'stand by her man'? For days, the anchors hyperventilated, TRPs sky-rocketed and the gossip mills ground out one prurient copy after another.

Preeti Singh, like everyone in the country with access to a television, had been morbidly fascinated by the coverage. It had been disgusting. If the re-enactments on TV had not been enough of an outrage, there was the film fraternity and the national media's overwhelming sympathy for Randeep Kalra. She had heard her office assistant, herself a woman, say this on her phone, 'Why in God's sweet name would the prince even want to touch a nineteen-year-old waif of a girl, unattractive in every respect, when he can have the prettiest women in the country dance to his every whim?'

Though Preeti had kept quiet then, she had found it difficult to keep herself from screaming, from having to explain to the silly, old hen that rape had little to do with sexual attraction. It was the assertion of the most brutal and primal sort of power, power of the strong over the weak, a power whose malignant darkness had touched her personally.

A few days into the circus, the prosecuting lawyer had come to her chambers. That did not surprise her; she was after all one of the foremost psychiatric health specialists in the country.

Preeti had many faults. Modesty of course was never one of them.

The lawyer had wanted her to testify to the victim's emotional trauma as an indirect means for proving rape. Preeti had been glad to take up the assignment. Not that she let anyone know why, since that would call into doubt her objectivity.

The truth, however, was very different from what she had thought it to be. She had not taken much time to get to what actually happened, a little bit of hypnosis and a keen line of enquiry was all that had been needed.

Netra had been making the assault up, of that Preeti had no doubt. She had confronted her with the truth. The girl denied it half-heartedly for a brief while before breaking down totally.

The nineteen-year-old orphan had joined Randeep Kalra's service two years ago as a domestic help. Her job was to keep clean and ready for use an apartment on the tenth floor of one of Mumbai's high-rises. She called the place a 'love nest', where India's hottest matinee idol, newly married into one of India's most powerful political families, would bring starlets and wannabes for extended 'part readings.' For Netra, it had been a nameless, faceless existence, one in which her role was to tastefully leave the place when the master came in with his 'friends' and sit near his car parked at the bottom. There, Netra had become friendly with Kalra's driver. They had started talking. In a few months, she had started sitting inside the car rather than outside it.

It was there in the backseat of the parked car, on a rainy Mumbai evening, that the driver had suggested a big payday. She was poor and so was he and marriage was expensive. So why not get Randeep Kalra to sponsor it? It would hardly be even a pinch in his pocket.

The plan involved just a bit of play-acting, nothing that she could not handle. Netra would accuse Randeep of having raped her when drunk and, if necessary, have the driver back up her story. Knowing how much Kalra's reputation as a clean-cut married man mattered, this, they had figured, would lead to a quiet pay-off.

At least that had been the plan.

Things however had gone south from the moment the accusation had been made. Kalra, to Netra's surprise, had refused to pay up. In a last-ditch effort of arm-twisting brinkmanship, she and the driver had even gone as far as a police station. As luck would have it, there was a reporter from one of the channels there. She had pounced on the story immediately and broken it. Within the hour, things had taken a life of their own. The point of no return had been crossed; she had to stick to her story.

Randeep Kalra was in the courtroom, dressed in a spotless white shirt tastefully hugging his Adonis-like body, that fine-stringed instrument of sexuality that had launched a hundred brands and fluttered a thousand hearts. The only sign of discomfiture that he betrayed was his boyish frown. *Just a sign of irritation at having his time wasted so needlessly in a non-airconditioned room.*

Ever since she had first set her eyes on him, he had reminded her of Vicky. They were strikingly similar – cocksure of the power their looks and money gave them. Both were natural-born predators of women. For both, a girl meant nothing more than a disposable lighter, good for a few strikes with the thumb. She despised the type, more so because she had loved one of them, loved with all her heart.

And then Randeep turned slightly to the right. For a second, just for a second, maybe reminded of some private joke, he smiled before the veneer of contriteness was pulled up again.

Why shouldn't he smile? He is confident that he will be let off. He has a great team of lawyers. Plus, he is innocent.

Innocent?

What a fucked-up word.

Strip the innocence away from poor girls and stay innocent. What a fucked-up world.

So, what if that cock-weasel had not raped Netra? If not now, then he would later. Some other Netra. Why even later? He already has raped. Those struggling models and actresses – did they have any choice but to submit to him if they wanted to survive?

Guilty. Guilty. All those bastards. Randeep. Vicky. And Vicky had gotten away.

All those nights of screaming into pillows, all those days of staring silently at the clouds... was no one going to answer for them? Would there be no justice?

Yes, there would.

Someone would pay. Someone. Of that she was definite.

The lawyer looked at Preeti and coughed. 'Should I repeat the question, Doctor?'

'No need. I have no doubt in my mind that Ms Haldar was raped. Every symptom she displays is consistent with that of extreme sexual trauma.'

A murmur went through the benches. Her eyes remained locked on the person in the white shirt. Now he too was looking at her, unblinking, the lines of his jaw visibly hardening, the arrogance of invincibility shorn off him in an instant.

Revenge. At last. She kept looking at Randeep throughout the deposition, her eyes gleaming like triumphant diamonds.

I will never be caught off guard. Ever again.

And then her head was spinning. The courtroom was becoming a blur. Preeti Singh had been ripped apart from the world, watching helplessly as it drained away, swirling down like water in a sink. Pitched forward through time, she was now at a different place.

Leaning back in the bamboo chair that belonged to her father, Preeti felt relaxed and rested. The morning was slightly chilly, unusual for the time of the year. A newspaper lay on the side table. She picked it up with her right hand. The left held her coffee.

And there it was, on the front page, right next to the renewed violence in the Gaza strip.

Randeep Kalra commits suicide in his jail cell. He had cut his wrists with a blade he had managed to smuggle in.

Preeti sat silently for a while, slowly circling the bitter Arabian coffee in her mouth. Never before had it ever tasted this sweet.

She felt herself steadily floating away again, a feeling of languidness washing over her like a warm blanket.

Where was she now? This was no longer her living room. Her surroundings had dissolved away, leaving her suspended inside a chamber of impenetrable darkness. Then she was thrown again, careening back through the hollows of time.

The fluid moved about in her mouth. It was sweet and intoxicating, relaxing all the tension in her body with its subtle warmth.

What drink did Vicky give me? This is really nice.

Kicking off her heels, she leaned back onto the bed, supported by her elbows. The strap of her black cocktail dress slipped down her shoulder.

Vicky had been coming on strong the last few weeks, pampering her with flowers, chocolates, mushy SMSes and expensively thoughtful gifts. She knew, of course, what all this was leading to. In the year they had been dating, she had never let him go beyond a bit of necking. She had been afraid of giving him all that he wanted. Would she become a slut if she did? Should she not save herself for marriage, as good girls do? And what if he lost interest in her after going the distance?

But Vicky did deserve something special... so maybe tonight being special. Her birthday. Today was her birthday.

He had booked one of the VIP rooms above the club, telling her that it was for a little after-celebration. She had said yes, despite being well aware of the kind of celebration that happened in these rooms. Looking around at the mirrors on the wall and the ceiling and the red-blue diffused light, she giggled and took another sip of the drink.

God, I have been such a cocktease. I have to be pricey, else Vicky will not value what he is going to get tonight. I won't go all the way. That I cannot do. But I will take care of him. I really will.

But where the hell was Vicky? He had left about an hour ago saying he was going to get a surprise. Doesn't he know not to keep a lady waiting?

Maybe it was just the music that was making her impatient. She hated death metal. Blaring through the wall speakers, it was way too loud, its thumping beats disorienting, surrounding her in an envelope of sound.

Anoint yourself for the blood bath The Red Angel roars in his wrath.

The room was swimming now, shimmering like an asphalt road on a hot day.

She wanted to get up and turn the wall speakers off. It was then that she realized that her legs were not responding. She tried again and yet they still stayed where they had been. She tried to push herself up from the bed using her elbows. Her body remained still, as if frozen into a block of solid ice.

What was going on? Was there something in the...

She tried to cry out for help, but the sound died in her throat. It was as if someone was muffling her with a pillow. The room was also closing in on her steadily like a trash compactor, the music getting louder, invading every crevice of her mind, drowning out all thought. Preeti was being dunked headfirst into an ocean of mind-numbing fear and there was nothing she could do about it.

Open yourself up, open wide. There is no place left to hide.

Then the rape started, Preeti's breath yanked out of her lungs by its savageness. She could not see. Darkness roamed her body, outside and inside, tarnishing every inch.

Each one of her other senses had been heightened to the point of an overload; every brutal thrust rattling her entire being.

The ceiling sunk its teeth into her flesh, its acid breath scorching her insides.

Open yourself, release your force. And let the evil run its course.

The song went on and on, going back on itself in a bizarre loop of devilishness, till at last Preeti lost count.

The lights were back, glowing dimly still like fireflies. Her eyes cleared enough for her to realize that was a shadow there, hiding in the darkness. She cringed, moving back to the corner of the bed, curling herself into a foetal ball, expecting another assault.

But there was no attack. The shadow stood still for a second. Then a person materialized in the light.

It couldn't be...

Randeep Kalra was standing in the room in a white shirt sliced to ribbons, the red light dripping over him like rain.

Blood, fresh and raw, bubbled out through the razor cuts on his wrists, dribbling down in thin rivulets towards his elbows. Thrusting them right in front of Preeti's face, he whispered, in a breath that smelt of death.

'Why? Why? Why me?'

Doubled over Preeti's body, Karan Rathore held her wrist and frowned, the crease lines criss-crossing his forehead like cracks on dry mud. 'Her pulse... it's almost as if she is running a marathon.'

Preeti Singh had been sitting at the chair silent for so long, staring fixedly ahead. Now all of a sudden, she had keeled over to the side, off her chair. Her head barely missing the corner of the table, she lay on the ground, legs splayed at a near impossible angle, head thrown back, arms taut as if in the middle of a seizure, mouth twisted to the side, her eyes, framed by the purple rings, closed and fluttering rapidly.

'It's a dream-seizure. I dare not try to snap her out of it... her heart may just stop.'

Sitting right next to Preeti, Akshay massaged her fingers tenderly.

They stayed rigidly extended as if caught in an electrical socket.

'Agent GX, isn't it?'

Karan Rathore looked sideways at Anjali Menon. She had been pacing up and down the room. The cause of her agitation was clear – she wanted to get moving.

'Would seem so.'

Anjali turned her head around with great speed and was about to speak when Preeti Singh sprang bolt upright. 'Help me. He is coming. Help...' she screamed, looking hysterically from one face in the room to another.

Akshay leaned forward, still sitting on the floor, tentatively trying to embrace her. 'It's all right. Just a bad dream. Nothing more...'

Preeti trembled, 'She was right. Lilith Adams was right. I have to answer for what I did.'

Akshay ran his hand soothingly over her back. 'I told you, it's just a nightmare... a stupid nightmare...'

'No, it's not.' Preeti clutched Akshay's shoulder, her nails digging into his flesh. 'She was right. Justice will be served here and now.' The last word was shouted out at the top of her voice.

Akshay looked around helplessly, hoping someone else would step in. Karan asked, 'What kind of justice?'

'Many years ago, I killed a man,' Preeti's voice cracked. She hesitated. 'No. I... I didn't really kill him... I sent him to his death.'

'Look at me, Preeti. Look at me.' Akshay held her hands together, moving his face right in front of hers. 'Nerve-gas has been let loose in this building and it's fucking with your mind.'

He tried to give Preeti a condensed version of the discussion that had gone on when she was unconscious. She looked straight at the light, not hearing a word of what he was saying.

'Randeep Kalra... remember him?' Akshay looked puzzled. 'We don't have...'

Preeti screamed again. 'I asked you. Do you remember Randeep Kalra?'

'Yes, of course. The superstar who committed suicide in jail. It was big news many years ago, but why him, all of a sudden?'

'I set him up with false medical testimony. I killed him,' Preeti lowered her voice. It was calm now, almost as if her agitation had passed. 'I felt good doing that.' Her head was now slanted unnaturally to the side, resting on her right shoulder.

Karan Rathore asked, 'Did you see him in your dream?'

'Yes, I did.'

'And he wanted to know why you did it?'

'Yes.'

Akshay interjected angrily 'You aren't helping things here Doctor. Surely you can't be...'

Karan looked thoughtful. 'Just like Jaal's victims. That question – "Why?"'

Preeti ignored Akshay and looked straight at Karan. 'I can feel his presence close by.'

Akshay made yet another attempt to calm Preeti down. 'There is no one here but us. Everyone else is dead.'

'The past is not dead here. It walks. I saw it just now. Randeep Kalra was there for me...' She started sobbing again. 'The blood... oooh the blood... blood all around.'

Akshay once again held her close. 'No one will take you away. You get that? Just trust me, baby.'

'Not to sound like a bitch here but can we stop this lovefest for a while? Isn't there someplace you need to go to?'

'Lovefest? What the fuck is that supposed to mean?' Akshay propped Preeti's back against the nearby wall and then stood up. He had had enough of this lady.

'In case all you men forgot, I have a daughter here paralysed from the waist down. Just perhaps if she has not been taught to flutter her eyelids and play the part of the distressed damsel, it doesn't mean she counts for more than her.' Anjali folded her hands mockingly. 'Now, pretty please, can you two get moving?'

'Stop using the cripple as your sympathy chip, lady.'

'What did you just say?' Anjali's chest bellowed out straining against the white shirt, her shoulders drew back as she clenched her fists tightly.

'You heard me well enough the first time.'

Anjali had put her hands on her waist, looking down at the ground, like a bull raking up the dirt with his hooves before readying for a charge. Plainly, she was putting in an intense effort to stop another physical assault on Akshay.

'Stop using the cripple as your sympathy chip, lady.' Akshay broke every word distinctly as if speaking to someone hard of hearing.

That was it. The dam had been breached. Anjali moved frighteningly quickly towards Akshay, brutally kicking away a chair in her path with one swift motion.

'Who did you call a cripple, you twat?'

Akshay took three steps back, nearly tripping over his own heel.

'Stop it, both of you. Right now.' Karan Rathore materialized between Akshay and Anjali, gliding smoothly like a trained dancer changing partners. There was not a trace of emotion in his voice. Yet its icy coldness seemed to freeze Anjali right as she had crouched, ready to spring.

Karan addressed Anjali directly. 'Fighting him won't help Anya. It will only make things worse.'

Akshay would not stop. 'Yeah, listen to the man. What he is saying is that I am the only person who can get you through the blast doors. So better be nice to me.'

Samar said, 'That's enough from you too. Remember you are not the only one valuable here, not the only messiah. You need me as much as I need you.'

Anjali had a smile on her lips, like an open bottle of cyanide. 'Yeah, I will be nice to you. Real nice. Just file this at the back of your mind: my time will come... it always does.'

Karan Rathore patted Akshay on his back. 'There never is any provocation for violence. Accept my apologies on behalf of Dr Menon.'

Samar turned around to see Anjali's face. She had however moved away to the farthest corner, like a boxer at the end of a round.

Akshay had once again bent down, holding Preeti's face in his hands. His voice was firm and reassuring. 'I need to go now...' Preeti tried to say something, but he had his finger on her lips. 'I have to get something that we all need in order to break through the door. It's just down the hall. I won't be gone for long. You be good now.' Giving a gentle squeeze on her shoulder, he turned towards Samar. 'Coming, oh my messiah?'

No matter what he said, Samar knew that their lives were all now in the hands of Akshay and the marvellous device he had claimed to have seen. This of course meant he himself was no longer in absolute control. That worried him a lot. Stepping to the side, he bowed in mock deference, 'Lead on into the night, dear friend. Lead gently on into the night.'

'That tomb-digger lady sure hates me.'

'Maybe calling her daughter a cripple has something to do with it.'

'Well, someone had to tell hysterical mama to shut up. In any case, wasn't it she who went for my collar in the first place?'

Just the first person to go for your collar, Dr More. I am definitely in line.

Samar did not like Akshay, and that was an understatement. There was something rather infuriating about the man, like a fly buzzing around the ear. Was it the arrogant smirk? The superior curl of the lower lip? That ceaselessly condescending way of speaking? No. That was not it.

The more he thought, the surer Samar was. It was Akshay's whole tough-guy Clint Eastwood act, as fake as the three-headed boy at the village carnival, that was so grating. He had seen those eyes, rabbit-like in fright, when Anjali had seized him by the throat. He had seen Akshay dancing around the room, like a scared fighter expecting a blow, every time Anjali made a sudden movement. A wimp, a lip-shooter. Samar hated the type. He had worked under too many of them.

Akshay though was, right now, the least of his problems. Getting out alive was all that he cared for. This place was massive, even more massive than he had remembered the last time he had walked this way. It filled him with awe and a sense of dread, the same way he had felt when he had first seen the Karakoram range on a hiking trip. There was a reason behind all this vastness, up in the world above and down here, one which he felt he was too small to comprehend.

There would be time later for philosophical reflection, thought Samar. For now, he kept scanning the surroundings, his expert eyes trying to spot turrets, tripwires and the other telltale signs of danger. Akshay walked a few paces behind him. At least he has a good sense of self-preservation, thought Samar wryly.

'All you guys think I am mixed up in this somehow, don't you?'

'Well you did forget to mention the small matter of nerve gas in the labs. You must accept that is kind of suspicious.'

Akshay's dry laughter rolled through the empty passageway. 'I guess I can say this to you now. Yes, there was a reason for that.'

'Wow. I would never have guessed.'

Akshay ignored the sarcasm. 'I have some shit on my balance sheet. A mortgage I can no longer afford, some gambling debts, some money borrowed from bad people. I need a lot of money. A lot.'

'So, you made a deal on the side with Lilith Adams to not reveal the whole nerve agent thing. Some extra frosting on the top of the cake. I get it. As a matter of fact, I should have gotten it a long time ago.'

'Hear me out, oh wise one. I do a bit of reading on germ and nerve gas warfare, enough to know the value of the military technology they have here. And that too just in one lab, the only lab I had access to. A prototype smuggled outside and shown to the right people would be worth a fortune. Only problem is, this isn't the type of house where you can just walk out with the plate and spoon and not have the dogs rip you to bits.'

'That's what I said. Quid pro quo. Your silence for a little party bag that you take home.'

'See that's where you are wrong. *There was never any deal.* I tried to talk to Lilith Adams to see if we could work something out, strictly off the books of course. I called her on the communication device and she said, and I remember the exact words, "We will have time enough later to talk about what you need. For now, do what is best for you." So that's exactly what I did – the best I could for myself.'

'You actually thought you could push a deal with her after you had submitted a favourable report?'

'What can I do? I am an optimist. And optimists live longer.'

Samar rolled his eyes. 'Make sure the tomb-digger lady doesn't find out that your professional opinion wasn't really professional at all. Else it will be your tomb she will be digging. Being an optimist won't save you from that, I guess.'

'Do you think what I said or didn't say would have made any difference to what happened in the end?' There appeared to be a whiff of regret in Akshay. Or perhaps not, he was too arrogant for that. Akshay was immediately back into attack mode. 'Well at least I have been honest. I wish I could say the same for you.'

'I told you the reason why I know my way around back there. I was given the passwords and I have covered...'

'That's not what I meant.'

For the first time, Samar cast a glance back over his shoulder. Akshay stood a few paces behind him, his eyes sparkling like that of a cat which has just chanced upon an unguarded bird's nest.

'You are on some kind of anxiety-controller, aren't you, strong enough to put an elephant to sleep? I'm going out on a limb here. But I also think you have skipped a dose or two.'

The blue pills. How did he know about them? Am I showing withdrawal symptoms?

'I am not a junkie, if that's what you are trying to imply. I have prescriptions for what I take.'

'That's what they all say. That's what they all say once they get busted.' Stretched from one ear to the other was a mocking vicious parody of a smile.

'I notice things, Spy Man, small things that others don't notice. Like the way Karan Rathore speaks.'

'What about it?'

'Have you ever met a man whose voice does not modulate, not even a little?'

'Yes, I have.'

'No, I am sure you haven't. Not like this. Normally when we speak, it's like a yoyo – low-high, high-low sometimes high-higher and then low-low. Not this man. When he talks, it's like...'

'So what he has a flat voice? Won't sing high notes well, is that the problem?'

'Just think about this for a second. A man comes to know that he is trapped inside a mine. No way out. Almost everyone else dead. He is breathing in a nerve gas which will kill him. He is smart enough to know that when that happens, it will be anything but a peaceful drift into la-la land. And yet, and yet, not once does his voice show a bit of excitement, a bit of fear.'

'If Karan Rathore was in Lilith Adams's pay, which is what you are hinting at, he would pretend to be frightened. Fright, like yawning, is contagious. So they say.'

Lilith Adams wanted them to be scared, that much Samar was sure of. Not, of course, for the reason she had given. It was too fantastic to be true. But then so was this situation, even more unbelievable than the craziest thing one could think of.

'I was not saying that Rathore was an agent of Lilith Adams. I just meant, and I know I sound gaga here, he seemed to me... kind of dead... dead from the inside.'

'Oh, I get it. Lilith Adams: dead and yet alive. Karan Rathore: alive and yet dead. Where exactly are you a professor of again?'

'What we do not understand, we make fun of.' Akshay mumbled.

'Excuse me?'

'No, nothing... nothing... just something someone told me, not so long ago, down there, down at that accursed place.'

Samar and Akshay stood a few feet away from the door of Lab Delta. Samar had been worried that the room would be locked. It was not. The automatic door had been kept open, giving them a full view of what was inside.

Lab Delta was a huge circular stadium-sized room with rows and rows of transparent chambers, all of different sizes, each lit from inside by blue light coming, oddly, from the floor. Each chamber had equipment that looked like it came straight out of a science-fiction movie, along with blinking terminals, wires crawling between them and transparent storage cabinets.

Akshay said, 'When I first saw it, I thought the guy who designed this lab wanted to make a disco, with the under-lighting and all. Now I know what was on his mind. He was thinking of a jewellery store: lines of glass showcases and inside them... diamonds and gold.'

Samar though was reminded of Reshmi's glass doll's house. Anita had found it in an old Parsee-owned antique shop near New Market, the one she would visit every Sunday. Lab Delta seemed to be like that doll's house, square glass rooms with beautiful things inside them.

Aah. That glass doll's house. He had never liked the idea of Reshmi playing with something so easy to break.

She had loved it though and that was all that mattered. Then, one day he had come back from work to find Reshmi weeping, sitting at her pink table. The doll's house lay on the ground, smashed to fine dust. It must have come close to the shelf's edge and then that accursed cat, fattened by the prime cuts of fish that Anita would spoil it with, must have knocked it over, like it had the heavy vase in the living room a few months ago.

'Fix it daddy, put it together. Please. I promise to check every day so that it stays away from the edge.' She had said between sobs, hugging him close.

It had taken every bit of fatherly eloquence to explain to an eight-year-old that there are some things that cannot be put together.

'Not even by Daddy?' She had asked, pearl-shaped drops swelling beneath her eyes.

'No. Not even by Daddy.' He had sat with her, wiping the tears away with his fingers. Samar had thought of going to New Market to see if he could get another one just like it. Then he decided not to. Reshmi needed to learn to let go, to realize that there were some things that would never come back.

'Hey, stop, what are you doing?' Samar had been brought brutally back to the present by the sight of Akshay striding eagerly forward, like a kid running towards the circus gates while his father fishes around in his pocket for the ticket money. Samar clasped Akshay firmly by the wrist, making him stop immediately. A step more, and he would have been inside Lab Delta.

'There is a high chance the entrance is booby-trapped. Don't move unless I tell you to.'

'If we didn't see any on the way here, why do you think there is one right at this spot? Something you know that I don't?'

Samar looked to the side, up at the ceiling and at the floor. Nothing seemed to be dreadfully wrong. Glass everywhere and well lit, not a place to hide a trap. Still, he needed to scan every quadrant visually and it was better that he kept Akshay engaged in conversation while he did so.

'Have you ever had your house infested by German cockroaches?'

'Mmm... No.'

'You can thank your lucky stars.' Akshay looked blank.

'Well, I personally have had that misfortune. What you do then is put a thin layer of boric acid under the pipes and near the sink – any place essentially where there is water. The pests can live without food for days but they need water every few hours. So, you know they will have to come that way sooner or later. Once they do, you can hope, mind you just hope because they are hard bastards – that they get the boric acid on their feet and take the poison back to their nests.'

Samar remembered how much he despised cockroaches. Anybody would have, if they had lived in the vermin-overflowing shitty apartment that the Indian government had put him up in for six months during his training at Quantico. Despite the visceral hatred for German cockroaches, he had developed an admiration for their resilience and determination to live. You could smash them so that their insides came out and yet they would run.

'Booby-traps are planted on the same principle. They are placed at bottlenecks, points where you know your prey has to go through.'

'So, what are we? German cockroaches searching for water? Or rats on a wheel? Was that not what Lilith Adams called us?' asked Akshay.

Samar was now confident enough to move ahead. He took a step, gingerly placing his toe on the floor in front of the door. Nothing happened. He looked around once again and then gestured to Akshay to follow him.

'I know that when there is not enough to go around, cockroaches eat each other. So, if we are cockroaches, I suppose we will be doing the same.'

Samar ignored Akshay's attempts at morbid cleverness. They walked a few paces in silence.

'Would you look at that?' Akshay whistled softly, pointing to a gigantic metal contraption in one of the glass rooms.

Samar's eyes flew wide. 'What? Is that what we are going to carry with us?'

'No. That's in the room next to that. But just look at this for a second, will you? This, Spy Man, is one of the latest, greatest and most powerful industrial lasers you will find. The design for this would be worth many millions of dollars if you could only just get it to the right people.'

'Too heavy to steal it seems, even for you.'

'Some things even I cannot do. Sadly.' Akshay pointed forward. 'And there is what we came here for. Agent Astra, the killer acid.'

Behind the glass were three transparent cylinders lying next to each other on an elevated platform. Each had two metal-lined chambers filled with different liquids, one glowing greenish-yellow and the other shimmering like mercury. On the side of every cylinder was a keypad with a small display unit.

'What you do is enter a password through the keypad. Once the password matches, the diaphragm inside the cylinder dissolves, the two acids mix, a super-acid is formed, and with that super-acid one can melt through virtually everything. I asked one of the scientists why they needed something like this. He said that sometimes when you need to blast through rock-faces, a conventional explosive device could trigger a rock-fall. Something like Agent Astra carries the punch of many sticks of dynamite but does its work silently, without the shock waves, say, that monster laser gun would cause.'

'So, you know the passwords to those things?'

'That's the fun. These are absolutely new devices. So, they do not have any passwords set.' Winking conspiratorially at Samar, Akshay put his hand on the door's sliding knob and gave it a sideways shove.

Samar looked down at the door sliding through the channel. It seemed to jam for a fraction of a second before it opened.

It was then that it hit him.

Swinging his hand out, he grabbed Akshay's forearm, wrenching him back from the door. Caught unawares by the suddenness of the backwards jerk, Akshay lost his balance, his feet flying out in front. He looked up to see Samar also diving down, right on top of him.

'What the...'

The ear-piercing sound of plexiglass shattering drowned out Akshay's sentence. A bolt of humming red heat whistled past his neck, followed by a series of louder crashes as his shoulder hit the cold hard floor with a dull, painful thud.

And then silence reigned once again.

Both of them lay on the ground, collecting their breaths, their eyes fixed on the laser gun. It stood there, silently ominous, the only trace of it having fired being the slight vibration of the machine.

'Holy Mother of God...'

Akshay lay pinned below Samar, trembling, breath coming in ragged short gasps. Samar disengaged himself from the tackle-down position and shook his head in disgust.

Damn, I did not see that coming. Like that truck that rammed me from the side. Like the man in the shadow.

'What the...? After all that speech about cockroaches and booby-traps, this is what you do...' Akshay still remained on the ground, seemingly too scared to move, his face paper-white with fear.

Samar's heart was still beating too fast to reply.

'Wait... do you have any idea of what you are doing? Or are you just a dopehead who somehow got mixed up in this?'

A part of Samar wanted to shout at this ungrateful prick whose miserable head he had just saved from being drilled by a laser beam. But another part of him felt guilty, monstrously guilty, like the dad who cannot put together a glass doll's house.

The trip wire that set off the trap was placed in the channel. A good trick but you should really have anticipated that.

'Sorry. I should have been more careful.'

Samar's quiet acceptance of defeat took Akshay by surprise. He was going to say something but then kept quiet.

Silence again.

'Let us hope that the laser has not damaged the cylinders,' said Akshay, dusting himself up.

He now moved into the chamber, over the pile of debris and shattered plexiglass, not waiting any more for Samar's directions.

'It wasn't meant to.'

'What?' Akshay seemed genuinely puzzled.

'I am saying that the purpose of this defence system was not to protect the cylinder. It was to vaporize whoever opened the door. This is active defence. In passive, you lock the door from inside so that the thief can't get in. In active, you let him enter and then lock it from outside.'

'Fucking sadists.'

'Well, at least we now know for sure that we are on the right track. We were definitely supposed to be here.'

'You still think we are in the middle of a military experiment, don't you?' Akshay asked.

'What else? Or does the whole fear-mining thing make more sense?'

'Considering how shit scared I am, I have to accept it would make business sense, if they could actually tap it.' Akshay smiled nervously. Samar was not looking at him, his attention drawn to the object that had hit his foot. Lying on one side, amidst the debris, was a medium-sized chainsaw.

Akshay noticed it too. 'A chainsaw? Strange, I did not see this the last time we were here. But this is good, isn't it? We might need it in order to cut through some of the lighter barriers.'

Samar stayed grim. 'That chainsaw was placed here because they wanted us to find it. We are doing exactly what they expect us to do. That worries me.'

'So, you suggest we let it be?'

'No, we have to pick it up. We need it after all. Right now, we have no option than to play by their rules. But I don't like it. Do not like it one bit.'

Akshay lifted up the chainsaw, brandishing it above his head playfully. Its sharp serrated steel edges gleamed cruelly in the light. His body doubling up in forced laughter, Akshay pulled the chord, humming the chainsaw hysterically to life. 'So, what are we now, then Spy Man? Cockroaches looking for water? Rats in the maze?' He paused, his white teeth as jaggedly cruel as the chainsaw. 'Or simply lambs to the slaughter?'

'Is this man absolutely crazy? Or just a twenty-four-carat asshole?' Anjali Menon threw up her hands in exasperation and then started pacing about the room, punching her palm with the other fist.

'Better an asshole than dead,' Akshay said, keeping his hands crossed cockily on his chest, though careful to be at the opposite corner of the room from Anjali. 'Why pretend? I don't trust any of you. And I am sure none of you trust me either. I need to take precautions.'

Samar and Akshay had come back to the conference room without incident. The excitement however had started once Akshay had put the three Agent Astra cylinders on the table. Instead of programming the three cylinders with one common password, as Samar had suggested, he had insisted that each cylinder be 'owned' by a specific person, with only that person knowing the password to the cylinder and no one else.

Karan asked, 'How does this have anything to do with not trusting us? Have you considered what would happen to a cylinder if the person who owns it... well, if something happens to him?'

'Of course, I have. That is precisely why I insist on individual ownership. I just want to make sure that everyone here has an interest in protecting everyone else. Any one of us die, the rest get locked inside. Good enough incentive to work together, no?'

Akshay patted Samar on the back, in a show of mock camaraderie. 'Some while ago, Spy Man here saved me from becoming an overcooked sausage. Why did he do that?'

Samar stayed silent. *No use in arguing with this man. I know what's coming.*

'The answer gentlemen and ladies is self-interest. He knows he cannot afford for me to die, not before I have had the chance to show him how to programme this thing. Right?'

Samar knew enough not to be provoked.

'At this moment, you need me. All of you. Otherwise, you could have just hit me on the head with a chair and taken the cylinders away. Why, I think Anjali here would just as well do it right now.'

Anjali Menon ignored the taunt though the quivering nostrils did give away how close to the truth Akshay was. 'Very funny. But have you considered a few things? There are five of us, three cylinders and three doors to break down. So, which...'

Samar interjected. 'Correction. There are actually two doors. I believe once we break down the second door we can get to Lilith Adams' chambers and reverse the lockdown. If we cannot, then even the third cylinder would not be of any help. That's because the main lift to the surface would still be stalled and that is the only way up.'

Anjali looked at Samar balefully, not appreciating the interruption.

'My point being that two people are going to be left without their cylinders. How do we decide who those two will be?'

Akshay was ready with an answer. 'Preeti must have a cylinder. She is the weakest among all of us right now and without this kind of protection, I am afraid you guys won't lift a finger to save her should a situation arise.'

Preeti did not even acknowledge the mention of her name, sitting at the table with her head nestled on her chest. She had spent the last hour, alternating between long bouts of uneasy silence and incoherent mumblings.

'You think she is in a state to remember a password?' asked Anjali.

Preeti suddenly looked up, left eye hidden by her locks of unruly black hair. 'I haven't gone crazy, if that's what you are trying to say. Even if I have, I still have the right to live.'

Everyone looked at her, surprised at the chilly stillness of her voice. She almost sounded sane. Almost.

Akshay held Preeti by the shoulders from behind, gently squeezing them together. 'As long as I am here, no one is going to take away that right.'

Preeti moved the hair away. The blackness beneath her eyes glowed wet with tears.

Anjali rolled her eyes impatiently. 'No need for the drama again please. She gets her password. So now it is two out of four. How do we decide now? Lottery? Eenie, meenie, miney, moe? Anyone else wants to break down?'

Akshay said, 'Let's start off by asking who does not need to own a cylinder. One person clearly does not – Spy Man.'

'Excuse me? Why, Your Majesty? Why am I deprived of the right?'

'Because you, sir, do not need to have a cylinder to maintain your value. We cannot get by without your help in detecting booby-traps. Not that I have a particularly high opinion of your expertise but at least you are better than the rest of us. Plus, you know the place well, having gone everywhere inside this installation.'

'I do not need a cylinder. You can have mine.' It was Karan Rathore. Anjali tried to say something, but Karan thrust his hand out. She stopped. He continued, 'I refuse to accept the premise of Dr More's little insurance scheme, that humans help others purely motivated by self-interest and for nothing else.'

Akshay sneered dismissively but stayed silent.

'Cynicism is a crutch, a crutch that justifies the worst in us by pointing to the worst in others. I have lived my life on the shoulders of a simple principle – trust my fellow man to do the right thing. I believe, should the time come, you too will do the right thing. As a matter of fact, I know it. Even though you don't.' Karan stopped, his voice losing its strength for an instant. 'I now leave it up to you to decide for yourselves who will take the cylinders. I am out.'

Samar was no Boy Scout. Listening in on phone conversations and sifting through emails as part of his life as a spook, he had seen how friends turn on friends, mentors sell out their disciples and lovers leave the objects of their affection hung out to dry. He had no doubt that Karan Rathore's belief in the basic goodness of humans was grossly misplaced. And yet there was no escaping the genuine courage on show here. It's one thing to take a principled stance over cups of coffee on a relaxed afternoon. It is quite another thing to stand by one's convictions while buried alive underground. *Crazy old fool. Must be feeling the effect of the gas, the way he choked up.* God knows how long he has.

Samar said, 'Akshay is right. You guys do need me till the very end. Preeti, Anjali and Akshay – hope you three are happy with your cylinders now.'

Anjali shook her head. 'There is still one problem. In which order do we use the cylinders? Who is going to volunteer to lose their help-me ticket first?'

Akshay said, 'Just to show I am not as big a prick as you think I am, I volunteer to be first in line.' He turned towards Karan. 'How's that, old boy, for the best in humanity?'

Samar was looking at Anjali, expecting her to respond to Akshay's gesture. She stayed silent, her lips pursed into a straight line, her hands holding firmly the handle of her daughter's wheelchair. She was not volunteering to go next.

The shameless pause when the waiter drops the bill on the table and no one wants to go for it, delaying the pull for the wallet just so that the other one does it first.

Anjali won out. Preeti blinked. 'I will go second.'

'Seems the old boy's little speech shamed all except Dr Menon here.' Akshay's sneer now smelt of triumph.

Anjali yet again made no eye-contact, bending down to explain something to her daughter.

'It's then decided – first me, then Preeti and Anjali has the backup. Now all of you set your passwords.'

Akshay then started talking to Preeti in hushed tones. Meanwhile, Samar had sided up to Karan. 'You all right?'

Karan Rathore said, 'Just felt slightly faint once or twice. Don't worry about me. There is plenty of life still left in these bones. Plus, I need to make sure that Anjali and Anya make it up to the top; it's the least I owe Nikhil.'

Samar made a mental note to keep an eye out for Karan. Anjali Menon could not care about anyone but her daughter. Akshay was soft on the Preeti girl. Nobody seemed too concerned for this man. Perhaps if he had been bent with age and shrivelled, Karan would have commanded sympathy. But he looked too fit for his age, too much in control of himself for people to 'awww' him.

'You are a good man, Dr Rathore.' Samar wanted to assure the doctor that there was at least one person looking out for him.

Karan's eyes twinkled impishly 'I will watch your back too. Don't underestimate the power of this old man, still a lot left in these bones.'

Samar chuckled to himself. There was definitely something about this man, something quite unique.

A distant rumble came from downstairs. It was time to start.

The six of them walked together – Samar at the head, Karan, Anjali and Anya following closely, while Preeti and Akshay lagged behind the rest. Those who had cylinders carried their own with the exception of Anjali. She pushed Anya's wheelchair and Karan carried hers, without complaint.

Pain hung heavy in the air like a poisonous mist. They proceeded softly, the clicking of their shoes on the metal floors echoing through the empty, dimly lit halls.

Samar kept scanning for ambushes, careful not to have a repeat of Lab Delta. It was tough concentrating though, knowing that the poison was coursing in his veins, steadily eating away at whatever that made him *him*. From time to time, his eyes would wander over to Anya. The more he saw her, the more he was reminded of Reshmi. They were very different in all ways. Reshmi was a bird – light on her feet, floating through the air, her laughter like a hundred tiny bells pealing joyously. Anya, in contrast, was serious, her large eyes soaked with the sadness of silence and loss.

'I am sorry to be so blunt, but I could not help seeing how you have been looking at Anya. Do we have a problem?'

Samar was taken aback. Not usually the person to struggle for words, he fumbled for a second. *Damn, she thinks I am a paedophile or something*. 'I... I... well... she just reminded me of my own daughter.'

Anjali's gaze showed no sign of softening, burning into Samar with a piercing ferocity. Samar felt obliged to allay her suspicions, more so because she was very clearly on the edge. And so, despite it being a topic he rarely, if ever, shared with anyone else, he told her briefly about Reshmi and her disappearance.

After the story was finished, Anjali's expression clearly showed a change, the aggressive mother-tiger scowl replaced by something akin to embarrassment. Looking down at her feet, she said 'I am sorry for... suspecting. It's just that this place and this... I have not been myself of late.'

'I absolutely understand. As a mother, you have to keep an eye out for her. All the time,' Samar paused, holding Anya's feeble hand in his. 'Unlike you, I took my eyes off my daughter, got so wrapped up in the little things of life that I never realized when I had lost her.'

For a second, an image of a shadow in the trees fleeted past him. Then it vanished as suddenly as it came. 'Guilt is the throbbing nerve centre of grief. It is also a blessing – without guilt, there is no acceptance of responsibility. And without the acceptance of responsibility, there can be no redemption.'

Samar had not noticed when Karan had moved into the conversation. Karan said, 'Death is God's little touch of the devil. It is not easy to deal with or even understand.'

For once, the flat gravelly tone of Karan's voice struck Samar square in the chest. With a sudden burst of steely passion, he said, 'My daughter is not dead.'

Karan took a step back, raising his hands slightly in a gesture of surrender. 'Sorry if I suggested something I should not have. I was just...'

Samar knew he was correct. His was a father's heart and a father's heart is never wrong. Reshmi was alive.

Somewhere. But maybe he should not have reacted to Karan. Intrusive empathy though got his goat; Samar preferred his grief 'on the rocks'. He opened his mouth to say something and then thought better of it. Silence once again enveloped them uneasily.

Samar stopped.

In front of him lay the power-generation sector, the hub of the entire installation. Its gigantic turbines gleamed sinisterly in the diffused light and the steady mechanical hissing of flowing coolant sounded malignant, as if the massive reactor pipes that encircled the room were animals of prey, crouching for the unwary to come their way.

Get a control over your imagination, Samar told himself.

Turning back to the rest, he pointed forward. 'Listen up, people. At the end of the power-generation sector is the ramp up to the door that will take us upstairs. From here to the door, our journey becomes more dangerous. While there were at least eight paths by which we could have reached this place, from now on there is only one way to the next floor up. And that passes through this massive room.'

Akshay interjected, 'Aaah, the path of the cockroach below the sink. The traps start here.'

Suddenly, out of nowhere, Anjali's voice trembled theatrically.

Then, grating loud on hinge of sickening sound,
The Underworld's portals open wide. O, dost thou see
What sentinel upon that threshold sits,
What shapes of fear keep guard upon that gloom?

'Excuse me?'

'This is how Virgil describes Tartarus in the *Aeneid*.' There was a smile on Anjali Menon's lips. She was enjoying Samar's look of confusion.

I hope this dame too isn't going to go hysterical on us. I don't like that smile.

Anjali added helpfully, 'According to Greek myth, Tartarus is a dark, gloomy abyss, located even below Hell. It is a place of eternal damnation, a torture chamber for the worst kind of sinners, those that sin against God himself. "For God did not spare the angels who sinned but threw them down into Tartarus and delivered them to be kept in chains of darkness till the day of judgement".'

'That's from the Bible, isn't it? So, are we the angels who have sinned?' asked Karan.

Anjali turned towards Samar, who looked as confused as before. 'I am not going crazy, don't worry. Just couldn't help noting the similarity of this place with Virgil's description.' Seeing Samar's face remain impassive, she added, almost defensively, 'At the very least, give an academic the privilege of getting the last word in, will you?'

'May I have your watch please?' Samar stretched out his hand towards Karan.

'Excuse me? What?' This time it was Karan who looked surprised. 'Something I have to check.' Samar impatiently waved his fingers.

Karan unclasped the bulky old metal watch and handed it over to Samar. Without warning, Samar threw the watch into the room and stepped back. As it hit the ground, bluish-white sparks bolted across the polished metallic surface, turning the watch instantly into dark ash.

'Ah well, never did quite like that watch I suppose.' Karan shrugged morosely.

'The fuckers have electrocuted the floor. Just awesome. Now what? Now what?' Akshay threw up his hands in a mixture of panic and despair.

Samar stood watching the floor, which was still crackling like a frying pan. This time, he had been smart enough to have anticipated the trap. Not that it was rocket science; throwing an object on the ground was one of the standard procedures to test for vibration-sensitive traps like mines and pressure-bombs. But still he had done it. He was once again in control.

The surge of relief was momentary as the reality of their predicament sunk in. No way were they going to be able to move over an electrified surface. They were stuck and from the looks on everyone else's faces, they all knew that.

Anjali asked, 'Can't we kill the power to the room?'

Samar said, 'The circuit breakers are on the other side. The master controls of the whole installation are in Lilith Adams's room upstairs.'

'So, it all ends here then. Damn, fuck, why didn't they just kill us before?' Akshay groaned.

'Exactly. They could have killed us before. But they did not. They would not have allowed us to get the Agent Astra cylinders unless there was an opportunity to use them. Stopping us now defeats the experiment.' Samar's faith in his theory remained firm. The way out lay somewhere, he only needed to find it.

Karan remained as deadpan as ever. 'I like the fact that you stand by what you believe.'

Was he mocking him now? Or was that genuine admiration? Samar had no time to deliberate on the question. Something else was eating away at him like a hungry rodent, something about this place that he should remember.

During his security review, Samar had spent quite some time in the power-generation sector. It made sense since if anyone was working to sabotage the plant, they would definitely try to compromise this place. The old foreman with thick white eyebrows who had showed him around had been polite and helpful but very obviously scared of his own shadow. Samar had asked him about Asgar since they belonged to the same division. He remembered the foreman pointing upwards, and how he manipulated his own arm, mimicking the way Asgar's body had been mutilated.

'The more twisted they are in life, the more twisted they become in death.' He had said about Asgar, hushed terror soaking through every word. Samar had followed his finger up, if only to avoid the maniacal gleam in the man's eyes.

Up. Upwards.

It was then that he remembered what he had seen up there, something that had since totally slipped his mind. 'There is another way to get across this place.' Samar pointed up.

'What's there?' asked Akshay.

'Look carefully. I know it's almost totally hidden by those pipes. But if you stand tiptoe, you will be able to see a cable car there, the kind you see at ski resorts.'

Akshay shouted shrilly, like a teenager who has just caught sight of a rock star. 'Yes, there... there is something!' He held Preeti's hand in his but she remained morosely calm, looking down at her toes.

'But... but that's hardly a cable car. It's just a bench strung up by thin wires. Two can barely sit on it at once,' said Akshay, his enthusiasm whistling out like air from a punctured balloon.

Samar said, 'It's just a small thing, used by maintenance personnel to do work on the machinery at that level. Won't take us all together, need to go in batches. The important thing is that cable car leads to an enclosure on the other end of this sector, which has access to the ramp. Once we take it to the other side, we will actually be quite close to the door.'

'How do we get up there?' asked Karan.

'There is a very steep access stairway to the side, outside the room. Getting up should not be a problem for us except that someone has to take Anya on their shoulders and someone else has to take her wheelchair. I volunteer to carry Anya.'

Akshay said, 'I would have taken Anya, but I am not going to give my cylinder to anyone else.'

Karan signalled he would take the wheelchair.

Akshay started, stopped and then finished his sentence. 'I know you people think I am an asshole. But I am not... I really am not.'

Karan replied, 'You have assumed the worst about us and that is why we have seen the worst in you. I told you once before, you never lose out when you trust your fellow human beings.'

Akshay clutched the cylinder to himself, the feeling of guilt, fleeting as it was, replaced once again by naked suspicion. 'Save those lines for the self-help book. Or put it on a fridge magnet. Just spare me the lecture,' he drawled.

The side stairs were narrow and steep, the edges like metal blades, positioned chest high. Moving up in single file, they trod carefully, securing their footing on one step before raising their leg for the next. Samar concentrated on each breath of his. The little girl he carried in his arms was his responsibility. He would not fail, not again. He had failed too many times for one lifetime.

To his surprise, Samar was invigorated; propelled up the stairs by a lightness he had not felt for many years. He felt possessed in a good way, almost as if by the spirit of himself, as he had been years before, from a time when he yet did not know what being bitter was.

He knew the reason for this change. Anya.

Samar did not believe in destiny. He never had. But perhaps there was a reason behind why he was here. Perhaps he needed this – this walking toe-to-toe with death, just to know that he still valued life.

The climb was now over. Samar stood on a small metal platform with the others. Two solid cables stretched out in front of them, vanishing into a dark square hewn into the opposite wall. The other side seemed an eternity away. The focus of all their hope, the cable car, was parked on the platform. It looked rather flimsy, not something one would like to trust their lives with, so many feet above the ground.

Akshay had moved close to the precipice. Putting his hand on the metal railing, he asked with mock cheer, 'Well what do you think, Doctor? What will kill us first – the fall or the crackle once we touch the ground?'

Karan seemed to have taken him seriously. 'You never know. I have seen people survive big falls. There was this young kid on campus who tried to commit suicide by jumping off from the ninth floor. His backbone had been shattered, his shin bone had gotten stuck into his thigh and his left arm had... remember him, Anjali?'

Anjali gently pleaded, 'Please, Karan, let's not make Anya even more scared than she is. Please.'

Karan still finished his thought. '... and yet he was alive. But yes, the shock might kill you if the fall does not. Having your heart stop on the way down is merciful, much better than dying slowly in little pieces or being fried by the electricity.'

'So, who goes first?' asked Anjali.

Karan said, 'We could do it by splitting ourselves into three groups. Each group carries one cylinder across. In this way, we distribute risk as much as possible. If the rope snaps, we lose just one cylinder. Of course then, the ones who have not made it across will be stuck on this end. And those on the other side won't have the cylinders to make it through. Unless of course, the rope breaks on the last pass, in which case...'

Akshay held his head and said, 'This is sounding like one of those aptitude test questions – the boat, the wolves and the goat. Let's just do this simply. Every person who owns a cylinder goes across with his or her own. Two people on each pass. Leave the rest to luck.'

Preeti, with the sudden determination of a child who has decided she will have only vanilla ice-cream and nothing else, squeaked, 'When I go, it will be with Akshay. No one else.'

Akshay added, 'And I am not handing my cylinder to anyone else.'

Anjali yelled, 'So if you go together, that will be one pass with two cylinders? That means if the thing breaks, we lose two cylinders and...'

'You don't like that? Lodge a complaint with the management,' Akshay shrugged.

The nerve in Samar's head throbbed with an angry intensity. For a split second, he felt his muscles stiffen, an impulse of intense violence surging through him.

What next? A fight over who gets to sit near the window?

He had had enough of the two drama-queens. Samar was about to let loose when his eyes fell on Anya, soulfully trusting, looking back at him in silent faith, almost as if entreating him noiselessly to stay calm. He had to keep it together. Every second they spent arguing here, Samar reckoned, was reducing their chances of making it out. They had heard explosions throughout their journey and at any time the fire could burst through to this level. What weighed down on him even more was that they had been forced to take this risky path, one where they could be more easily ambushed than in the huge room downstairs. All it would take would be the cable of the cable car to snap. A single, very convenient, point of failure.

'Fine. I am not going to try to talk you two out of this. But you are going last with those two cylinders of yours.'

'Preeti, you and I have been naughty. So, Uncle Samar wants us to go last.'

Samar sought to explain the situation patiently. 'If there is an explosive attached to the trolley wire, it is going to blow the moment the wheels touch the triggering device. The first journey across will be the riskiest. You understand, right? Since, if anything is going to snap, it will do so then. Because you two will carry your two cylinders, and there is nothing I can do to change your mind, it is best you go last. That way, even if the lines blow out, you two will still have a chance of making it through the doors. How you will get to the doors, of course, is another matter.'

Akshay nodded. 'So, by that logic, the first two across should be you and the old doctor. Next Anya, her mother and their cylinder. And finally, me and Preeti with our two. The more cylinders each group has, the more valuable their lives are. I like that.'

Samar turned towards Karan, the only man in the group who seemed to be in his senses. 'Yes. The only two idiots without cylinders. And so we go first.'

Even before Samar had completed his sentence, Karan was already stepping into the cable car. A nod of his head, an adjustment of his silver-framed glasses and he was strapped in. Samar joined him. There was a small control panel on the handle. He flicked the red switch. The overhead motor sprang to life. Stiff gusts of wind gushed out from the overhead air conditioning vents, rocking the cable car slightly.

Samar leant over. 'If you believe in god, now might be a good time to say your prayers.'

'Why? Don't you believe in Him?'

'No, I never did. And now might be a bit too late to start.' Prayers? God? He could hardly believe these words had come out from his mouth. 'I just said that to make sure you are ready, in case we...'

Karan remained as placidly stoic as always. 'Of course, I am ready. Every moment we live, we move one second closer to death. No bigger truth than that. Is there?'

Samar stayed silent, feeling the strong aura of Karan's peace. The cable car lurched slowly forward, gently rumbling into the vast void ahead.

Preeti hated many things about her mother though nothing more than her impulsiveness. Quick to fall in love and equally quick to fall out. Quick to lose her temper. Quick to trust those that did not deserve to be trusted and quick to suspect everyone else. Quick to cut people out from her life. And equally quick to insist they accept her back into theirs, expecting things to go on as if nothing had happened.

She remembered that autumn morning when, suddenly out of the blue, Ma had showed up at her boarding school, driving a distance of two hundred kilometres. Their annual social was the next day and Preeti, as the Head Girl, was in charge. There was no way she could leave, and neither did she want to, but Ma convinced the nuns to let her come with her for a few hours. She had sulked in the passenger's seat as Ma kept on rambling about how much fun she had in Istanbul, what wonderful hot springs she had been to in Prague, almost as if she genuinely expected Preeti to care.

Then suddenly Ma had taken a detour without telling Preeti, driving off the highway onto a dusty country road. She had caught a glimpse of a Ferris wheel and just had to get on it. Preeti protested; being in Class Ten, she felt she was too old to ride in one. Her protestations, though, fell on deaf ears. Once Ma wanted something, she usually got it.

There had been a light shower a few hours before. Everything around them had been drenched in rain – from the rays of the sun to the wood on the seat. Preeti had sat, scared stiff as the wheel spun them high into the blue sky. Ma however seemed to be having the time of her life, impervious to Preeti's state of fright, her arms outstretched towards the heavens, chestnut-brown hair flying in the wet breeze, eyes closed in delight.

And then she had felt Ma's hand in hers, surprising in its warmth. 'Don't worry, I am here,' she had said. Then Ma had shouted, 'Wheeeeeee, I am flying.'

As the cable car inched forward slowly through the vast emptiness, images of that afternoon came flooding back to her, fresh like strawberries in June. Maybe it was just the feeling of being suspended in space, as scared as she had been on the Ferris wheel which had triggered the memory. Or maybe it was that just now, standing at the cusp of life and death, she had finally realized that Ma had cared, in her flawed little way.

'Forget it honey, why do you want the pain to drag? Let it go,' she had said in that singsong way of hers, as casually careless as if she was talking about a dress with a wine-stain. 'By the way, I met this man in Vienna and he was so...' There was no one in her world, except her. And pain never breached its walls, especially when it was someone else's.

Preeti remembered that last night in the hospital. Ma had sat propped on the pillow, her face ravaged by illness. 'Too many cigarettes, too much gin and way too much cocaine' was what the doctor had said. A beautiful woman once, she was just a pale shadow of herself. Ma's entire frame had shrunk and shrivelled, like a raisin out in the sun for too long. Preeti had got the news weeks after Ma had been admitted. Ma had not wanted to inform her. Nor did Preeti want to come for that matter. But yet she had, out of nothing more than a sense of duty. The unpleasantness had only gotten worse through the evening, Ma had berated Preeti for having wasted her life and she had shouted back, blaming her for being a selfish tart. The exchange had become so heated that twice the nurse had come in, the first time coughing pointedly and the second time asking Preeti to not let her mother get so agitated. Ma had shooed the nurse away with a dismissive 'My daughter is like that.' So typically Ma.

After an hour of the back-and-forth, Preeti had had enough. About to leave, she had made it to the door when the distinctive sound of sobbing caused her to pirouette around. There was Ma with her thin disease-ridden hands stretched out, just like they had been on the Ferris wheel. Her words had struggled out amidst the flood of tears. 'I am so sorry. I am sorry for everything. Can you please find it in yourself to forgive me, Pitu?'

Preeti had stood silent for a second. She felt no pity, not even the slightest desire to run into her mother's arms for the hug that she was expecting. All that raged through Preeti was blinding anger. 'No, Ma, I will not. I want you to know that no matter what happens, I will never forgive you. Never.' And she had stomped out.

The call had come that night at 4 a.m. Ma had passed away in her sleep. To her surprise, Preeti felt nothing except a sense of closure. Ma had cried in the end, not her. The knowledge that she could make her feel pain made her somewhat happy.

I will never forgive you. Never.

The words were coming back now, in another voice, murderous and masculine. Only this time she could feel their sharpness, as Ma must have felt them. Ma, the only person in the world who cared to hold her hand when she had been scared. She could see those large eyes even now, shimmering with regret, as Preeti had walked away, without turning back even once.

How can I expect to be forgiven by a stranger when I myself could never forgive the only person who truly cared for me?

Preeti tried desperately to keep the tears away.

If only I had hugged Ma that day. If only I had told her it was all right. If only I had not...

'Are you all right?' Akshay asked. They were sitting together, clutching the cylinders to their laps, squeezed close by the smallness of the bench, as it bobbed slowly down the cable. Samar, Karan, Anjali and Anya had already reached the other side safely, they were the last. 'We are almost there, just a few minutes and this part is over', Akshay continued being comforting, leaning even closer, pressing against her soft shoulder.

Preeti stayed silent, coldly unresponsive.

'Nothing can possibly go wrong, not till we reach that side. There, of course, I have to deal once again with that crazy woman. And that scares me a lot.' Akshay said with a bit of a smile.

Preeti was drowned in herself, scarcely listening. When she spoke, the words came out, quickly tripping over each other. 'How does one expect to be forgiven when one has herself never forgiven? How can I deny someone their revenge when revenge is all that has driven me?'

'Jeez, will you please stop obsessing about that dead movie-star? He is not going to come out from the shadows and strangle you.'

'But I did kill him.'

'No, you didn't. He killed himself.'

'I took away his life, in the same way Vicky took away mine.' Preeti looked down at the room below her, shrouded in bluish light, feeling the void below her feet. 'Have you ever taken something that you could not return? Something that was not yours to take, something so precious that...'

'Oh will you...'

'Have you ever felt so angry that you no longer cared who exactly suffered, only that someone did? Have you ever felt good really hurting someone you loved? I did. I loved the way Ma cried before she died. I loved the look on that Randeep guy's face when I screwed him good.' She paused for breath. 'So, you see, nobody knows more than me, how pleasantly fun revenge will be for him.'

'We will have time to regret and make things better once we get out. For now, I don't see what any of this has to do with what's going on...'

'No, this has *everything* to do with where we are. And why we are here.' Preeti looked over her shoulder towards where they had come from. She lowered her voice to a hoarse whisper, almost as if talking loudly would snap the cable, 'He is watching us like we watch lobsters in a tank. You know how it is: "Hey waiter, give me that one." He is going to point at me, any time now. And I am going to be taken out from the water onto a hot...' She breathed heavily once, trying to swallow her fear. 'I sound crazy, I know. But there is nothing wrong with my head. As a matter of fact, I have never experienced such clarity. It's as if the gas has washed away all the cobwebs in the attic. I can remember things now, things the rape drug blotted out.'

'Agent GX does strange things to your brain. I would not be surprised if it brings back suppressed memories.'

'The rape. I had forgotten all about it. I don't mean I had forgotten what was done to me, I wish I could. But the act itself had been wiped clean off my mind by whatever thing that fuckface had mixed in my drink. Now it's back again. I can see that room, feel the darkness and touch that man again. His spirit is close by, real close... and he wants answers...'

'If it helps Preeti, I am scared too, very scared. And that's just because this place is booby-trapped, and we are people who cannot be trusted.'

Preeti turned to look at Akshay, her eyes softer and kinder than he had ever seen them, mellow like honeyed milk. 'I can trust you. You have been a great friend, these last few hours.'

'Thank you... it's nothing...'

'It is something. Perhaps the only thing left in this place. Friendship.'

Preeti cradled her cylinder in her arms, like a child. 'There is nothing I can do right now, except to give you the most precious thing that I have right now: my password.'

'You don't have to.'

'It's your name Akshay. A-K-S-H-A-Y.'

'I... I... well... I am honoured that you would choose my name as the...'

'It's nothing. I would not have made it this far had it not been for... I just wish I had known you during college, perhaps things could have been different.'

'I wish that too. You have no idea how much I wanted it. But I guess I was just too ordinary for you, then.'

'See that's your problem. It always is for people like you. You try too hard to make yourself extraordinary.' Holding the cylinder in one hand, she reached out and touched his sleeve with the other. 'Who wears such threads unless they are going out to dinner at a fancy place? Or this watch for that matter? Way too showy. And do you know the most ridiculous thing of them all? Your American accent.'

Akshay raised an eyebrow good-humouredly. 'Oh, really? People "like me"? But before that, what's so wrong with my accent?'

'It's totally fake. You know how I know? Cause it changes from time to time. When you are scared, it's gone. When you are trying to impress someone, it's back. Don't tell me no one ever told you this before.'

Akshay nodded his head. 'Not like this.'

Preeti said, 'All I am saying is don't try to hide where you came from. You are a pretty special guy as it is. It's not the worst thing, to blend into the crowd, to be unremarkable.'

'And how does that help?'

'It helps you to be forgotten.'

'But isn't the whole point of the expensive clothes and the watch and the accent to not be forgotten?'

They were almost at their destination. On the raised platform where the cable ended, stood the other four people. Akshay looked towards them, as the trolley gently ground to a halt on the platform. Reaching out his left foot, Akshay anchored it to the metal edge. Standing up on the platform, he put his cylinder down on the side. Then he turned around and gallantly offered Preeti his hand. 'It's a difficult thing to balance, this revenge thing. A part of you wants to leave no trace, just stand in the darkness and watch the fun. But there is this other part that wants to be remembered. Not by everybody of course, just by the person you hate.'

Preeti held his right hand in hers. Wrapping her left arm around the cylinder, she stepped onto the platform. Akshay's chemical-scarred hand shimmered in the light – liquid, red and raw.

He completed his thought. 'Because revenge is never complete till they know it was you.'

The heel of Preeti's shoe hit the metal with an audible clank, turning her ankle slightly. Akshay gripped her firmly, preventing Preeti from falling face down on the surface. 'Hey, watch it...'

Even as she tried to maintain her balance and keep the cylinder from falling out of her arms, Preeti's focus stayed fixed on his hand. A flash went off in her brain like a thunderclap. And another, and yet another. A set of images, bathed in white light, burned into her mind in rapid sequence.

She was back in that nightmarish room. A shadow figure was pinning her down with the weight of his evil. His shirt, white as the starched light, was open down the front obscenely, like a gaping smile, laughing at her helplessness. His torso was descending on her in slow motion, stuttering between each successive flash.

She felt the pain. She felt the scalding heat. But most overwhelmingly, she felt the hate.

And yet through all this, her focus stayed fixed on the hand. The hand of the attacker. For the first time in her life, she could remember what was so special about it.

The hand had been burnt – liquid, scarred and very raw. Just like the man.

Samar was relieved that all of them had made it across the chasm. In front of him, a few metres away, was a metal door leading to the ramp. A minute's walk up that ramp and they would be at the sealed hatch that separated them from the floor above. He certainly had not been expecting the journey to be so painless. Not that he was complaining.

Just at that moment, from the corner of his eye, he saw Preeti stumble.

Reflexively, he reached out his hand to steady her. 'Mind your step there.'

Akshay, having got off the trolley at Preeti's side, reached her first. He clasped her wrist firmly, enabling her to retain her balance. Still bent but moving forward, she looked straight up. As their gazes met, Samar stopped dead, hand still outstretched. Preeti's once-pretty face had become contorted like that of a rabid dog's. Froth guzzled out from the sides of her lips and the eyes were glazed over, glowing almost purple.

Samar had not recovered from the shock of what he had just seen when the Agent Astra cylinder Preeti was carrying hit the ground with a loud clank. His first reaction was to brace for the acid to come splurging out. But the cylinder took the impact.

The moment of relief turned to horror as it started rolling towards the precipice. Samar leapt forward, throwing himself parallel to the ground, trying to grab the cylinder as it teetered on the platform edge, bouncing slightly. As he did so, he saw Preeti crouching, ready to pounce. Samar's focus remained on the cylinder. It had now rounded the edge and was about to topple over when his hands shot out blindly, and the receptacle of acid settled between them perfectly.

Samar lay there on his stomach for an instant, his heart pounding like the pistons of a steam engine. There was no time to catch his breath though. A shriek ripped through the air, echoing through the huge metal chamber, a primal cry of pain and anguish. Akshay had gone down on his knees at the corner.

He was clutching his face, trying to push off Preeti who had pounced upon him like a dog on raw meat.

And then she screamed, each word hanging clear and heavy in the air: 'You raped me.'

Karan was the first to recover from the shock. Striding purposefully, he pulled Preeti away from Akshay, holding her from behind at her waist, pinning her to him. No match for Karan's considerable physical strength, she kept throwing her hands and legs about, in a desperate attempt to break free and claw at Akshay's face.

Anjali and Anya were still in a corner of the platform, Anya in her wheelchair, and Anjali, hand on her open mouth, as if turned to stone. 'Oh my god...'

Akshay was crawling away from Preeti, like a wounded insect, using his right elbow to drag himself forward. His left elbow was raised, the palm covering his left eye. Dribbling down the forearm were torrents of blood, like a spring of pain gushing out of a cave.

'My eye... my eye...' cried out Akshay.

Preeti's words drowned in spit. 'Rapist... you motherfucker... all these years... it was you... you all along.' She swung her elbows with all the force she could muster, trying to burst loose from Karan's hold.

'Cool down, Dr Singh. Please...' he said, coldly patient despite the battering he was receiving.

'Fuck, fuck, fuck... the bitch gouged it out...'Akshay said, tottering upright, his legs unsteady. The door leading to the ramp was right in front of him. He leant on it for support. 'Get her away from me. She has gone mad...'

Preeti tried to speak but the dribble of spit and tears choked her. 'You are dead. You hear me... you are dead.' She twisted her head back to look back at Karan, trying to bite at his wrist, struggling to break loose. Her eyes squinted with effort, the words came out baked in hate. 'Let me go, you old pervert. You're enjoying holding me like this, aren't you?' Her spit landed on his shoulder. 'Getting you hard, am I?'

Karan tried to move her away to a corner, even as she kept flinging herself forward. 'Please, please get a hold on yourself.' Karan looked at Samar, wordlessly asking him to take over the job of restraining Preeti. 'I need to take a look at Dr More. He is seriously hurt.'

Samar left the abandoned cylinder propped near Anya's wheelchair and walked up to where Karan was restraining Preeti. The transfer of the frenzied Preeti into his arms was not easy. As Samar took Karan's place, Preeti rammed her heel onto his toe. He felt the nail splintering inside the shoe yet held on despite the pain.

Akshay was now careening crazily forward into the corridor. Unlike the platform, it was lit brightly. Karan caught hold of him by the shoulders. 'Move your hands away. I need to look at your eye,' he pleaded. Akshay refused, shaking the doctor away violently.

'She is seeing things. It's the gas.' The blood was still dribbling down, a trail of red pain marking his every step.

'You need to let me look at your eye. Please. Maybe we can do something about it.'

Preeti turned towards Anjali, hoping she would help her. 'This man... he raped me. Don't let him get away by telling you that I have gone crazy.'

Anjali had picked up the cylinder that Akshay had propped on the platform. Moving closer to where Samar was still struggling with Preeti, but still maintaining a safe distance, Anjali said,

'Then please stop trying to get at him. The more violent you are, the more everyone will think you are crazy. If he has indeed raped you, we can get you justice once we reach the outside.'

'Hey, hey, you guys aren't actually believing any of this, are you?' Akshay gave yet another ferocious shake to his body. Karan gave up trying to help and stepped back. Akshay moved towards the huge, circular metallic hatch-door, sealed tight, that marked the end of the passageway. 'I swear, a second ago, she was coming onto me. And now, all of a sudden, she has got this into her head.' He was now standing level with a slender black column that reached to his waist. On top of the column, was a touchscreen. The lectern-like structure was the security console for the metal hatch. In normal circumstances, that was where one had to enter the password to open the hatch door. Right now, it was just a blank blue screen with the touch buttons flickering steadily.

Preeti stopped struggling with Samar. Once again, she appealed to Anjali, 'I can prove it. Right here. Right now.'

Karan still kept trying 'This is not the time for this. Nor the place. Please. There will be plenty of opportunities later on for proof.'

Preeti pushed forward slightly. Samar kept his hold on her, but much lighter than before. 'He told me he has chemical burns only on his hands. But now I remember, I remember everything. The marks are everywhere – on his chest, on his cock. The bastard took it all off when he was raping me.'

Akshay took another few steps back.

Preeti laughed hysterically. 'I remember everything now, you bastard. Everything. This place has brought me back, back from the living dead. I am going to live now, you son of a bitch. I am going to enjoy it too, just to make your life hell.'

Anjali walked towards Akshay holding his cylinder. 'Take your shirt off. We can solve this right here.'

'Surely, you guys are not serious.'

'I am serious. Do it.'

'Absolutely not. By the way, who do you think you are? Mother Justice?'

Anjali did not waver. The edge was unmistakeable. 'Why are you afraid to take your shirt off? Surely there is nothing to hide, is there now?'

'Because I refuse to put myself on trial on the basis of a crazy woman's words, that's why. She framed an innocent man once and killed him. Don't you see, she is trying to do that once again?'

'It's all very simple. Your shirt.'

Akshay looked towards Samar for support this time. 'This rape that she talks of – I was not even there at the time. All these years, she has accused her boyfriend of having done it. And now, it has become me.'

Anjali was not prepared to let it go. 'You said it yourself, did you not, that the gas in the air opens up neural pathways? Maybe she has remembered something that had been long forgotten. Maybe she has gone absolutely crazy. I don't know. But still, she is making a claim. There is no way she would know about the scars you carry on your penis, unless it was you who raped her. So, let's start with the shirt.'

Samar broke his silence. 'Really, this is between these two. We shouldn't get involved.'

Anjali hissed. 'I am not dying to get into this mess either. But both of them own cylinders and we absolutely need one of them. So, I think it is in my best interest to resolve this as quickly as possible. Now, Dr More, please, just do it and we can all move on.'

Akshay moved his hand away from his eye and leaned on the wall to the side. Samar wondered whether he was actually going to take his shirt off or whether he just needed the support. His eye was clearly visible now – a mangled blob of orangish-red flesh, misshaped and swollen, like an egg that had burst while boiling.

Karan's voice boomed unexpectedly. 'Anjali is right. Why don't you just take it off and get it done with? You are not helping anyone here with all this drama.'

'Drama? She just tore my bloody eye off, and I am the one doing the drama…'

Akshay once again covered his eye with his hand. 'She has gotten to all of you, hasn't she? All her life, she's been doing this. Acting the victim. Getting away with murder.'

Preeti had been slowly advancing all this time. Samar had stayed near her, his hand gently near her waist, prepared to grip her tight if she made any sudden movement. Suddenly he slipped, losing his hold for just a fraction of a second, as his shoe slid over something smooth and viscous. He knew what it was without looking. Akshay's blood. That fumble was all Preeti needed. Like a horse bolting, she surged forward, given wings by the hatred that burnt inside her. Karan was too slow in reacting this time. Flying past his effort to stop her, she leapt in the general direction of her target, screaming incoherently.

Anticipating the attack, Akshay stepped deftly to the side, but not far enough to avoid the full thrust of Preeti's weight. Off balance, he stumbled against the wall. Preeti's hand lashed out, this time clutching his collar. The momentum of her forward lunge ripped the white shirt clean off. As she stumbled, her legs hit the large panel, the one that controlled access to the door, with a loud smashing sound.

All eyes were now on Akshay. His chest, revealed in the bluish light, was rough and striated like the skin of a serpent, brown and red in its stark chemical-burnt ugliness.

'See, see, he has it everywhere'. Preeti's eyes glittered. 'I told you. I told you... It was him...'

A heavy rumbling sound drowned out her voice. There was no time to move. No one did. The entire place trembled as a solid block of metal, the size of a large refrigerator, ripped out of the ceiling and slammed onto the ground, right where Preeti Singh had been kneeling a sliver of a second before, triumphant in the moment of her vindication.

A huge lake of shimmering liquid red now spread out slowly from that very spot. Preeti lay crushed beneath the boulder, flattened like an ant by a heavy boot.

The only thing that struck out from below was her right hand, its index finger still accusing, pointed dead ahead at Akshay. It seemed to tremble once and then once again, like a broken watch spring, before finally becoming deathly still.

'Twenty-seven minutes late. Twenty-seven, you fucking sewer rat.' Sonda spat the words out viciously, the veins in his forehead throbbing with wild rage. 'Can't even blame you, I guess. It's in the blood. Your dads eat the shit that comes out of our asses, us honest taxpayers. Then they settle down on our land, turn it into stinking holes, and breed with she-mice whores. And out come sewer rats like you.' He gulped down the spit that had flooded his mouth. 'You know what the solution is? Take some rat-poison and put it in the slum water supply. Wouldn't that be awesome? But, of course our government pussies won't do it. Too many votes in sucking up to rats...'

Akshay More stood in his sparkling white club-attendant uniform, looking down at his shining black shoes. No one talked back to Sonda, or even made eye-contact, when he was in one of his rages. It didn't take much to trigger one – poor people, half-wits, fat whores, government handouts and, the worst of them all, people who stole his time. Akshay had stolen his. Precisely twenty-seven minutes, as he had pointed out, his brutish finger tapping the thick, diamond-studded gold watch wrapped round his gigantic, hairy wrist.

Sonda's time was valuable. After all, he was the owner of Elixir, Pune's hottest club where the filthy rich and the filthier powerful danced, drank and doped. Sonda was not his real name. No one knew what name was on his birth certificate, if he had one, or how he came into so much money. Remo, the bartender, said that Sonda had once been the bodyguard of Mumbai's most famous don, now in exile in Pakistan. But Remo... you could never trust that bastard, especially after he had snorted some white powder. What Akshay did know about Sonda was that he could bench-press a hundred kilos, that he had no qualms punching employees in the face, that he had a wife and two mistresses and that the police called him 'sir'. You did not mess with Sonda in this town.

Akshay kept looking contrite. He did not want to lose this job at the club; the timings here suited his college schedule, since the parties were always in the evening. More importantly, it paid him four times more than his last job as a shop assistant at Shirtains. Akshay needed the money badly. Mother had been sending longer letters and that meant he was expected to send more back home. Not that he much enjoyed cleaning the bar, mopping up spills, serving drinks in the rooms above and taking orders for martinis and Manhattans. But it still beat, by a long margin, folding clothes, measuring the waists of obese men, lifting and stocking supplies and then being paid peanuts at the end of the week.

Sonda shook Akshay by the collar, his breath smelling of whiskey, chicken and hate. 'That's the second time I've caught you sneaking in late. Last time, it was fifteen minutes. This time, it's double that. You better hope, fucking hope that this does not happen once more.' The material of the shirt bit into Akshay's neck, yet he did not dare look up. 'I hire you for one simple reason. The girls here like to have smart-looking, English-speaking pretty boys wishing them Happy Valentine's Day with a fucking rose and a free drink. And you do look kind of like a faggot. But don't kid yourself. You are not irreplaceable. Get that? Now stop looking at your limp dick, and make yourself useful, you pathetic piece of low-bred shit.'

'I am sorry, sir, won't happen again,' Akshay said, before backing out of Sonda's blast radius.

A few minutes later, he was arranging the glasses at the bar, like a robot. Remo, long and wiry, sidled up. For some reason, he always reminded Akshay of a tapeworm. 'Why do you do this every time, this coming late? We have a good thing going here; don't ruin it, dude.'

Akshay had half a mind to tell Remo what had happened. He had left college early enough. About halfway to the club, on the open country road, it had come back again. The chemical-burnt nerves on his chest, crotch and arms had roared to life, strong in their anger. Head spinning in intense agony, he had driven his bicycle off the road onto the grass at the side. Frozen beneath the tranquil sky, he had lain there, white spittle gurgling out from the corner of his mouth. After what seemed to be an eternity of spasming without control, the attack burnt itself out, leaving behind only its dark shadow and a promise to return.

No. He would never talk of the pain to Remo or anyone else for that matter. He never went to the beach, just to avoid the stares and the questions that would follow if he took his shirt off. The only time he mentioned the accident was if someone noticed his hands. Even then he brushed it away, never revealing how pervasive the burning had been. The scars were his shame, mocking him every time he looked in the mirror.

Remo whispered, 'You got the stuff, right? The club's gonna get hot tonight.' Akshay pointed to his backpack, propped up behind the bar counter and winked slyly.

After the accident in the lab, he had been warned against doing any more experiments alone. One more time and he would be rusticated. But he had continued, bribing the old guard to let him work after the doors closed. The lab was his ticket to the big-time and no one, not some dipstick with 'principal' written in gold letters on a piece of wood, was going to keep him from that.

He procured the raw materials from local stores. The Internet provided the manuals. Thus equipped, he would sneak into the college lab and manufacture recreational drugs, which could then be sold on the streets. It was not just the rupees and the paise that brought him back every few nights to the lab. Akshay just loved the challenge. Since he never had all the chemicals or the sophisticated equipment the processes required, he had to continuously innovate and improvise – and it was this that kept him awake for nights on end. He loved chemicals, loved playing with them, loved the way the colours changed, the way powders spluttered like angry serpents when sprayed with liquids and the sudden, magical changes in temperature. Most of all, he loved being God, creating something valuable out of nothing. It was the only time he felt truly in control of his life.

The problem, of course, was moving the stuff. He had sold some during the annual fest but it was too risky. Demand was low on campus, nothing compared to what it was in the clubs – clubs like Elixir. That is why the job meant so much to Akshay. He could not sell directly, though. Everything had to pass through Remo. He made the contacts, slipped the stuff to the boys and girls in the club and collected on the payments. Akshay knew Remo ripped him off on his share of the cut, but then that came with the territory.

'I have the usual. Make it count tonight, Remo.'

The 'usual' was what Remo had been selling as Ecstasy. Producing euphoric highs among all-night revellers, it was the drug of choice at Elixir and the rich kids paid well for the 'foreign stuff'. What they did not know was that the 'foreign stuff' was being made by a second-year college student, right here in Pune.

Today, however, Akshay had something else in his backpack, a new drug he had developed. This was his greatest creation yet. He had to keep it hidden from Remo. His plan was to sell it here direct, without giving the cheat his share, now that he had his own contacts among the regulars.

'Don't worry, you rat. We will rob the bank today. Now take this vodka to that long-legged bitch sitting there.' Pursing his lips in a mock whistle, Remo ogled. 'Would you look at those fuck-me heels? The bitch is in heat... you can bake a loaf of bread there...'

Akshay took the tray, his mind still preoccupied with how to start selling his new product. Remo caught him by the shoulder. 'And oh, don't ask her for money. Her boyfriend called and told me to put her drinks on his tab. It's the bitch's birthday. Fuck, man. Would love to see her as naked as a baby...'

Akshay nodded and set off towards the table. The good thing about Remo was that once the partying began, he started taking the stuff himself. That was when Akshay figured he could walk about, push the stuff, and Remo wouldn't even know.

He bent down and set the tray on the table, absentmindedly glancing up. His stomach clenched tight. Sitting there, in a kill-me short black cocktail dress, was Preeti Singh.

Akshay's first reaction was one of shame. They were not students in the same college anymore. She was the customer and he, the server. *Wait*, he thought, *there really is nothing to be ashamed of.* Working here in Elixir was considered cool and it wasn't as if she'd seen him wiping the floor or getting slapped around by Sonda.

He smiled at Preeti and said, 'Hi.' Preeti made eye-contact in the haughty way that was oh-so-Preeti-Singh. She said nothing, but looked at him with a 'Do I know you?' expression.

Akshay realized his mistake. Of course, she did not recognize him. Who would, in this white suit he was wearing and the crazy red bow tie, which he always felt made him look like a back-up dancer in one of those 80s movies.

'Remember? We met during the prize-distribution ceremony two months ago. You were Miss Sandham College, and I was getting the President's Gold Medal.'

She still kept looking at him.

'We were sitting next to each other. The Dean pronounced my name wrong. You laughed... Remember, I was joking how boring his speech was, and you...'

Yet, she kept looking. There was an uncomfortable second of silence.

Then another.

Finally, Preeti smiled that winning smile of hers, the one which always stopped Akshay's heart dead. She had finally recognized who he was. Of course, she would. Who forgets the guy who came first in college?

'This has to be the weirdest way of asking for a tip. Look, whatever your name is, you don't need to make up these little stories. I'm a good tipper, as any other waiter here will tell you. Plus, it's my birthday, and I am in a great, great mood.'

Akshay had been called many things in life from a rat to a shit-eating pig. He had never taken them to heart; being called names was not really the worst thing about being poor. But never, ever, had he ever been made to feel so insignificant, so small. It was as if being the college's best student, considered worthy of sharing a stage with her, counted for nothing the moment he put on a waiter's uniform. It wasn't that Preeti had a bad memory; it was just that her brain could not make a connection between a person whom she spent two hours talking to and the server with the tray that stood before her. The uniform had reduced him to a faceless cog in society's wheel, a man who was yet not a man. Akshay fought back the tears, without much success.

Even then Preeti did not notice. Because, as he now realized, she had never once ever looked *at* him. She had always looked *through* him.

Digging through her purse, Preeti asked, 'How much do I owe you?'

Akshay found his voice, choked, cracked and trembling. 'Ma'am, it's been paid for.'

'Oh, Vicky must have called. He has been so sweet these last few days. Well, here is your tip then.' Her slender fingers held up a fifty-rupee note, dangling at the extremities of her long, red-painted nails, then put it onto Akshay's tray, right next to the coaster.

Akshay used his shoulder to wipe his tear-soaked cheeks. 'Happy Birthday,' he mumbled as he started walking away. She did not even acknowledge him, turning her eyes away towards the glittering disco globe that spun overhead, round and round.

'Jesus! Why don't you watch where you are going, you stupid oaf?' Vicky looked in anguish at the wet streak from a martini snaking down his black silk shirt.

'I am so sorry, sir. Come with me to the bathroom and let me take care of that.'

'If this does not come off in five minutes, I am going to make Sonda take it out of your pay cheque.'

Akshay shook his head, immensely apologetic, leading Vicky into the restroom while holding his drinks tray in one hand. Panels of wall mirrors, elegant marble washbasins, luxuriant arches and a chandelier... Akshay had often wondered how many of the families, including his own, who lived in the run-down rows of tenements in Mumbai, could be accommodated inside one of these rooms.

Vicky was grumbling loudly in his ear. 'You have no idea how much the shirt costs, do you? Many months of your salary...'

'Please, sir, take the shirt off.' Vicky threw his shirt at Akshay and stood bare-chested, glowering aggressively. Akshay rubbed his fingers rapidly on the stain, taking some of the hand soap and plucking a lime wedge from the side of a glass. He kept the tray on one of the huge marble panels. 'Sir, while you wait, please take as many drinks as you want. My compliments.'

Vicky took a drink from the tray. Gulping one down as fast as he could, he reached out for another. Then something made him stop.

The tap was on. But the waiter was not holding the shirt under the water.

Instead, he was watching him from the corner of his eye. 'What are you looking at me for? Go, wash the shirt.'

'Just seeing you gulping down one free drink after another,' Akshay said with a disarmingly pleasant smile.

'What, for fuck's sake, is that supposed to mean?'

'Just wondering how there is not much difference there between me and you. Rich or poor, we all like freebies. We all like to take that which is not ours.' Akshay was now putting the white waiter's gloves back, working his fingers into them with cold deliberation.

'Are you messing with me, boy?' The last words came out slurred. Vicky's tongue weighed a tonne. The waiter was flickering in front of him like a bulb about to blow its filament.

'Y... you will pay for...' Vicky felt his knees buckling. As he stumbled backwards, Akshay stepped forward quickly and caught him from behind. Vicky's body slumped into his arms.

'No, you fool, it's you who is going to pay today.' Akshay paused, looking down at Vicky, passed out limp. 'And it's gonna be me who gets the freebie.'

'Take these cocktails upstairs to Room 211. If you can get a peek in past her boyfriend, you might even get a glimpse of heaven. Fuck, he must be having the time of his life.'

Remo nudged Akshay in the ribs. The floor above the bar housed what were euphemistically known as 'private party rooms', luxuriantly furnished with funky lighting and fancy speakers, that were used for one thing and one thing only.

Time of his life indeed, thought Akshay. *Does being kept in a walk-in closet on the second floor, in deep chemically induced sleep, qualify as a good time?*

Akshay had been waiting for exactly this order all evening. A wet chill of excitement ran down his spine. He was drunk without a single drop, high without a single hit of white. Yet he had never been so calm before in his life, never been as sure of what he had to do. He had played it perfectly till now. Remo, that sneaky bastard, had no idea that Akshay had any interest in the girl in the black cocktail dress. He also thought that her boyfriend was, at the moment, in her room. In case questions were asked later, Remo would provide the perfect alibi.

Throughout the evening, while serving drinks, Akshay's attention had been solely on the corner table where she'd been sitting. The boyfriend, Vicky, arrived soon after she had tipped him. They had then sat there in the shadows together. Around an hour later, he had received a call, kissed Preeti and left. Akshay had been close enough to catch his parting words: 'Wait for me upstairs, honey. Something just came up.'

She'd had another drink at the table and then gone up. Akshay had followed her with his eyes. She was moving funny, with an exaggerated swagger of her hips.

Drunk. Perhaps.

In heat. Absolutely. Perfect.

About forty minutes later, he saw Vicky come in through the main door. The club was crowded, the dance floor packed. No one noticed his arrival. Akshay did. He had been looking out for it. Slipping upstairs, into the darkened corridor, he waited with the tray. The 'accidental' spilling of the drink, the fake show of subservience, the entry into the bathroom had been smooth. As smooth as the fake call placed earlier to Vicky's phone.

Details. The devil was always in the details and Akshay had remembered to keep the devil happy. To make sure that they would not be disturbed by a random visitor, Akshay had stuck an 'Out of Order' board outside the door beforehand. Vicky had been so distracted by the conversation that he didn't notice the sign. Nor had he noticed Akshay locking the bathroom door shut behind him. Once he had gulped down two glasses, rich-boy hadn't taken much time to pass out, collapsing like a sack of potatoes. Akshay had then 'stored' him in the janitor's closet.

But what about when he came to? Surely, he would remember who did this to him? No, he would not. That was the genius of the whole thing.

The stuff that had been slipped into his martini was Akshay's masterpiece, his Mona Lisa. He had produced it in the lab, using commonly available stuff bought from the corner-store chemist outside campus. This was what he had been planning to sell on his own in Elixir. The rich kids would love anything that got girls into the sack. And this one was a sure shot. In small doses, it made people lose their inhibitions. In medium quantities, it left gigantic gaps in memory. And Vicky had been given a large amount, enough to make even an elephant forget. *If I want, I could wrench this guy's teeth out with pliers and he would just wake up a few hours later wondering how he had aged so fast.*

Akshay smiled. Like a well-designed experiment, everything had been set up perfectly. The reaction was now chugging along. There was no going back. For now though, he put the arrogant prick out of his mind. More important things remained to be done. Returning to the bar unnoticed, he busied himself wiping the glasses, waiting, waiting for the inevitable order to go up with complimentary drinks. It would come soon enough and when it did, he would be ready.

Luck had never been so good.

Akshay stood at the door of Room 211. A second passed. Another. The powder swirled into the drink from the sachet in his hand. A moderate dose would suffice for Preeti. He did not want her to pass out cold. She needed to be in her senses, just enough to feel everything.

You forgot me because I was too insignificant. Well, not after tonight.

From today on, you will remember me. Except that you will not be able to.

That will be your tragedy. That will be your curse, Preeti.

The door opened slowly. Inside, Preeti was reclining on the bed, twirling a high-heeled shoe on her toe seductively. 'Vicky... what took you so long?' she slurred.

'No, ma'am. I am here with the drinks.'

'Oh, the boy. Keep it on the table. Now where has Vicky vanished to?'

Akshay walked in and held the tray in front of Preeti. She took the glass by the stem without looking at him. Her purse lay on the side. She fumbled for it.

'Ma'am. No need for a tip. You have already given me enough.'

Akshay felt strange. It was like watching a chicken moving around in a cage, unaware of its fate, while the butcher sharpens the knife at the side. She was drinking deeply, once again no longer conscious of his presence. He backed away, closing the door, out into the shadows.

The drug would take two to three minutes to act. He looked up and down the corridor. No one had seen him. Turning the knob, he re-entered. The door locked behind him with a silent click.

Preeti Singh was propped on the bed, her eyes still, like those of a fish.

She was now under his spell.

Akshay unbuttoned his shirt. The waiter's uniform slid noiselessly to the ground. He stood naked, gazing with pride at the dark crevices and red troughs on his chest.

The mirror at the head of the bed covered the wall from one end to the other. Reflected back at him was a powerful dragon, marked by the fiery fingers of fate, one that would take whatever it wanted from the world, without apology, without scruples. And those who stood in its path would be scalded.

He ran his fingers over the scars. No shame. Not anymore. Akshay mounted the bed.

Looking down on Preeti Singh, he felt a blinding rush of hatred, as intensely enlivening as the blood rushing into your leg after it has gone to sleep. Akshay bathed in it, letting it drench him to his core.

Fuck you, bitch. Fuck your snottiness. And fuck your tips. All my life, I have served your kind. Now it's your turn to pay me back.

Then he started, slow and hard. She gasped for breath, drowning in his naked aggression.

All my life, I have been screwed by the world. Now it's my turn.

He looked in pleasure at her eyes, open wide, seeing, yet not registering, feeling, yet not comprehending.

How does it feel to be a bit of meat?

Finally, it was over. He was still shivering, panting with excitement, his entire body engulfed by the flames of his wrath.

His training had taught him that most accidents happen at the closing stages of an experiment. This meant he had to wrap things up perfectly. He opened the door slightly. The closet was nearby. He dragged Vicky's unconscious body by its armpits and put it in Room 211.

Akshay surveyed the scene in front of him. Vicky would not remember anything of what happened. Neither would Preeti. Hell, she had forgotten him even without being drugged.

He clinically wiped out all traces of him having been there. He loved reading about forensic science and knew exactly what the cops would look for – if they came, that is. They would not. Sonda would hush this up, he was sure. It would be bad for his business if the word got out that rich bitches were getting raped on the premises.

Smiling at the two figures sprawled on the bed, he could not help but think of what that big rhino had called him earlier in the evening. A rat, one that lives in a stinking hole.

Maybe being a rat was not such bad a thing after all – steal the cheese and simply vanish into the darkness.

Never to be found. Never to be remembered.

Karan Rathore sat still on his haunches, looking at the metal block that almost completely covered Preeti Singh's crushed body, oblivious of the blood lapping gently against the black leather of his shoes. 'It was the control panel, wasn't it? That's where they set the trap.'

Samar stood right in front of the control panel, shaking his head sadly. 'Yes, it was. She hit the panel with her foot. That set off the trigger, sending those tonnes of metal falling on her head. A modified deadfall, that's what this is.'

The deadfall, thought Samar, *one of the oldest traps known to man*. A heavy boulder is kept tilted at an angle and supported by branches. When the animal runs into one of the branches, it triggers the boulder's collapse right on top of it. The mechanism here was, of course, way more sophisticated than that, but the basic principle was the same.

Anjali was still standing where she had been when Preeti died, clutching Anya to her breast. The girl was trembling in fear. It must be horrible not to be able to scream, thought Samar.

'You murdered her,' said Anjali, in an almost matter-of-fact way.

Akshay remained silent, his right cheek now a swollen bloody mess, still looking fixedly where Preeti Singh lay buried beneath the metal, as helpless and immobile as she had been when he had left her, so many years ago, in that hellish room. The blood was spreading in all directions. He caught his face reflected in the trembling puddle of red. The dragon no longer roared back at him.

'You murdered her,' Anjali repeated. She was not going to let him go without an answer.

'She set off the trap. I had no hand in it.' More blood came down from his eyes, down over his cheeks.

'Disgusting pig,' Anjali mumbled.

Akshay kept looking at the Preeti's index finger, still in a trance. The words came out dry and flat. 'Thank you. Rat or pig – no problem being any of that. I have been called worse.'

Many years ago, while he used to work for the government, Samar remembered catching this guy, Kumar. An attaché at the Prime Minister's Office, he had been passing sensitive files to the Pakistanis. Since it was Samar's surveillance tech that had brought him in, he was part of the interrogation team. At the table under the overhead light, Kumar clammed up at first. Then his old boss, Sunderan had taken out his 'Human Rights Box.' Samar hated violence, so he had sat outside the room, smoking and playing solitaire while Sunderan and Iqbal worked on Kumar. Around dawn, Sunderan had called Samar in.

When he entered, he could barely recognize the man that had walked in earlier that afternoon. They had broken him down physically and mentally. When Kumar spoke, he was barely coherent, his words coming out slurred like he was drunk. Rather than answering any of the questions, he kept going on and on about why he had done what he had, trying to justify to these strangers around him that he was not a bad man.

Akshay seemed to be in a similar state of utter breakdown. He kept rambling on about Preeti, what she had done to him, how she had set up the actor fellow and then once again repeating what she had done to him. To make things worse, Anjali kept arguing with Akshay throughout and Karan, whom he was expecting to end the conversation, remained silent, almost as if interested keenly in the exchange.

Samar had to snap them out of it. 'What Akshay did is none of our business.'

'A rape? A girl killed? None of our business?'

She has forgotten amidst this outrage, Samar thought, that it is her daughter for whom time was of the greatest importance. It might have slipped her mind, but not his.

'Preeti is gone, and we can't bring her back. I don't care how unfeeling and cold-hearted this makes me sound, but arguing over this is a waste of time.'

Karan nodded. 'He is right. We don't have time. And now with her death, we don't have her cylinder. Two acid capsules and two doors now. No more backup.'

Anjali pointed at Akshay viciously. 'If only this man hadn't insisted on not having one password for all of them.'

Akshay took off the remains of his blood-soaked shirt and dropped it tiredly on the floor. 'Preeti told me the password before she died.'

'Thank god,' Anjali folded her hands in prayer.

'Time I made myself useful,' Akshay stood up now, his face twisted in pain from the effort. Taking Preeti's cylinder, he approached the gigantic circular metal hatch. He explained to no one in particular, 'The way this works is that you stick it to the object which you want to burn through.'

On one side of the cylinder was something akin to a seal. He pulled it off. 'This now exposes a strong industrial adhesive.'

Samar wondered why Akshay was suddenly being so professorial, almost as if he was demonstrating an experiment in class. Maybe this was his way of fighting the anguish, his way of shutting out the dead body lying at his feet.

Akshay stuck the cylinder to the hinge. Despite its rather considerable weight, it remained effortlessly attached in a horizontal position. 'There, gentlemen, you have it.' Akshay punched in the password. Immediately a sharp chirping beep started. 'And now, thirty seconds to detonation. So, I better get moving.'

Akshay started running back, quite quickly for a man who was so visibly in immense physical discomfort. The rest of the party also scrambled back, seeing how far from the cylinder Akshay had run.

The acids were now flowing into each other, swirling and glowing angrily. The canister shook. Then it exploded, but not as violently as Samar had anticipated, almost as if someone had overturned a shelf full of glass plates.

Had it misfired? Samar could not see past the dense grey fumes that covered the surface of the door. He waited. He waited some more. Each second seemed to be an eternity. The smoke slowly dissipated, becoming more and more transparent, till the wisps of acid died away, leaving behind a clean, though uneven hole in the metal. Blue light from the floor above streamed in, flooding them all with hope.

'It worked. Oh my god, it worked.' The excited happiness in Anjali's voice was barely concealed. She had seemingly forgotten all her anguish. All of them stood for a second, watching the solid metal totally dissolving in front of them. There was space now for a man to walk through.

Akshay had once again sunk to his knees, holding Preeti's wrist limply. 'This sounds crazy, I know. But I really loved you, all my life. If only you knew...'

Suddenly conscious of Samar's surprised gaze burning into the back of his head, Akshay turned towards him. 'Sometimes the only thing you want in life is to be accepted, you know, accepted by this one really special person. But when you find out that that person doesn't care... hell, doesn't even acknowledge your existence as a human being... the love that is inside, it twists,' Akshay thumped his chest theatrically, 'into monstrous hate.'

Samar looked the other way, totally cold. As far as he was concerned, this man was rambling on like a mad dog. Then his eye caught Anjali Menon. She was looking furtively at Akshay, gently shaking her head, almost as if in silent empathy with what he had just said.

Samar wondered why.

The waters of the lake, dark and ominous, shivered in the light breeze. A fog had descended from beyond the blue mountains, smothering like a heavy pillow. Far away in the liquid vastness, a small raft bobbed up and down. On it a stood a girl, back turned to the shore, looking upwards at the looming hills. Samar cried out from the shore, once and then again. Reshmi, all alone in the middle of the lake, was unaware of her danger. She needed to be warned. But no matter how much Samar shouted, long and clear, she did not seem to hear. Or perhaps she did not want to.

Then she turned.

The sound died in Samar's throat. His daughter's eyes had turned to silent stone, her face as sternly still as the grey sky, hair swirling in the breeze like angry serpents. Streaming down her cheeks, as if in stop motion, were clear drops of red blood. Yet her expression changed not a bit, remaining icy and impenetrable.

Samar tried to wade into the lake but it seemed to move away from him. Then, all of a sudden, the entire sky turned crimson. The waters bubbled and hissed in rage as the lake dissolved into black flames.

Reshmi was gone.

But the silence had been broken. A booming voice filled the world, lilting in its African accent, familiar and yet so forgotten: Save me, sir. Save my son.

The journey had become more difficult. The sheer vastness of this level tightened around Samar, suffocating all hope.

He had been alert enough to spot two potential traps in the last hour. But the intensity could not be kept up, not indefinitely, not the way he could feel himself sinking. His head was spinning, as if he had just stepped down from a fast merry-go-round. Long-forgotten faces crowded around, walking noiselessly over from the dream world into the real and back again.

The effects of the chemicals, he reminded himself, touching his forehead.

He was burning up with fever.

'It gets worse every second. Doesn't it? Those visions?' The gentle voice of Karan Rathore brought him back. 'Memories of Sierra Leone, perhaps?'

First Lilith. Now him. How does everyone know?

Karan smiled knowingly. 'I still remember the way you gave a start when Lilith Adams used the word Sierra Leone in the first meeting we had. It wasn't so much the fact that her eyes were turned on you that made me notice. It was how your slouched shoulders suddenly stiffened to attention, almost like a deer does when she detects a tiger in the vicinity.'

'You notice much.'

'Any good doctor does. He has to. Most patients, they don't really know what bothers them. All they know is the pain.'

Karan rubbed his chin thoughtfully. 'Don't worry, it wasn't just you that she fingered. She did it to the others too. Dr More, for instance. While talking about safety precautions in the Mine, she had said something on the lines of *how scarring a moment of carelessness can be*. Then there was a time she said she expected the judgment of the team to be fair and not be influenced by personal prejudices. Guess who she was looking at then?' A smile crossed Karan's lips. 'Of course, all this strikes me now as I think of it. Though I have to say, no one there quite reacted as obviously as you.'

Samar slowed his pace. He looked around to see that Anjali, pushing Anya's wheelchair, and the limping Akshay had fallen quite a distance behind, out of earshot for the moment. With some irritation, Samar asked, 'So what's the point you are trying to make?'

'You would have seen it yourself by now had you still not been clinging to your idea of this being a military experiment, even though we haven't any evidence so far to back that up.'

'And your hypothesis is...?'

Karan said, 'Everything Lilith Adams said has so far come true. The girl paid for her sins. So did Dr More – with his eye. He's never going to see again, that I am pretty sure of.'

'That's bullshit. I may be getting screwed in the mind by the gas, but I'm not so fucked that I am going to buy this retribution crap. Preeti got killed because she was running all over the place in a mine-field and hit her foot on a trap. As simple as that.'

'So you feel no fear? No fear at all for what you did in Sierra Leone?'

'Wait... Wait. What did I do in Sierra Leone? What do you know about what I did there?' Samar's raised voice made everyone else look at him. The smile on Karan's face got broader.

'Nothing. I know nothing except what the fear on your face tells me every time that place is mentioned in your presence.'

Samar felt he had to defend himself. He really had nothing to hide. 'All right then. So here is what happened in Sierra Leone. Fourteen years ago, I was working a contract job at a diamond mine, in charge of electronic security and video surveillance. Two months into the assignment, there was a miner's mutiny. It was not pretty. They killed three guards, grabbed their guns, and went after everyone else. I ran into the mountains, along with a few others, on foot. There I stayed for a week hiding in the thickets. Then, the owners sent in the heavy artillery. A private army of mercenaries swooped down on the miner's villages and they... well... they burnt them to the ground. Killed a lot of innocent people too. Just to teach a lesson.'

'And no one knew about this? No one was ever brought to justice?' asked Karan.

Samar shrugged. 'I never talked about it to anyone. Not even to my wife. All my assignments, in any case, are top-secret. So yes I was surprised when Lilith Adams mentioned it.'

'Don't you feel even a little bit guilty that you kept silent? That you let mass murder go unpunished despite being, by your own admission, a witness?'

'What bull! Do you know what kind of a place Sierra Leone is? Killing and counter-killing is the law there. What do you think I should have done? Filed a police report at the local station about death squads?'

'I know that many of these warlords in Sierra Leone were tried by special courts set up by their government together with the United Nations. Made quite a bit of news. I know that they all got off because there was no one to give witness against them. Did you ever try to find out what *you could have done*, Mr Bose, considering that you have knowledge of them killing a lot of people, innocent people as you say?'

'No, I did not. It was not my business.'

'Ah, "not my business",' said Karan loudly, before dropping his voice to say, 'How delightfully evil.'

Samar found himself gasping for breath. He suddenly felt very weary, like a brown leaf in the winter breeze. Karan's eyes were gleaming once again and this time he found them infuriatingly piercing. 'Evil? Are you calling me evil?'

'I understand evil is a very offensive word. It is... how to put it... too dramatic. But I did not use it lightly.' Karan adjusted the sleeves of his shirt. 'Allow me to explain. Consider people like our friend Dr More here.' Karan looked to see Akshay was still some distance away, struggling to walk. He lowered his voice even so. 'What he did to that woman was so clearly horrible that we can all point and say "Yes, this man is evil." Easy.

'Things are less straightforward when we come to people like Preeti Singh. She is, after all, a victim. Awww, poor girl – that's what we say, isn't it?' Karan brandished his index finger, swinging it from side to side. 'I say no. She is evil, some may say even more evil than Dr More. After all, he took revenge on the person who hurt him. Even animals bite if you poke them. But

Preeti? She took her revenge on an innocent man just because he bore a resemblance to the one she thought had hurt her. How senseless is that?'

The rest of the group had now caught up with them. Karan looked at them to acknowledge their presence. '*Transference.* One of the evils of the modern world, Mr Bose. I am weak. I cannot get back at the one who hurt me. No problem. I just take it out on someone else, someone who is weaker. And no, that does not make me bad. I did it because someone else "made me" do it.

'When I was a child, there was an old man who would come to our neighbourhood, going from door to door, selling eggs. Sometimes in between, he would sit quietly on the sidewalk polishing his eggs. They shone white, I tell you, that's how much he cared for them. Then one day, a group of Muslims set a Hindu family on fire over some land dispute. Riots broke out in the city. The old Muslim egg-seller must have known how risky it would be for him to make his rounds in a Hindu locality. But even then, he still came. Maybe he had to sell those eggs before they rotted. Maybe he thought everyone knew him and so he was safe. I don't know. All I remember is walking to the corner the next day and only seeing a large number of eggs, clean and white no more, lying broken on the bloody footpath. Now, if this kind of misdirected revenge is not evil, you wonder what is.

'The worst form of sin is, of course, still not transference. It is the acceptance of sin. Every bit of food we eat, everything we wear is obtained through some form of exploitation – of farmers, weavers, labourers, miners – someone, somewhere deprived of his fair share so that we may get ours. Yet, we are comfortable with it. We might as well be, because it is just the way God built this world. Makes you wonder whether God himself is evil. Or whether what we consider the design of the devil is actually nothing but the will of God?'

Samar shook his head. 'So what's your point?'

Karan ignored the interjection. 'I, too, have lived my life not asking the uncomfortable questions – whose plate goes empty tonight so that I can have my roasted chicken on a bed of tender rice; which child never goes to school for the sake of my Persian rug; which man groans in agony so that I sleep snug and comfortable in my warm bed. When I see children begging on the streets, I roll up the car windows and turn up the airconditioner. When I come across dishonesty, I pretend not to notice, taking the high road. Each and every time though, I have an excuse ready for this cowardice, a line which I believe, Mr Bose, is one of your favourites. *It is not my business.*'

The whole party had now stopped. Everyone was looking at Samar. His face had gone dark. He understood perfectly well now what this lengthy monologue had been leading up to. The rage was rising up in him, slowly but surely like a well of acid. He was about to let loose when an unearthly shriek preempted him.

Akshay was looking past them with his remaining good eye, at the shadows high up on the giant turbines that ran across the room. He was trying to say something but only a terrified gurgle came from his throat. Their eyes followed his gaze. There was nothing there except rotating ventilator fans.

Akshay screamed, 'P... P... Preeti... up there. She...'

Since Preeti's death an hour or so ago, Akshay had been steadily sinking. His handsome face, bloodied and beaten up, looked like a can crushed under the tires of a monster-truck. The arrogant strut was gone. Every few seconds, he would stop to look over his shoulder, mumble something under his breath, and then shuffle on, almost tripping over his shoes, cradling his Agent Astra cylinder like a dead baby in his arms. Sometimes he would say something out loud, but none of the party would turn and respond.

Karan now did. 'We do not see her. But I am not going to call you crazy. I am convinced that you do see her because that vision is real. For you and you only.' Akshay was trembling, still looking up, rivulets of cold sweat streaming down the side of his neck.

'She is coming for me.' His words came out in pained gasps.

Karan gripped Akshay's wrist. 'All of us here have their own little visions of hell. Your friend Preeti had hers. Now it's your turn. I wish I could comfort you. I wish I could tell you everything will be all right.' The gentle smile had now been replaced by an expression of intense sadness. 'But I can't.'

Samar realized that they had at last reached the entrance of the ramp that led up to the final floor. It beckoned in front, a dark hollow with a flickering green light. He knew there would definitely be a trap between here and the hatch opening to the upper level, as there had been in the last level. He reminded the party not to make sudden movements, to keep behind him in single file and to walk very, very slowly.

Suddenly, Samar felt a tug on his shirt at the elbow, a small weak pull followed by another, more insistent, one. Turning his neck, he saw Akshay standing right behind him, stooped forward. One look at the hideously deformed face from this close, and Samar had to turn away. Almost involuntarily, he gave his elbow a jerk, breaking Akshay's frail hold on it, like one does to a stubborn beggar. The shirt now felt wet at the forearm. He knew with what. Revolted, Samar took a few decisive steps forward, so that Akshay could not touch him again.

'Take it.' Akshay said, pointing to his cylinder, fully conscious of the revulsion in Samar and yet no longer caring for it.

Anjali sidled up to Akshay. The conflict between her hatred for the man and pity was flush on her face. Pity won. 'Don't give up hope. Put your trust in God.'

Akshay just looked down at his boots. Smiling sadly, the words coming with surprising coherence, he said, 'The more trust I put in God, the surer I am that there is no hope.'

Samar stood still, pondering in disbelief.

How could this be?

They had made it through to the last level without any further drama. Samar had been quite sure that there would be a trap guarding the level access, just like there had been last time. Perhaps they had avoided it. Remembering what had happened to Preeti, every one of them had been very careful, treading as if on eggshells. The sound of heavy breathing, the smell of sweaty fear and of course the palpable presence of Death seemed to heighten their alertness. That had somehow saved them.

Perhaps not.

The last heavy metal door had dissolved away at the brutal touch of the acid from Akshay's cylinder. Perfectly.

'This room just gives me the creeps.' Anjali clutched hard at Anya's wheelchair.

Samar had to accept that it did. The hatch door had opened into Extraction Chamber 7. Here, the mined ore passed through gigantic metal pipes while jets of air, ejected in concentrated bursts from the valves that lined the pipe, would remove the impurities.

That, of course, was what they had been told. Now they couldn't guess its purpose. All they saw was a giant hall full of serpentine pipes twisting in on themselves, a mythical python in repose. As the air blew, the pipes bellowed and shook, making the whole place wheeze heavily like an asthmatic patient.

Anjali picked up speed, pushing the wheelchair. Samar cried out, 'Please still be careful... for now... we have to...'

He could not finish. Akshay, still lagging behind all of them by quite a bit, had sunk down to the ground on his knees, hitting the metal floor hard with a loud thud. He groaned, 'The pain... it's just too much.' He sat propped against a pipe, his knees drawn in, curled into an almost foetal position. 'Give me a minute... please.'

Karan turned back towards Akshay. 'Not now. We cannot wait.'

Akshay looked like he was pleading. He tried to say something and then fell silent. Karan went on, sternly steady. 'Remember what you said yourself. Our worth is determined by what we have. You no longer have your cylinder. So, we have no more use for you. You see, Dr More, when you expect the worst of the world, expect the world to think the worst of you.' He paused, then added, 'All I ask is that you keep pace with us.'

Akshay still sat there, his head drooping.

Karan's voice betrayed immense impatience, like someone tired of repeating himself. 'Do not expect any pity. If you were in our position, you would have kept walking. Why should we do anything different?'

That seemed to have spurred Akshay to action. He reached out his hand to grab the side of a pipe and tried to get up with a forward thrust, but his knees wobbled, and he fell off balance. Intensely conscious of the stares on him, he tried once again to rise.

'Wait. I will help you.' Samar started to walk towards Akshay, his hand outstretched. Somewhere deep down, he felt guilty for that moment of revulsion at the gate, when Akshay had reached out to touch his elbow. He remembered the look on Akshay's face when he had recoiled away, shaken by his hideousness. A criminal he was, an unlikeable asshole, but still, he was a human being.

Akshay's eyes lit up seeing someone coming back for him. He reached out, struggling still to get his footing, his face black with the pain, trying to support his body's weight on the side of the pipe.

'T... Thank ...'

And then Samar heard it. A soft musical voice from long ago, floating through the deserted corridors of his memories and whispering in his ears.

Daddy, Daddy... danger!

Samar froze. Right at that moment, the pipes, which stretched all around him, burst into violent convulsions, straining violently inside their giant clamps. A swirling sound, like one hears inside a shell, but with none of its gentle sonorousness, flooded the room, blotting everything out.

Akshay reacted first. His eye squinting in terror, he yelled out a warning. Samar heard nothing. All he saw were Akshay's lips moving before the pipes on either side of him cracked open with a deafening metallic rumble.

And then Akshay was airborne, carried upwards by the swirling vortex coming out of the pipes. There he remained suspended for a fraction of a second, as he threw out his arms and legs in an impotent attempt to touch the ground.

Samar could not move, his feet immobilized as if frozen into concrete by the terror of what he saw in front of him.

Caught up in the arms of an invisible monster, Akshay floated in a sea of agony. Then, as they all looked on in shocked silence, his right arm was sliced clean off its socket. Then the left flew away to the other side. Finally, his legs were ripped and thrown to the side as if caught in a monstrous meat-cleaving machine.

Akshay tried to squeeze out a word but lost to the force of gravity that brought the stump of his torso to the ground. There his limbless body stood, macabrely balanced upright on its mangled and bloody base, not toppling over. His head was turned upward, thrown back through whiplash, one eye bloodied and closed, the other death-white and open.

Akshay's splattered blood, warm and still alive, dripped down Samar's face and neck. It trickled down the sides of the metal pipes. It blew as a light mist, on the puffs of air that still came out, in tired spurts, from the ruptured valves.

No one moved. No one said anything. Time held its breath.

Anya's muffled groans brought Samar back to reality. The little girl was shaking in her wheelchair, eyes blinking rapidly, arms drawn close to her chest. Anjali had tried to turn her away from the grisly spectacle but had stopped midway, frozen in shock, leaving Anya to witness Akshay's last moments in all their terrible goriness.

Samar ran up to her, going down on his knees. He thought of comforting her. There was, of course, nothing he could say. There was no way he could pretend that he, or any of the other adults, was in control. He felt fear. He knew she did too. Silently, Samar took Anya's palms in his and rubbed them gently. Warmth returned to the deathly cold fingers. They connected in a closed loop of soundless support. Strength returned.

Karan had rushed towards the stump that had once been Akshay More. He spoke in bursts of words, too distraught to form sentences. 'Oh my god, they just cut through him, the polishing air-jets. Did you see that? They broke through the pipes – concentrated air at that velocity – sharp as platinum blades. Unbelievable.'

They all stayed silent for a while, looking at the body of Akshay. Then Anjali turned towards Samar. 'Still hanging on to the military experiment theory, are we?'

Samar was taken aback by the vicious tone of accusation in her voice, almost as if Anjali suspected him of deliberately misleading them. But he did not show his surprise. 'I have not found anything that disproved the theory in what happened. You saw what happened. Akshay put his hand on the side of the pipe. That set off the booby-trap...'

Anjali rubbed her neck, trying to wipe away the few specks of blood that had splattered onto her. 'Let me get this clear. The trap trigger unleashed those streams of compressed air with such pinpoint accuracy that they cut through his arms and legs with surgical precision. Aren't there easier ways of trapping or killing someone?'

'Well, as to the accuracy, it may have been controlled centrally by those monitoring us...' Samar realized he was not making much sense. He was in over his head, as impotent intellectually as Akshay had been when caught in the air draught. 'I... I don't know...' he said, struggling for words, still trying to come up with an explanation he himself could believe. He had always admired his capacity for self-delusion, an umbrella of comfort that he would use to shut out the light of inconvenience. After all, he had managed to convince himself all these years that Reshmi would come back. But now, for the first time in his life, even that escaped him.

Anjali still obsessed over the blood, wiping her neck even though it was already clean. 'Please. Let us not keep insulting our intelligence. Recognize the situation for what it is and for who is causing it.'

'And that would be?'

'The shrine downstairs. Lilith Adams. One and the very same.'

'What new mumbo-jumbo is this?' Samar had been wondering about Anjali for some time, whether she was all there. He had noticed her looking over her shoulder nervously several times. He was sure it was not out of concern for Akshay lagging behind them.

Anjali was running her hands through Anya's hair and then tugging the blanket around her securely, as if the reason for the little girl trembling was the cold. 'My scientific training keeps my mind open to alternative possibilities, even the most extreme ones. The way things stand, the facts do not support your hypothesis. They do mine.'

'And that hypothesis is what? That the shrine is killing us one by one?' Samar kept his eyebrow cocked sarcastically.

'Do you remember the carvings on the dome? Those frescoes of women being killed in elaborate contraptions? And the words below them?'

'The words... no, I didn't even know there was something written below them.'

'Ah, but of course. I had forgotten you didn't hear a word of my briefing.' 'It wasn't the most sparkling present – well, just repeat it for me... if you please?' said Samar, raising his hands in a show of angry mock surrender. They were going down one by one, and this lady still had the time for this.

'One of the panels had a very angry woman, sitting with a judge's hammer in hand while a hammer descended on her head from behind. Underneath was written "Those who judge shall be judged".' Anjali's voice trailed away. 'Preeti Singh. Crushed to death by a boulder. Or perhaps I should say, a giant hammer?'

Karan said, 'The angry vengeful woman who judged an innocent...'

Anjali continued, with an approving nod, 'Right next to that panel was, "Those who ravish shall be ravaged." And the punishment shown is that of a woman...'

Karan completed the sentence, '... tied to four horses and being pulled apart.'

All of them looked at Akshay's stump, his arms and legs lying around him in a circle of bloody mayhem.

He had ravaged. No doubt about it. Samar gave a shudder.

Anjali breathed hard. 'I am well aware of how fantastic this hypothesis is. But looking at the similarities between the carvings and what has happened to those two, this is, by far, the more believable explanation.'

Samar was not ready to accept the possibility suggested, despite the feeling of despondency churning his gut. *This could not be true, what she was saying, and yet...* 'What about the nerve gas in the air? It made Preeti remember. I have felt its effects too.'

'Remembered things you had forgotten?' asked Karan.

'Yes, something like that.' Samar tried to ignore the penetrating gaze of the old man. He was fingering him once again, of that he was sure.

Karan said, 'Maybe it's the shrine that sets off these visions. Maybe it wants us to stew in fear, make our punishment not so much violent death, but the terror that the anticipation of it releases in our minds. Like what happened to Jaal. It will happen to us too.'

Samar realized that this line of reasoning was futile. 'So, following that logic, there must be a panel for each of us in this group and for the rest in the Mine. If that is the case, why were there so few panels on the dome? After all, this place had many, many people.'

Anjali said, 'Remember, we saw only a small fragment of the dome, there is no telling what lay beyond that. Perhaps we were shown only what we were meant to see... maybe the workers saw something different, something relevant to their fates.'

'So, we are all dead. Right? Why don't we all just give up and wait for the end? Even better, smash our heads against the wall and get it done with.'

Anjali shook her head sadly, looking at Anya. 'I could never give up. I am a mother, after all.'

Karan gave Anjali a light, friendly squeeze on her shoulder. 'Indeed. From the time we were born, we have lived with the inevitability of death. Yet, we have not stopped moving. Why do so now?'

Anjali came closer to Akshay's body. 'It's not the end that scares me. There are fates worse than death, like being trapped in a state of perpetual pain – neither alive nor dead.'

The word rolled off Karan's tongue slowly, 'Tartarus...'

Anjali said, 'Yes. Every legend of Tartarus is like that. Sisyphus rolling a boulder eternally up a mountain. Tantalus, forever thirsty, bending down to drink and the water shifting away before he can reach it. Danaides, carrying a jug of water with sieves in the bottom, never being able to finish his task.'

Karan interrupted. 'I always thought of these legends as excellent metaphors for the human condition – we are forever cursed to run around in repetitive cycles of futile endeavour, our goals always a mirage, neither dead nor, as you said, alive. Of course, my idea of Tartarus has never been of a place buried deep inside the earth, but one perched right on top, in plain air, under the sun, the ultimate testament to God's hatred of mankind.'

Samar had had as much as he could take. Not that he was squeamish about death, but he wanted to move away from the dead body that still looked, macabrely, alive. 'Are we going to keep talking funny? Or are we going to start moving?'

Karan said, 'I see you are still not convinced. No matter. There is yet more for you to learn. And that means you still have more time to live.' He tightened the chainsaw that he still carried along with him and patted the back of Anya's wheelchair. 'Let's go.'

Suddenly, he stopped. 'It occurs to me that, before Preeti and Akshay died, they had seen ghosts, the shadows of their pasts, to use Lilith's words. None of us have, so far. I, for one, definitely have not. So maybe, just maybe, there is hope...'

Samar said nothing. Have I been seeing ghosts? *The lake? The mountains? Reshmi. The forgotten voice from Sierra Leone?* He did not want to answer the question. This is all bullshit.

Anjali tittered nervously. 'Seen ghosts? Oh, yes, I have. Ever since we left the room downstairs.'

Karan asked gravely, 'So, why did you not tell any of us?'

'Because I did not want to make Anya any more scared than she already was. Now I guess it's too late... too late for so many things...'

THE END

His room on Level 5 seemed different from the way he had left it. It was still as small and the black tabletop still gleamed as coldly. There, on the single bed, lay the large handbag turned over to the side, thrown open, with his clothes half-out, infuriatingly untidy as ever. Yet there was something that was not the same.

Never mind. There were things to be done. Samar leant over onto the bed, reaching for his bag. He turned it over and emptied its contents onto the table.

'Excuse me, but did we take that long route around just so that you could come to your room to pack?' asked Anjali, in a tone that betrayed disbelief.

One of the things that had dropped onto the table, with a sharp clang, was a shaving razor. It was of the old type where you had a blade between two metal plates. Samar unscrewed the plates and took the blade out from the razor. 'Have any of you thought of what we will do once we leave the place?' Samar took the blade in his hand and reached into the bag. 'There wasn't a bus out to civilization from here, last time I was up there.'

Karan said, 'I guess I never thought we would get so far. So never bothered...'

With one fast twist of his wrist, Samar dug the blade into the soft leather and started ripping the lining apart. 'Now that we are almost there, maybe it's time we started thinking.'

Anjali grunted, 'Almost there? I wish I could share your optimism. We still have no idea if the lift to the top can be activated from Lilith Adams's room – the controls might be deactivated permanently or behind a password, for all we know.'

Samar had fished out something from the destroyed bag. He held it on the tip of his index finger.

Karan asked, 'Is that a transmitter?'

Samar nodded. 'One of the smallest homing devices in the world. This one sends a high-powered encoded secret signal with its geographical coordinates to the Indian Air Force's Command and Control Centre's spy satellite. Standard ops dictate the Air Force would send out an aircraft to the source once they get this signal.' What Samar did not say was that this used to be standard operations three years ago, when he had done a private job for the Indian government. If they had changed the encoding of the signal or the protocol since then, they were all screwed.

Anjali arched her eyebrow. 'How did that get past their scanners when you first came in?'

'That's the magic of this little thing. It is perfectly protected from any kind of scanning technology that uses...' Samar stopped. The penny had dropped. Anjali was not looking for a technical answer.

'Am I under suspicion?' He asked, not looking at her, a smile of indulgent amusement lighting his face.

'You have chosen our paths. When you have asked to stop, we have stopped. Whenever you have asked us to move, we have. And yet, following your every instruction, two of us are dead. Can one be blamed for thinking that you took us exactly through where you knew those traps were? Now you claim you got this... God knows what it is... through that kind of security. Nothing personal, but if you were in my place would you not think the same thing?'

Samar took a pen from the table, twisted its end and pressed it to the device. The smile remained. 'Here is what I would have done had I been in your place. I would have made up my mind and stuck to it.' The pen made the connection he sought. 'Some time ago, you were going on about the shrine. The carvings and how Akshay and Preeti died in exactly the same way as shown in the panels. Now you seem to have come around to my hypothesis that this whole thing is an experiment, except you think I am on their side, facilitating the experiment. Before, of course, you suspected Akshay. Now it's me. Make up your mind.'

Karan had come around to look at the device. 'That's enough, Anjali. There is nothing he could have done to save those two. Their pasts had sealed their present.'

'There. I just activated it. Signal transmitting.' Samar exclaimed with a flourish. 'Now, if everything goes according to plan, we should have an escort waiting for us outside the door.'

No use in further grappling with this lady. Let her think what she wants.

Samar was about to turn away when his eye caught something. It was the brown stuffed teddy bear lying on the bed, the one he always carried along with him. Thoughts of other times, happier times, flashed through his mind. Only for an instant though, as half-understood memories of a shadowy figure on a winter afternoon overpowered him, once again, with a feeling of guilt. There was something down here, something he had missed. Like the lyrics of a forgotten song, it scraped gratingly away at his mind.

As Samar squeezed the teddy bear into his pocket, he avoided Karan's sympathetic look. 'Pain sometimes becomes a comfort in itself... which is why letting go might be...' Samar did not respond, merely pointing tiredly towards the door. It was then he realized what had changed from the last time he had been here.

The glass of the large overhead square light, fitted into the ceiling, had cracked. The fault lines, radiating out in crooked lines, together with the incandescent white centre, seemed to Samar to be a glowing spider, sitting at the centre of a web. Waiting.

The eyes. Watching him relentlessly.

He had felt them before too, burrowing into the back of his neck on those lazy mornings in the garden when he would stretch out on the bamboo recliner, reading the newspaper. He would stop while walking up the stairs, feeling the chill of a secret gaze, only to find nothing but the white curtains fluttering in the breeze. He had once told Anita of this goldfish-in-tank sensation and she had immediately laughed it away. 'Oh, Mr Spy, you are soooo paranoid. Who would dare snoop on the country's number one snooper?' He had tried to say something but then she had pressed her lips to his. And once that happened, he would invariably forget.

Maybe Anita was right then, maybe he had been paranoid. The nature of his profession had probably made him that. But today he was sure – the eyes were very much there, following them every step of the way.

What were they doing? Measuring their progress in this military experiment? Ticking the dead off against a scoreboard? Have we behaved exactly like they thought we would? Or have we gone further than they had expected?

Right after they had left the living quarters, Samar had to make a choice. Should they take the only passage to Lilith Adams's room or go through the maintenance shafts in the walls? The straight road would be the natural way to proceed. Hence, it was likely to be riddled with booby-traps. The shafts made more sense, though a crawl through them would be tough with Anya. The only problem was that access to these shafts was restricted by metallic mesh grating.

The chainsaw. It would cut through the grating like butter. Perfect. But too perfect, thought Samar. It was as if the eyes wanted to shepherd them in that direction. Perhaps that was why 'they' had left the chainsaw in that room for them to take.

So, Samar had decided to take the main passageway. Not doing what they expected them to do – that was the key to staying alive. And in doing this, if he had been double-bluffed, then, well, at least he tried. The good thing was that within half an hour, if he did not trip over a trap, they would be in Lilith's room, and their ordeal would be over.

One way or the other.

Over the last few minutes, the temperature had risen sharply, swallowing them in a bubble of throbbing oppressiveness. Karan took out his handkerchief and wiped the side of his sweat-drenched throat. 'I guess this is what they mean when they say "hot as hell".'

'Well, at least this place isn't as claustrophobic as the shafts would have been. The ceiling must be six floors high.' said Samar.

'What is this huge place for?' asked Karan.

'From what I was told, this handled the power for the top of the Mine. Those giant metal cylinders house the turbines and those...'

Samar had been watching Anjali. Her hands were on the wheelchair pushing it forward and yet her eyes were mostly turned upwards and sideways, almost as if avoiding something that lay in front. Samar felt the need to make small talk so that her mind could be taken off whatever she was trying her best to avoid.

'... those steel things hanging upside down from the ceiling, like stalactites, they are used for transmitting power – or that was what I was told...'

'They look like teeth. And so far up they are,' said Anjali, before lapsing into silence.

Small talk would not work. 'Anjali, please do not lose your focus now, when we are minutes away from escaping this place. You owe it to Anya and you owe it to yourself. Just look where you are stepping and nowhere else... understand?'

Anjali kept looking everywhere shiftily, 'So, tell me, do you think the dead hold dominion over the living?'

Oh dear. Here is the supernatural sing-song yet again. Samar deliberately feigned misunderstanding. 'Excuse me?'

She cleared her throat. 'I meant do you think the dead hold the living accountable in the world that lies beyond?'

Karan said, 'The *memento mori* downstairs – that's what you are thinking about isn't it?

Anjali had stopped. Looking down at her hands, she said, 'Yes, I am. "We were in your past. Your futures will be with us." That's what it said. That's what Lilith also implied.'

Samar shrugged his shoulders. 'I don't bother myself with what lies beyond. What does concern me though, is what we do in this life.'

Karan interrupted, 'Like shutting out the genocide in Sierra Leone? Like not ever trying to find out how you could have brought justice to those dead? The hottest places in hell are reserved for those who in times of great moral crises maintain their neutrality.' Now Karan's smile reflected the shine of the chainsaw that glimmered sinisterly on his shoulder. 'Before you get angry, I didn't say that. Dante did.'

'It seems that what happened at Sierra Leone bothers you more than it does me,' said Samar.

'There, perhaps, lies the tragedy of it all.'

Samar was sure of Karan's technique now. Throw the bait and see if someone jumps for it. To his chagrin, he realized he had fallen for it every time.

Anjali seemed to be oblivious to their exchange. She continued, seemingly hypnotized by her thoughts, 'Death and its legacy. An archaeologist deals with it every day as a part of their profession. So that's not what scares me. Nor, for that matter, does the possibility of being judged by the dead.' She now sank down on her knees, turning Anya's wheelchair around to face her. 'What scares me is having to face up to the living...'

Samar looked quizzically at Karan, unable to understand this dramatic change in Anjali.

'We grow up being told that lies are bad. As a mother, I told that to Anya too. But then when we do grow up, we come to realize how merciful lies are, how they are perhaps the only measure of control we have in this crazy world.'

Karan tried moving towards Anjali. 'What's gotten into you? What is...?'

Samar looked into Anjali's eyes. They burned with a silent smouldering flame. Her lips pursed into a determined grimace, as if she had made up her mind after much deliberation. 'The greatest fear in this world is the fear of the truth, of having to say it.'

Anjali took a deep breath, stood up, turned Anya's wheelchair around and rolled it down the walkway. Samar felt relieved – the madness had passed.

Then he felt it: a strong whoosh of air, like that of a giant bee flying past his ear followed by a hideous wail of pain.

He turned around to see Anjali Menon suspended upside-down by one leg, her head a few feet above the ground. She was dangling at the end of a metal wire that had reached down from above, catching her like a fish on a hook.

A disembodied metallic female voice droned, 'Security device malfunction. Error code 78x12.'

Anya tried to leap out of her wheelchair, reaching for her mother, trying to catch Anjali's flailing arms as she swung crazily to and fro like a human pendulum. But the paralysis in her body bound her to her chair. In helpless agony, she tried to scream, but only a frenzied gurgle came out.

'It's ok, baby, it's ok...' Anjali reached out her arms, struggling in vain against what had pulled her up, her eyes squinting in pain.

Samar had rushed over and was holding Anjali by her thighs, trying to steady her. 'Steady... steady... This thing will dig further into your ankle the more you struggle.'

Karan had also caught hold of Anjali's waist, clutching her hard, holding her steady. 'What the hell... what...' Karan's words drowned in the panic of the moment.

A metallic clamp, with serrated teeth had sprung around her ankle, its steel edges now stained dark red with the fresh blood dripping down the back of her heel and over her leg in three rivulets. Samar tried to put his finger in the metal hinge. He said, dismayed, 'It's an electronic bear trap planted in the ground with the metal cord camouflaged, and triggered by the pressure of her stepping on it. Again, yet another ancient trap but with a wicked new twist.'

The voice once again said, 'Security device malfunction. Error code 78x12.'

Samar held the metal cord in his hand, looking up towards the ceiling. 'This was supposed to retract the moment she got caught, pulling her up. As you can see, that part has not worked. But this part has – the clamps have locked shut.'

Steadied by the two men, Anjali had been able to reach out and hold Anya's face in her hands. The little girl was bawling uncontrollably, her eyes pursed tight with the force of her outburst. 'Look at me, look at me... please listen to me... for the love of God,' Anjali whispered, the sweat carried downwards over her temple by the force of her tears.

Anya still kept on shaking her head.

Anjali screamed, flailing her hands. 'I don't have time. Please...'

Anya stopped, silent. Anjali dropped her voice to an unreal softness, speaking slowly with deathly emphasis. 'Please, baby, don't be scared. Please. Nothing is going to happen to you. Trust me. This place only punishes the wicked. And you are not... you are not... wicked.' Tears overpowered Anjali. She struggled to get the words out.

Karan tried to calm her down. 'You don't have...'

Anjali shrugged him away, a reserve of final determination giving her back her voice. 'There is no easy way for me to have to say this. But I have to…'

'Security device malfunction. Error code 78x12' the voice repeated. Karan said again, 'This is not the time, nor is it the...'

'He wants me to. Why do you think he has followed me every step along the way?'

Karan shook his head sadly and turned his face away.

Anjali fought back the tears. 'Death is not punishment enough. I have to tell my daughter the one thing I had hoped she never finds out. I have to tell her this, so that she knows why, why her mother is going to die... *why she has to die...*'

She grasped Anya's face as firmly as she could, fingers pressing hard against the soft cheeks, glistening now with tears and snot. 'Your father... I lied…'

So engrossed was Anjali in her *National Geographic* that she had not noticed when the ticket-checker had entered the compartment. Now that there was some commotion, she looked up from her magazine to see what was going on.

The only other passenger in her coupe had opened his suitcase on the berth and was rifling through it, tossing clothes out, making an apologetic whimper from time to time while the ticket-checker, a lumbering man with tobacco-greyed lips and a brutal gaze, stood towering over him.

'I am sure I had my wallet with me.'

'That's what they all say once we catch them.'

'Trust me I would not lie over a train ticket. See here is my ID card, I am a professor at…'

'Do I look like I care?' The ticket-checker shook the man by his arm. 'We are getting down at the next station and you can do your explaining to the rail police.'

Anjali took a look at the man who had introduced him as a professor. Outsized distinctly unfashionable glasses, shirt buttons tied in the wrong way, the collar of the blazer folded back improperly, an almost puppy-like head of hair, unruly and uncombed, there was something endearingly boyish about him, almost as if a twelve-year old had woken up in the body of twenty-five.

She wondered what subject he taught. That sharp nose, the soft lips, the frail, slightly feminine handsomeness.

Poetry? Romantic languages? There would be time to find out.

'Excuse me, sir, what seems to be the problem?' Anjali stood up and approached the ticket-checker.

The ticket-checker's gaze moved over her, scanning from top to bottom. She saw his eyes. They had gone from hard to soft.

Predictably.

'Madam, this gentleman is travelling without a ticket. Now he is pretending to have lost his wallet.'

'No honestly… I had my ticket. I had 10,000 rupees too…,' the young professor was almost on the verge of tears.

Anjali tossed her head to the side, 'Please sir, can't I pay for his ticket?'

'No madam, he has been caught travelling ticketless. There is a fine. We need to make a report. It's not as simple as that.'

She leant forward slightly, 'I know sir. But surely we can settle this among ourselves.' Popping open her purse, she brought out a small wad of notes, of considerably higher value than a single person's ticket. This she then slowly inserted into the checker's shirt pocket, lingering her index finger there for a second longer than she knew she needed to.

'Madam you are too kind. But let me warn you. You are making a mistake saving this scum. We see their kind every day.'

'Thank you so much. Do you want to see my ticket?'

'No madam, that won't be needed. I still say you made a mistake.' He slipped out of the compartment stealthily, taking one last appreciative look at Anjali.

A drop of a smile wetting her lips, she looked intently at the professor. 'So, what's your story?'

'I had my ticket. I swear.' He pointed to his open suitcase. 'I thought I put it in the wrong trouser pocket. But now it seems I have lost my wallet and with it my ticket.'

Anjali stretched out her hand. 'Anjali.'

He looked at her for a second, uncomprehending. Then he realized she was introducing herself.

'Nikhil. Nikhil Menon.' Shaking her hand, he then rummaged through his suitcase and fished out a notepad.

'Please give me your address and phone number so that I can return the money once I get home.'

Anjali asked, 'Do you have a pen?'

'Pen… yes… pen… damn I keep losing those blasted things.' He patted his shirt pocket and then the back of his trousers.

Conjuring a pen from her purse, Anjali almost snatched the notepad from his hand.

'So professor, what is it exactly that you are a professor of?'

'Microbiology.' He cleared his throat. 'I lied to the ticket checker. I am not really a professor. Just a lecturer. Finished my PhD two months ago.' Then he paused and almost as an afterthought asked, 'What do you do?'

'Besides saving professors from the rail police you mean? I am doing my PhD in archaeology. Third year.' Handing back the pad, she now sat down and stretched her arms lazily.

'You haven't had your lunch yet, have you Professor Menon?'

'I will buy something at the next station.'

'Buy? I thought you had lost your wallet.'

'Oh yes. So, I have. Not a problem. I will have something when I get home.' He clutched his palms together and looked down at the floor, not caring to hide his embarrassment.

'I don't know what I would have done today if you had not been here. How can I ever thank you?'

Anjali brought out a large metal tiffin-carrier from a basket that was hanging from a hook on the train wall.

'You can thank me by sharing these *aloo-paratha*s I made.'

'What?'

'*Aloo-paratha*s? You don't like?'

'Oh yes. Of course. I love them.'

Professor Nikhil Menon's eyes fixed hungrily on the *paratha*s, his glasses sliding carelessly down his nose.

And at that moment, that very precise moment, Anjali wanted nothing more than to reach out and run her fingers through his unruly mop of hair. She controlled herself just in time, knowing fully well that it would only be a matter of time before she lost control.

The marriage registrar had a strange type of face, like a giant pancake that had been burnt at the edges. Supremely disinterested in the tenth vow that he had to solemnize since morning, he turned towards Anjali and asked, 'Do you take this man as your lawfully wedded husband?'

Anjali's fingers tightened around those of the person to her left. In a blue sherwani, he looked a prince, slightly confused and overwhelmed, but still a prince.

Their families had wanted a big social wedding. Only son, now a division director at the prestigious Pujara Center, rapidly rising in his world, they were proud of him. She had however insisted on a simple affair. 'Tell me what you want', she had asked, 'a Bollywood wedding or a cheap one?' He had, typically, just said, 'Whatever you would like.' So, it had been her way, with just closest family and friends around.

She had a plan of course. She always had. With the money they had saved, they would be off on a dream honeymoon – to Cambodia. Having been there before on field trips and written papers on its ruins, it was her most favourite place in the world.

Which is why she wanted to share it with the man she loved the most. History. Culture. Sex. And more sex. She had worked everything out perfectly. Seven days of heaven.

The registrar repeated, 'Do you take this man as your lawfully wedded husband?' the sleepiness in his voice now replaced by irritation.

'Yes, I do.' Anjali gushed.

It was then that she noticed his hair. Even on his wedding day, he had messed it up, like he always does. She thought of patting it down herself but then one look at the registrar's furrowed brow made her reconsider. Plus, she kind of liked him like this.

Anything else would not be Nikhil. Anything else would not be her husband.

The sudden draft from the door made Nikhil Menon look up from the computer terminal.

Anjali stood at the entrance to his office. She looked dressed as if to go to a party – chiffon sari, a plunging spaghetti blouse and a matching set of gold necklace and earrings.

'Do you remember what day it is today?' Her voice was glacially cold.

Nikhil stood up from his chair, surprised. 'What are you doing here in the lab?'

'Do you remember what day it is today?'

'Of course. It's your birthday', Nikhil sighed, 'I know we were supposed to go out. But something really important came up. One of our clients… but forget that. Why don't you just sit down?'

Anjali walked forward and stood facing him, on the opposite side of the table.

'Important enough to keep me waiting at the restaurant?'

'I tried calling you on the cell phone. But you had kept it off, didn't you?' She brought a cell phone out from her purse. 'How come there is no missed call from your number then?'

'Oh damn. I must have forgotten.' He touched his lips contemplatively. 'We have a sudden deadline here today at work. So must have slipped my head.' Nikhil stopped and then added as an afterthought, 'Why don't you go home, and we can do your birthday tomorrow or Saturday?'

Anjali's lips, red and lightly glittered, stretched into a harsh, thin line. 'My birthday is today. Not tomorrow. Not Saturday. Today.'

'Come on, Anjali. Act like an adult.'

'What did you just say?'

Nikhil repeated, 'I just asked you to act like an adult. Don't you think this "it has to be today" is a bit childish?'

'You… you… are now telling me to act like an adult? You, of all people?' Anjali banged her palm on the wooden table. 'Where would you and your career be if I had not babied you all these years? Cooking, cleaning and taking care of everything at home so that you could be the famous Dr Nikhil Menon? Huh? Where would you be if I had not acted like an adult when your father had a stroke? What did you do then? You simply called every day from London and asked "Is *Acchan* okay?" And what did I do? Stayed awake for nights on end, ran from pillar to post and that too with malaria.'

'Cool down, cool down, honey.'

'No. I will not. How dare you, who outside this lab cannot do one simple thing correctly, lecture me on being an adult? All this because you do not care for my birthday.'

'But I do. I do. You don't know but I actually bought you a surprise gift…'

'Yes. Yes. I know. You checked the cash-on-delivery option when you bought it online. When they delivered, your office's front desk would not sign for it because of course they won't pay. You were in Paris. So, guess what they did? They sent the delivery man to our house. I had to pay for my own gift. Do you think that was the end of it all? No. I then had to pay more to the delivery man so that he brings that thing back to your office. Why did I do that? So that I can pretend to be surprised when I get it on my birthday. Because I cared for your feelings. Like an adult.'

Nikhil held his head in his hands. 'I forgot to leave the money for them when I had left. Oh shit.'

'You said it right. Shit. That's what our marriage is.' Anjali was shouting now, her voice breaking and finding itself again.

'Anjali, please. We will discuss this at home.' She stood there, trying to hold herself back.

Nikhil pleaded, 'There are people here working late. Everyone can hear you. Even sir is in his room. Please don't make a scene where I work.' Nikhil started moving towards Anjali, stretching his hand out to touch her shoulder.

Suddenly she moved. Lunging forward, she picked up the laptop from his table and then, in one swift action, dashed it to the ground. As the case cracked, she lifted the flower vase from the table and threw it at the window. Shards of broken glass flew in every direction. Nikhil took two steps back in fear.

'I am pregnant, Nikhil. You hear? Pregnant. I wanted to give the news to you today. On my birthday. I thought it would be marvellous, I thought it would be special. But I think I will tell you tomorrow. Or on Satuday. Or any day you have the time.'

Nikhil looked around, once at the fragments of glass on the carpet and then at the laptop on the floor and finally towards the passage, where the lab-assistants and the post-docs were milling about, murmuring to themselves. He ran his fingers through his hair.

Anjali's eyes followed his fingers. And then she burst into tears.

Dr Nikhil Menon had had a tiring day. But it still was not over – hell, it hadn't even started. His watch said 6 p.m. Time for an early dinner and a dash back to the lab for an all-nighter. The experimental results would start coming out around ten. He had to be there in the lab when it happened. He used to love these moments of truth all his life. Now they filled him with dread. The whole project had been falling apart for the last few months. The results of the preliminary clinical studies had revealed damaging inconsistencies. The sponsors were furious. Just last week, he had to stand red-faced in front of the research review board, fumbling and mumbling, struggling for answers.

How had it come to this? Everything had been planned out in advance; the pre-clinical trials had been spectacularly successful. But then inexplicably, it had all gone bad. Horribly bad. He had no idea why.

Such things never happened to him. Not to Dr Nikhil Menon. Just today, he had thrown away a year-old issue of *India Weekly*, the one that had his face on it, smiling brightly in a white lab coat, above 'Changing the World: One Gene at a Time'. He had kept it all these months, perched on top of the reams of research papers that littered his table. Now the fluttering of its cover in the fan's breeze seemed to him a whispered giggle, mocking him tirelessly.

The world had turned its back.

Parking his car on a side street, Nikhil ran up the stairs, two at a time. Maybe he could get in by seven and revise the report once again before the results were reviewed. If he couldn't do it this evening, he would have to stay and do it tomorrow, after being awake the whole night. Not something he looked forward to. But then again, he could not get the review board angry once again. He just could not.

Strange. His apartment door was ajar. Not by much, just a bit, as if it had been left unlocked and then the wind had taken care of the rest.

Anjali must have come back. Just like her to forget to lock the door. What if Anya was at home – she would have walked out of the door and onto the landing! Such a hyperactive girl she is. But then all two-year-olds should be. Good thing she was at her grandparents today.

The moment he stepped in, he realized that something was not quite right. A low female voice came from the bedroom. Or was it from far away? He felt hurried movement. A loud thud – followed by a female groan, whimperingly long and musical.

Nikhil stepped into the bedroom.

Anjali Menon was nude, her heavy breasts plastered against the cold glass of the mirror. Behind her, almost covering her body, stood a young man, not more than twenty, his muscular hands holding her firmly by her waist. She ground back at him, her full hips making slow, sinuous circles. One of her legs curled up backwards enticingly, the anklet jingling in rhythm with her soft moans.

Blinded by her pleasure, she did not see the person standing at the door. 'Oh fuck, it's your husband...' The boy yanked backwards. By the force of sudden withdrawal, he temporarily lost his balance, slipping on Anjali's discarded panties.

Anjali turned around. Nikhil was holding on to the side of the door. She looked into his eyes, tried to say something, but the words stuck to her throat like glue. After all, what can one say when caught having sex with a stranger in one's own home?

At the eye contact, Nikhil simply turned around towards the living room.

The boy dived into his jeans, hopping on one leg, trying to leave the scene as quickly as possible. He cannoned out, almost colliding into Nikhil, who said nothing, but simply moved considerately to the side.

Anjali came out, wrapping a bathrobe around her body, still shimmering with the sweat of the frenzied coupling. Nikhil had the fridge open, looking inside. She stood at the entrance of the kitchen. 'Look, I am... I need to... I didn't know you would be back so soon.' She felt stupid having said that. But it was the only thing that came out of her mouth.

'Do we have some leftovers from last night?'

'What?'

'Leftovers. It would be good if I could just heat them up and leave for the lab.' Nikhil leaned further in, his hands searching. 'Can't seem to find any. I was positive we had some...' Nikhil's voice trailed away.

She had come to this room expecting a lot of things. Maybe Nikhil would lose his temper. Maybe threaten to leave her. Maybe strike her hard. He had, of course, never done that before.

But then again, he had never seen her with her legs splayed wantonly, urging a man to enter her. What she had not accounted for was this uneasy normalcy, as if nothing had happened. 'Your dinner? Leftovers?' She simply repeated what Nikhil had said, still struggling to make sense of the situation. He was supposed to have been in a state of shock. But now, she was.

He brought his head out of the fridge. 'Seems to be nothing here. Can you make something for me quick? Like, real quick. Ordering pizza will just take too much time.'

'Do you... don't you want an explanation?'

Nikhil opened the cupboards on the top of the stove. There was an opened bag of potato chips. His face lit up. 'Aaah, at least there is something. So, really, can you please...?' His eyes pointed to a frying pan on the stove top.

'What the fuck, Nikhil. You just saw your wife, your wife of six years, you saw her... don't you have anything to ask me? Anything to say?'

Nikhil moved to the couch with his bag of chips. Adjusting his glasses, he reached in and took a handful. 'No, I don't. Really.'

'For the love of God. Say something. Get angry. Ask for an explanation. Don't pretend it didn't happen.'

'But I am not angry, Anjali.' He kept munching the chips, searching for the remote on the sofa. It had slipped between the two large cushions.

'You have to be... Don't keep it bottled up, please. Let it out. Please...'

'Damn, this thing doesn't have batteries.' Nikhil shook the remote, his arm stretched out fully. 'No, really. I am not angry, how many times do I have to tell you that?'

'Don't you care?'

Nikhil did not look up from his bag of chips.

'I am your wife. The mother of your child. Surely you feel anger. Surely you have to care?'

'Uh huh.' Nikhil was now obsessing over the potato-chip crumbs that had fallen on the sofa, collecting them into a small pile and sweeping them up with his hands.

'So, what do you care for, then?'

'My work. And it's not going too well.'

'Your work? You catch your wife in bed with another man and all you say you care for is work. For all you care, I could have been painting the house.'

Nikhil stared absentmindedly at the wall. 'Oh, that reminds me. Did the painter get back with the estimates for Anya's room?'

'We need to talk, we really do.' Anjali spoke with emphasis. 'I... there are so many things about me you do not know.'

Nikhil had left the couch and entered the kitchen. He was bringing vegetables out from the bottom of the fridge. Anjali still stood at the entrance of the kitchen, tears streaming down her flushed cheeks. 'I am not the same person anymore. Or perhaps I should say, I never knew the person I really was.' Anjali sniffled. 'Remember when you had gone to Holland, last October? I was very lonely, so I went to a club. And there I picked someone up. And then I kept going back again and again. Sometimes men, sometimes women.' She fumbled with her words. 'It's all so wrong...' Anjali closed her eyes, making an effort to form the words. 'But I just had to. I needed to. It made me feel good. *And wanted.*'

Nikhil had now brought out a few tomatoes and a big onion. One of the tomatoes rolled out from his hand and he stooped to pick it up.

'I knew... I knew, with the risks I was taking in public, one day I would get caught. Maybe I wanted to get caught. So that you would know, so that you would bring me back to you.'

'Could you do something for me, please?'

Anjali wiped her tears with the sleeve of her housecoat. 'Y-yes...'

'Can you just chop the onions? I can't get it right... the pieces come out all uneven and then the stupid thing fries unevenly.'

Anjali said nothing. She took the knife and chopping board from a shelf and picked out an onion from the fridge, trying vainly to sniff away the tears. 'I always knew your work was your first priority. But isn't there any corner of your heart for me?'

Nikhil did not reply, passively bored.

Anjali walked up to Nikhil. Holding him by his shoulder, she turned him around so that he looked at her.

'Forget caring. I am a cheap slut. I know that. But tell me, don't you want to fuck me anymore? Don't you want this anymore?' She whipped off her dressing gown. It dropped to her feet noiselessly. She held her naked breasts in her hands, thrusting them towards Nikhil. Her voice shook with passion. 'Tell me, these don't turn you on? Those kids at the grocery store whistle when I walk by. The guys in the club can't take their eyes off me. When I go on digs with the crew, everyone – I mean, every guy behaves extra nice with me, and I know very well why they do. Just for these. Now, tell me... that you do not want them. That you do not care who else squeezes these.' Anjali looked into Nikhil's eyes, their faces inches from each other.

His eyes stared back, silently still. No light – not of anger, of possessiveness or of any emotion – shone there. Nikhil was dead from the inside. Dead to her.

She sighed so deeply that it blew the curl of hair that fell across Nikhil's face, the one that gave him his boyish handsomeness. She remembered. Hiking in the Adirondacks, him walking in front with long strides. Walking through Angkor Wat, her explaining everything to him while he nodded along. Lying next to him, watching him sleep. Every pleasant memory, every smile, every word – all of it false. He had never cared. She only wondered why she had never seen this before.

'The onions. Please. I have to get back to the lab.'

Anjali nodded her head. Buttoning up her housecoat, she moved to the counter. Holding one end of the onion between her fingers, she started chopping, the knife hitting the board. Tap-tap-a-tap. Tap-tap-a-tap.

Nikhil was washing the frying pan. Shaking it to dry, he put it on the stovetop. The burner knobs, he always felt, were too tight. He used the small hand-towel to grip one. And then, from the corner of his eye, he saw the gleam. For a split second. The steel blade flashed in the kitchen light, before descending into the side of his neck, searing Nikhil in a burst of liquid burning pain.

Anjali stood there silent, tightly grasping the knife's handle.

Nikhil staggered backwards, his hand moving towards where the blood came flooding out, trying to dam it shut. The frying pan fell down with a resounding crash as his body hit the melamine handle that extended out from the side.

The knife came down again, this time with even greater force. It buried itself deep, deep inside.

Anjali stood watching as stillness descended in tortured spasms. Then she ran her fingers through that unruly hair of his, smoothing it down softly.

'Your father... I lied. He was not killed the way I said he was… your father... It was... it was... me. I killed him.'

The pain around her ankles and the certainty of fate tightened around Anjali. All around her danced images, of an evening long ago, in a place far away, of a shocked face, blood spurting from the side of his neck.

Anya kept staring at her mother, uncomprehending, frozen now in terror. 'Don't ask me, baby, why. You wouldn't understand. Not now. All you need to know is that your father was a good man, and I was wicked. And wicked people... I told you before many times... answer for their wickedness. But trust me, nothing will happen to you. Because you are pure ... innocent.'

She turned towards the two men. 'Take Anya and leave. Now. Don't let her look back.'

Samar had been fiddling at the metal ring around her ankle, trying to see if the locking mechanism could be disengaged. When it came to devising devices that cause harm, one had to appreciate the industrious ingeniousness of humans. There was no way to work this one off. None.

Karan held her hand. 'We have a chainsaw. We can use it to cut through the metal... can't we, Mr Bose?'

'We can try,' answered Samar. He took the chainsaw and pulled its start cord. It vibrated instantly to life. He held it against the metal cord, the kickback of the saw straining his shoulders. The serrated teeth buzzed against the metal, sparks flew blue white and Anjali's body swung to the side, bobbing up and down. And yet the cord remained unyielding. The material was too strong. Too strong for the chainsaw.

Samar kept trying, even though the futility of his actions was obvious. Waves of sweat drenched Anjali, sticking the shirt to her body. The blue jeans, tight against her legs, were streaked with blood. Anya kept bawling silently.

Finally, Karan stretched out his hand and patted Samar on the shoulder. This was going nowhere. He stopped, sinking to his knees in exhaustion. Karan took a deep breath and shuffled from one foot to another. He asked, 'Can't we cut through the ring?'

'No. The trap is clamped tight around her ankle, the metal too close to skin. I cannot direct this heavy chainsaw to just take the metal off without taking her ankle with it.' gasped Samar.

'Then there's only one thing to do.' Karan struggled to phrase the sentence and then gave up, giving it straight. 'We will have to take the risk. If she loses the ankle, well that's just what happens.'

Anjali shrieked. 'Are you crazy? Have you totally gone insane?'

Karan's voice boomed with an authoritative fullness. 'Let me tell you what's going to happen. As you stay hanging here, for God knows how long, more and more blood will flow to the brain. You will pass in and out of consciousness.' He tapped her on her forehead. 'The capillaries in your eyes will burst from the pressure. Yet, you will not die. Nor will you be able to kill yourself. All you can do then is to pray for hunger and thirst to deliver you from the pain. Does that sound any better?'

'Just go. Please...'

Samar could not believe this was happening. He had seen a horror movie a long time ago on television. Your life or your limb, the serial killer had asked his victims. Now this place was asking the same question.

Karan continued. 'Far better you try to cut the metal, and if the ankle goes with it, I can cauterize the wound. There are steam pipes nearby, so it's not impossible. Trust me, this is the only way.'

Anjali kept shaking her head from one side to another violently, like a child refusing to take her shots. 'Then kill me now. Do it. Cut my neck off. The chainsaw can do that... can't it?'

Karan barked at her, more roughly than Samar could remember him having spoken before. 'For once, for once in your life, think of someone else. Anya needs you – can't you see that? This pain you will feel is nothing... nothing compared to what she will go through in life, alone.'

Samar squeezed Anjali's shoulder reassuringly. 'As a father who has lost his daughter, I can say that if I was in your position, I would do it. Anything to be with my daughter. Anything.'

He meant it. *The greatest pain in the world was regret.*

Anjali still shook her head. She faltered, 'No, please. No... not that...' Karan said, 'Maybe this pain is the punishment. Maybe that's all that Nikhil wants. Maybe that's the reason why the trap does not work.'

Funny, thought Samar, how people managed to delude themselves. One would have thought that the trap malfunctioning was proof enough that there were human beings setting these off and not the devil in a dress. Evidently not. But this was not the time to debate over it. All the more so because Anjali had stopped struggling.

Karan held her face in his hands and turned it to look at him. 'Up there is life. Here, only death. Now isn't that worth something? Rather, isn't it worth everything?'

'Security device malfunction. Error code 78x12.'

Anjali closed her eyes, breathed hard. Once. Twice. She shook her head from side to side. 'Do it, then. Do it now, before I change my mind.'

Karan Rathore was already on the move. He had whipped off his belt and was tying it around her calf, twisting it round and round and tightening it hard. She kept crying, silently.

'Don't let her see this.'

Samar tried to turn Anya's wheelchair around. She protested wildly, flailing her arms, twisting and turning inside her confines. Watching strangers die violently would be enough to give her a lifetime of nightmares. But seeing her mother getting her ankle cut off without anaesthesia, would be on a whole different plane of trauma.

'Take your belt off, Mr Bose. We need to put one in her mouth so that she doesn't bite her tongue off.'

Anjali was howling uncontrollably now, shaking her head from one side to the other. 'No, no, please, no...'

'It's going to be all right. Just a second of pain. And then Dr Rathore will take care of the rest.'

With the belt in her mouth, all that came out of her were muffled groans of agony.

Karan adjusted his sleeves and lifted the chainsaw from the floor. The sight of its steel blade sent Anjali into another frenzy, her eyes popping wide open in terror. She shook violently against her ankle restraint, which merely clamped harder, sending a fresh torrent of blood dribbling down her leg.

Samar clutched tightly onto Anjali, making sure the belt stayed between her teeth. She bit so hard into the leather that it became drenched with blood from her gums. Karan wiped the sweat from his brow and pulled at the starting cord of the chainsaw.

Nothing. The serrated edges of the saw remained stationary. Karan pulled again. Still no familiar whirring movement. 'What the...'

Terror gave way to relief, giving way again to terror on Anjali's face.

'I don't know. It was working fine a while ago,' Karan mumbled apologetically.

There was something wrong. Something dreadfully wrong.

Which is when Samar realized what had been bothering him. The trap error message, that had been replaying itself periodically, had stopped.

Two things happened simultaneously. The chainsaw burst to life. And right on cue, a loud whirring sound came from above.

Anjali felt the jolt on her leg. She screamed, her eyes bulging white. The belt that she had been biting on slipped down from her mouth. Reaching out, she tried to touch Anya one last time. But all she saw was her back, turned as she was away from her, the handle of her chair out of Anjali's grasp. The next second she was gone, pulled rapidly up by the retracting metal wire. Her cry of anguish trailed away into the darkness above.

Samar, in a move of blinding quickness, shoved Anya's wheelchair from behind and then dived forward to avoid what he knew was coming down.

The crunch of flesh and bone hitting a barrier with hellish force shook the room. Then, as if someone had playfully thrown down a cache of red water balloons, blood descended from above in a shower of death.

Samar knew what he would see when he looked up. Yet he had to.

Anjali was impaled on one of the gigantic teeth that hung suspended from the ceiling, her head slumped forward onto her chest, curled up like a bird on a skewer being turned on a slow fire.

Karan had not moved, frozen in time. Blood dripping down, he turned his eyes upwards, almost as if in prayer.

'Those that are in passion shall be overwhelmed.'

'When you find yourself in a room full of crazy people, know this: the others are sane and the one that is crazy is you.' Old boss-man Sunderan and his maxims.

Maybe the world was sane, and it was he who was going crazy. How else could he explain the heavy Agent Astra cylinder he was still carrying on his back? He should have left the cylinder where Anjali had dropped it. After all, there were no more doors to melt through. Except, of course, the final elevator access hatch. But that could be opened simply by reversing the security lockdown from Lilith Adams's room. If, for some reason the controls from her room did not work, melting the final door would still be of no use since the elevator that lay behind it would remain stuck. To make things more ridiculous, he did not know the password for this damned thing. In all the excitement, Anjali had never told them. Yet, despite the acid canister being absolutely unusable, Samar still could not put the burden down.

He remembered, with a shudder, Anjali's face in those final moments, eyes opened wide in insane terror. But yet a light had shone there. He had recognized that gleam. He had seen it many times in the mirror these last few years, waiting to hear from some investigator with a promising lead or some cop claiming to be close to cracking the case. His hopes had been dashed time and again and yet the light had never been totally extinguished, flickering again in the next breeze of possibility.

Today, however, he had seen the gigantic fingers of certainty pinch the flame of hope in Anjali's eyes. It had been a sight much more viscerally terrifying than any of the bloodbaths he had witnessed.

And it was that accursed chainsaw which had administered that final torture. The torture of hope. That was why it had been kept for them.

Or had the chainsaw been put in their path so that he could cut through the metallic mesh grating of the maintenance shafts? Had he taken the wrong decision by not going through them? Had he been double-bluffed? Or would this have happened either way? He remembered what Karan had said. 'Their pasts had sealed their present.'

I am really going crazy. I am actually buying into the old man's claptrap. But no matter how much he tried, he could not bring himself to drop the cylinder. Nothing here had happened by chance, he reminded himself. The chainsaw had been kept for a reason. So, perhaps, this Agent Astra cylinder still had some role to play. What that was, Samar could not figure out.

He remembered that there had been something he had been meaning to ask Karan Rathore. 'You knew, right?'

'What?'

'You knew that Anjali had murdered her husband before she confessed to it.'

Karan did not reply but just pushed Anya's wheelchair slowly.

'You obviously knew what she was going to confess. You tried, at least twice, to convince her not to do it.'

Karan looked around over his shoulder.

Had he seen someone? Or does he just want to pretend not to hear. 'You are right, Mr Bose. I did know.'

Neither of them spoke for a minute. Karan looked tired, more tired than Samar remembered him. Through the long journey, he had been the most energetic of the party. Now he slumped his head forward. 'Nikhil would have won a Nobel one day. I don't say this lightly. But he made one big mistake in his life. He married her.'

Karan, once again, seemed distracted with something to the side. 'Oh, they looked beautiful. The handsome genius and the beautiful archaeologist.' Karan grunted a laugh of disappointment. 'But nature abhors perfection. Which is why the more beautiful something looks from the outside, the surer you can be that it is rotten from the inside.'

The whirring of the wheelchair rolling over the metal floor echoed through the empty hall. 'One day, I remember, she stormed into our lab and in front of the entire team shouted at her husband. Of course, when I say shouting, I am putting it as mildly as I can. Things broken, papers thrown about. All over something as trivial as forgetting some date with her.' He nodded his head sadly. 'Passion. Yes. She always lacked control, being a slave to what burned inside her. A grenade with the pin taken out. That was Anjali. That truly was Anjali.

'Then, they had Anya. She was a perfect little baby. But then as I said, the more perfect things look...' His voice trailed away. 'I am not the type of a man who brooks gossip. But one could not help hearing what people were saying about Anjali. The campus of the Pujara Center is a small place and things get around, when a married woman is seen at different places with different strangers. You understand...'

Samar interrupted. 'I get it. Forget I asked.' He did not want Anya to listen to this. She was too innocent to understand. But still, children – they can pick up negativity in a conversation pretty easily. Maybe one day she will find out why her mother did what she did. But today should not be it.

Karan ignored Samar. Perhaps because Anya had fallen asleep, burnt out by the excitement, her head resting on her shoulder. 'Nikhil had been working for a few years on a vaccine for the Ebola virus. It was exciting research and the initial simulation results had been spectacular. But then once we did a limited clinical trial, it went wrong. I mean really, really wrong.

'It's difficult to explain this, Mr Bose, but it was almost as if Nikhil had not done his homework. There were elementary mistakes in his procedures, totally unbecoming for someone of his talent. I say mistakes, but the independent review board actually accused him of having falsified data. This, I knew was impossible, but still there were valid grounds to ask questions. That was undeniable.

'He was very unhappy at the end. Everything he had worked for was vanishing away in front of his eyes. There was pressure to take him off the project. That, of course, I would not allow to happen. I was, after all, like a father to Nikhil...'

Karan shook his head with some force, the silver spectacles moving slightly askew from his nose. 'I saw him the day before he died, sitting in a corner of the lab, his glasses on the table, holding his head in his hands. He had been crying. I had never seen him do that before. So, I didn't enter his room. Now I wish I had. Really wish I had.' He stopped for a while, trying to get his voice to stop choking. 'Then that evening, Anjali calls me. I did not know her personally before that, so was surprised. She is hysterical over the phone. I can barely make out what she is saying, and so tell her to sit tight and not call anyone else. When I reach there, I find Nikhil dead. From what I could piece together, they had had a fight and she had killed him. Just like that. A knife to the side of his neck.'

Karan pointed to his neck to show exactly where it had gone in. 'She was, of course, ready to give herself up to the police. I stopped her.'

'What? You stopped her?'

'Yes. I did. I accept I did. Because sending Anjali to jail would not bring Nikhil back. It would only punish Anya.'

'What about the police? Did they not piece things together?'

'The police. Yes, we know how efficient they are, don't we?' barked Karan, the muscles in his jaw clenching tightly. 'I cooked up a story about a break-in and that became the official version. I pulled some strings and the file got buried. It bothered me of course, bothered me a hell of a lot. But I told myself that I had protected the little child. The greater good and all that. I was wrong. I had, in my arrogance, overestimated my power to control everything, little understanding how weak God has made Man. A few months later, Anya had this sudden bout of fever. And then a healthy girl became this...'

He looked at Anya sadly. 'The living have finally answered to the dead. Vengeance has been wrought. But at what cost? At what cost to the innocent?' Karan hands softly ran through Anya's hair. She still lay still, sleeping. 'Who will look after you now? Who will look after you once I am gone?'

Samar knew the answer. As a matter of fact, he was sure of it. He would.

Samar sat in the back of the pick-up truck, shoulder to shoulder with the other contractors. The ugly gash on the side of his neck burnt raw and fresh in the harsh Sierra Leone sun. The sweat of the other men soaked through their torn shirts, stinking steamily without the apology of decency.

It felt like Hell. It was.

They had just been rescued from inside the jungle by a 'security team'. They, too, sat with the contractors in their green fatigues.

Bulgarian mercenaries, their faces impassive, guns slung over their shoulder, scanning the surrounding landscape as the truck drove over the dirt road, shaking from side to side.

They were going back to the diamond mine that Samar and the others had run away from. How long had it been? Three days? Five? Samar could not remember. What he did remember was driving away from the revolt in a jeep and then making his way on foot into the jungles once the gas ran out. He remembered the fear. Of hiding from men. Of hiding from animals. Of wondering if there was any difference between the two. Of wondering if he would ever see his wife and daughter again.

At least the others, they had a God to believe in. He did not. He was smarter than them.

But smart men end up dead in Sierra Leone. George, their supervisor, had drilled it into them during their briefings. George was right. He himself had been one of the first men killed, hacked to death by the machetes of the rebelling miners.

The truck swung past one of the miner's villagers. Thick clouds of smoke swirled up. Fires crackled everywhere.

An old man sat on his haunches outside what seemed to have been a house, weeping in front of a dead goat. A naked woman lay on the side of the road, legs obscenely twisted.

Samar looked away in shame, but there was no direction that provided peace. Bodies were strewn everywhere. Some of them moved, some lay still. The 'security team' had mowed down every miner's settlement to quell the revolt. It had not been pretty.

Which is when he caught sight of Abebe. Abebe would hang around the contractors' quarters, promising to get them anything they wanted – cigarettes, alcohol, women.

His prices were good, his service prompt and he always delivered with a disarmingly joyous smile.

Abebe's smile was no longer there. Neither were his legs. They had been scythed away. But the man was still alive, reaching out ahead as he inched forward, crawling slowly on his stomach over the rocky path, leaving a trail of blood and entrails.

Samar clasped his hand to his mouth, trying hard to keep from throwing up on the men beside him. His eyes then turned to what Abebe was moving steadfastly towards.

On the road lay a small boy, not more than ten years old, turned to the side, wailing helplessly in a pool of blood and exposed bone.

As the pick-up came closer, Abebe turned his face up, hearing the sound of a motor. On recognising the familiar figure of Samar, he cried out loud, 'Save me, sir. Save my son.'

Samar looked furtively at the mercenaries. They had room in the truck. Perhaps the kid could be saved if they got him to the medical centre back at the mining colony. The doctor, he knew, was still alive. He was sitting next to him.

His hand reached out to tap the shoulder of the Bulgarian sitting in front. And then he stopped.

What was the use? It was not his business.

Not that these guys were going to listen in any case. Hell, they had possibly done this themselves.

And what if they got angry if he asked them to help these people? He was not stupid enough to find out.

After all, it was not his business, he told himself yet again.

The truck rolled on. He turned back to look at Abebe, who had finally managed to reach the boy. As the truck rounded a bend, the last thing he saw was him lying face down in the dirt, his elbows collapsed under the finality of fate, tenderly holding his son's palms in his hands.

Samar shifted uncomfortably in his seat. For the remainder of the journey, not once did he glance up, keeping his eyes firmly focused on his boots.

As Samar walked through the twisted corridor, that day long ago played and played again in his head. There was nothing he could have done then. Nothing he could have done later. Karan Rathore had been talking through his ass. Why was Sierra Leone his business in any way? Why wasn't it the business of any of the other contractors there? Why wasn't it the business of the people who had caused it in the first place? The people who had paid for the death squads? Why should he leave his life and give testimony in front of a tribunal? So, what if they had gotten off for lack of evidence? If no one else had bothered, why should he have?

All that was the past. The past had no bearing now. Or did it?

The devil's windpipe, thought Samar. That's where they were now, coming up and out from his belly to the mouth. Another fifteen minutes. Or would it be twenty? Lilith's room would be there. And then, the end.

He just hoped he would be alive till then. The gas was now fully absorbed; he could feel his arms and legs turning on and off, numbing down to gentle pins-and-needles and then blazing like petrol that has caught fire. His knees trembled and his forehead felt like a battlefield of neurons firing randomly at each other.

He stopped. Right on the bottom wall, a small red light was blinking. Samar would have missed it, had he not been looking precisely for something like this.

A laser tripwire. He let his eyes follow a line from the blinking light on the right to the wall on the left.

But there was no light on the left. At least, not straight across.

It was then that Samar realized what had happened. His heart sinking, he turned his head round to the left and downwards. There it was, the left blinking red light, two paces behind him. The tripwire had not been placed straight across, perpendicular to the passage as he had thought. It had been installed at an angle.

And Samar had already tripped it.

Yet nothing had happened.

'Stop... stop right now.' He raised his hands and turned around on his heel.

Karan stopped with the wheelchair, expecting some instructions. Samar did not know what to say.

What should I tell them? Will something come from the sky? Or from the ground? Or from the side? Should I tell him to run? Should I tell him to stay?

And are they in danger? Or am I?

Please let it be me. Please, not Anya. Please do not take her from me again.

They just stood facing each other, silent, waiting for the inevitable. Samar closed his eyes, surrounding himself with an icy mantle of darkness.

And for the first time in his life, he prayed. Prayed for his own death.

Then it came, rumbling down from above.

In the blink of an eye, they were gone. A gleaming metal surface reflected Samar's face back at him. A barrier had descended from above into the ground, sealing Karan and Anya behind it.

He rushed to the barrier, banging on the metal, solid and immovable. The disembodied mechanical voice was back. 'Inner security breach. Final protocols initiated.'

'Hey... you all right?' Samar shouted across the wall. Karan's voice came clear from behind. 'Yes, we are. You?'

Samar ran his hands over the smooth surface. Nothing to breach, not a single weak spot. 'Hang on, you two. I am going to get you out of here.'

Karan's voice came from behind the barrier. 'Don't worry about us.'

Still moving his hands over the barrier, Samar tried to keep himself as matter-of-factly as he could. 'Just need to get to the central controls in Lilith's room. This lockdown can be reversed. Don't lose hope.'

'I always have hope, Mr Bose. I have never lost it. Not once. This door will open. It has to.'

Karan kept his ear pressed against the door, the metal deadly cold against his skin, burning hot with the fever that raged through his body. *He wanted to believe. He so much wanted to believe. For his own sake.*

The last time he had seen this room it had been very different. Then it had been Lilith Adams's living quarters, just like the others, except it was larger. The size, he had figured, was merely reflective of the arrogance of its owner. The bluish-yellow light had then just been coldly antiseptic, like it was elsewhere.

Now the room was bathed in a violent red light, dimly luminant, bleeding out from the dark corners. Just like that shrine downstairs. Exactly like that place.

On the wall right opposite to the door was a huge monitoring terminal – a flat-screen touch-sensitive monitor. On it were displayed feeds from a large number of security cameras, laid out in a giant grid. All the feeds were offline, except five. Three streamed images of the dead bodies: Preeti Singh, Akshay More and Anjali Menon. One showed Karan Rathore and Anya – the little girl still asleep and Karan with his back to the camera. The final one, somewhere in the room, reflected Samar's face back on the screen.

The eye of the devil. I am inside it now. And I am seeing myself the way he does.

That is what Karan and Anjali would have said. Now he was saying the same thing. Samar could not resist a smile at how his way of thinking had changed. The neurotoxin had fried his innards, well and proper. His forehead clanged like a cymbal at a heavy-metal concert; his knees wobbled like that of a drunk after a night out. And his mind seemed to be all over the place.

I need to concentrate.

Samar sank wearily into the leather bucket-seat in front of the security terminal. The Agent Astra cylinder dropped from his hand onto the ground with a gentle clank. He looked around at the touchscreen in front of him, like a pianist before a performance.

Don't lose it now.

To the right of the touchscreen, was a blue button. On it was written 'Initiate Security Lockdown Reversal.' He knew what to do. Samar touched it with his index finger. The button glowed red.

The grid of camera feeds vanished away. In its place, rapidly scrolling down the screen was a series of system messages, each showing the status of different security mechanisms with [DEACTIVATED] written on the right. He hoped that the trap in which Karan and Anya were stuck was among the things being deactivated.

Wait! What was that he just saw? Samar's eyes lit up. [MAIN SURFACE ELEVATOR LOCKDOWN DEACTIVATED: ELEVATORS NOW ONLINE] They would be free now. He punched the air in triumph, his entire arm spasming in agony as he did so.

And then the screen went blank. What? What just happened? One second, then another, passed.

The black space dissolved into a dramatic crackle, replaced by the face of Lilith Adams, in the same blue business suit Samar had seen her wearing the first day they had met.

'Hello, Samar. Here you are again.' She smiled, with the warmth of an old friend one had run into after many years. Samar sat frozen, clutching the bottom of his seat.

'I am sure you have many questions. What is this place? What will happen to Karan and Anya? Why are you going through this when so many in the world, who have done far worse, are sleeping safe and snug in their beds? Why, indeed? Is it because the universe is fundamentally unfair? Is it because justice is something beyond your comprehension? I wish I could answer these questions. But, alas, I cannot. So, sadly, it remains your lot to go through life with most questions unanswered, to grope through the dark before finally stumbling on to the greater darkness beyond. If this makes things easier, I didn't make the rules. I just make sure you play by them. Here is what I can tell you, though. Nothing here happened by chance. Certainly not you coming here. Certainly not what you have seen. Nor is this final meeting between you and me a coincidence.'

Lilith became more sombre. 'Even if you forget everything else, remember this. The Mine isn't just a place underground. It's with you, inside you, everywhere you go, your own little personal hell below Hell, created from the shadows of your own actions. What I just said might not make much sense right now, but I know it will. Some day. And on that day, my friend, you will finally, finally, complete your journey.

'Goodbye. Forever.'

Samar's head spun. Had he just imagined what he just saw? But no...

The giant screen burst into green graininess. What came up was video footage from a camcorder, pointed towards a dirty ceiling. There was no movement on the screen, just iron beams and a stationary ancient fan.

But what made Samar jolt upright was the date prominently displayed on the bottom of the video feed, right next to the red recording dot. It was the day Reshmi left her house. For the very last time.

The camcorder jerked unsteadily. Someone had picked it up and turned it around so that the focus was now on a table.

The light was dim but still good enough to make out what was on it.

Knives. A long line of them, all laid out in an orderly fashion on a black leather cloth.

What was this?

And then Samar knew.

'Help... Please... no.' A girl's voice, faint but full of pain, came through, between bursts of sobbing.

Samar felt as if a cold steel blade had been plunged straight into his heart. Terror moved in waves through his body. It was a voice he had heard, in his dreams and in his nightmares. He had heard it through every waking second of regret.

Reshmi.

'Daddy, daddy...'

Then a man spoke, heavy and yet soothing. 'There is no Daddy here, baby. Daddy won't be here for a while.'

The camera shook again. Now it turned away from the table straight to the girl. Samar felt faint, his intestines twisting into a tight knot. Reshmi was tied to a chair, her white cotton dress drenched with sweat.

'I want to go home... please let me go home. I promise... I won't tell...'

The voice spoke again. 'I know you won't tell. Daddy does not have to know... does he?'

Samar wanted to close his eyes. But he could not. Not now. His heart seemed to be caught in a gigantic vice, collapsing in on itself.

A knife showed up on the camera. A jerk. A roll. Then a man, whistling to himself, looked into the lens. It all fit together now. The face he had seen that day near the gate, hiding in the shadows. The face which had revisited him in the Mine. The familiar face he could not place.

Asgar. The video footage of whose death he had watched and re-watched two days ago. The man twisted and battered up by the machine and left to bleed hanging down from above. The man whose death had brought them all here.

The camera now zoomed in to the serrated edge of the knife. Then the knife inched slowly forward in the direction of Reshmi's face, circling menacingly around her cheeks but not touching them. Her eyes were opened wide, following the slow dance of the sharp edge. A sudden gust of air from the side set her hair flying around her face almost if it was trying to escape, in a last frenzied attempt, from what was to follow.

She blinked once. And then with every last breath of life, she whispered, straight into the camera, her eyelids fluttering for the last time. 'Daddy, Daddy danger.'

The video died away to a white spot.

Samar still sat still. Was he dreaming? Was he awake? Did it matter anymore? There was nowhere left to hide, nowhere to run. All hope had been skinned away.

Asgar, the sick motherfucker of a child killer, was dead. There was no revenge left to be taken, no peace to be gotten.

Nothing. Nothing save a black void.

Reshmi, so alive, the day they had brought her from the hospital. And that morning he had dropped her off, her first day in school. She had wept and he had stood all through the scorching summer afternoon, outside the school, unable to leave or move his eyes away from the door. Then that day in December when they had all rowed down the river, the afternoon had been perfect. Reshmi playing in the flower bed at the back of his house, more beautiful than any rose anywhere. All those pleasant memories would now be lost, buried forever beneath that last image of Reshmi – her face contorted in terror, alone in those last moments, left to be brutalized in a way possibly even the devil would not imagine.

Doused in certainty for the first time since she had left him, Samar wept, his chest drawing back in a series of convulsive gasps.

But Lilith had still more left for him. The screen burst into life once again. This time, the video stream was from a different place, a room with a lot of light. The first thing Samar noticed was that this was not a hand-held handycam but footage from a sophisticated spy camera. There was no sound. That however did not make the scene in front any less bizarrely terrifying.

A man was slumped forward on the kitchen counter, a knife sticking out from his neck. Right next to him, with her face towards the camera, was Anjali Menon. She was fully nude, her elbows propped on a tabletop, her large breasts shaking from the thrusts of the man who was entering her from the rear with rapid yet rhythmic strokes. He was holding her savagely by the hair, forcing her to arch her back violently.

The man had his face turned down, almost as if surveying the carnage. And then he looked up towards the camera, triumphantly. 'I wish you had not seen that, Mr Bose. I really wish you had not.'

Behind Samar, leaning on the wall near the door, stood the man on the screen.

Karan Rathore was in the room.

Karan Rathore remembered it as clearly as if it was yesterday. Those beady dark eyes, the repulsive pink tail, the small furry body helplessly squirming inside the trap.

Just ten years old and yet he towered over it. A small kid Karan was to the rest, but in front of this puny rat, he was a giant. Bending down on his knees, he made eye contact with the little creature as it moved back and forth inside the metal contraption, unable to get out.

Asking for mercy, are you? Well, we will never know.

Then very coolly, he took a syringe out from his bag. Dad's compounder always left the syringes lying about. Pinching one from the box had not been a problem. Neither had been stealing a bottle of kerosene. The driver was always asleep with his feet on the steering wheel. He filled up the syringe with the black liquid, tapped it expertly on the side and then, with the clinical detachment of the physician he would one day become, injected the kerosene right into the side of the rat.

The rat stood still for a second and then its small eyes rolled around. Yes, there was pain there, he noted in satisfaction. Then he took a match and struck it against the phosphorous strip at the side of the box. The gentle fizz of the burning tip cast a circle of light inside the dark supply shed. Then, in one swift motion, he pushed the matchstick into the rat's mouth. At the same time, his left hand opened the clasp of the trap.

The rat burst out, fire leaping from its petrol-filled mouth, like a pathetically ugly dragon. He had expected the rat to burst like a little firecracker but what happened was even more fun – after twenty paces, its legs literally fell off, melting. Finally, it toppled over, belching petrol, a ball of burning pain.

Karan Rathore stood up breathing heavily, his knees quivering with a strange sensation, a sensation even more powerfully exhilarating than the one he had felt when he had chanced on his dad's stash of dirty magazines hidden in the old garage.

He would not understand, till many years later, what it had been that so aroused him.

Dad had sent him to a boarding school, where the sons of the rich went to learn how to behave, to waltz like gentlemen and speak in preppy British accents. Karan learnt all this. And more.

It was a dark, cold night just like most in Simla. The three of them had sneaked into the room of the new fat kid from Class Six, the one who peed in his pants at night. They then dragged him to the lake behind the residence halls. The fat kid had bawled like a little pig, jumping up and down and saying 'Sorry, sorry' pathetically as the three of them took off his pyjamas and shirt. They pushed him into the lake till he stood chest-deep in the water, buck naked, shivering and screaming.

'Come on Karan, let him go, we have had our fun,' said Amar, his best friend, the Home Minister's grandson, taking a puff at a forbidden cigarette.

Karan said nothing. He positioned himself at the edge, unzipped his fly and let loose. As the stream of pungent humiliation hit the fat bed-wetter square on the face, he looked towards heaven and closed his eyes.

Aaah, the power, delicious in its complete fury. He loved this exhilarating feeling of control. It turned him on, just like Ms Venkatraman's outrageous curves did Amar and Sandeep.

But unlike them, he did not just remain content with drawing dirty sketches of the principal's wife. Instead, he volunteered to work in her garden, after school.

What had been the most fun, he had often wondered.

Had it been pretending to be the innocent fifteen-year-old overwhelmed by the attentions of the older woman? Or had it been revelling in the power of standing tall like a little emperor as she sank on her knees in front of him, subserviently servicing him with her mouth? Had it been hearing the sound of their conjugal fights while working in the garden, knowing that the reasons for the breaking of crockery were what he had planted in her head? Had it been how she had convinced her husband to make him the Head Prefect of the school? Had it been when, on the last day of school, she had cried till her eyes became red or had it been him trying hard to stop from bursting out into laughter at her plight?

All of it.

He soon cultivated a taste for manipulating and getting his way. Women were easy. They liked to think they were in control. He let them work under that illusion. The flicking of the hair, the slight leaning forward, the deep sigh, the look over the shoulder, the fishing for compliments, and finally, the first and last weapon of their armoury, tears.

Karan knew all their tricks. They did not know his. That was his advantage.

The payoff was not just the sex, great though it was. It was the knowledge that he could make them walk, stand, roll over and finally burn in pain, all at his command.

Just like that rat.

But then, as he grew older, he bored of these kinds of conquests. He wanted more. He wanted the world.

Grandpa used to say, 'It's not the kings but the saints who conquer the world.' So, he spent his life being one. The kind, gentle-hearted doctor, the world-famous researcher, the mentor, the good uncle, the man whom the prime minister consults on health-policy matters, the philanthropist, the giant beyond reproach, the one to whom all bowed in respect – he became all that and more.

The perfect cover to play his real game, the one that he was born for.

Control. Oh, he so loved that word. In a way they all did, without realizing the essence of it. Preeti, that snivelling bitch, had enjoyed her moment of control over that innocent man, sending him to jail. Akshay – another nasty lot of goods. What was the rape if not the assertion of his power to destroy the most intimate possession of the object of his revenge? Anjali – she had thought her looks gave her control but when she realized how mistaken she had been, the knife had come out.

Hah.

Government, authority, wars, religion – all ways man has devised to maintain control, so that he may feel like what he calls God, the projection of humanity's ideal of power.

And then what can one say of the ultimate device of control in this world? Love.

He had simulated that emotion all his life. It had always been the source of his power.

Only once, just once in all these years, had he truly lost control over himself. Those few minutes of madness were now being projected on the giant screen in Lilith Adams' room. There he was, caught in his greatest moment of triumph as well of shame, a raw animal with all guards down.

A contented smile appeared on his face exactly at the same time that a teardrop rolled down his cheek.

Damn. Such is life.

Sighing softly, Karan Rathore said, in that flat and heavy tonc of his, 'I wish you had not seen that, Mr Bose. I really wish you had not.'

'I should have destroyed that video. After all, which sane person keeps a record of a crime? But this was such... how shall I put it... such a glorious moment in ways you cannot imagine that I just... I just could not bring myself to put it into the fire.' Karan Rathore sounded almost apologetic. 'Though how Lilith Adams got hold of this I cannot imagine. No one but me knew where I kept it. No one.'

Samar tried to get up from the black leather seat. To his horror, his legs did not respond.

Karan approached the table, moving slowly, still not making eye contact. 'Nikhil, that bastard. Too brilliant for his own good, solved a vaccine problem I had worked on for thirty years. In just three years... can you believe that?' Karan now looked at Samar with an expression of shocked innocence. 'I came to him, I did, asking for a joint publication. He told me, politely of course, in that greasy way of his, "No, sir." His own discovery, and he was not going to share the glory with me. Imagine the nerve of the idiot, I hire him, I fund his lab and then he wants me out... wants it all for himself.'

Anya. Where was she? Samar tried looking at the passage for her wheelchair, but Karan was blocking his view.

He looked up at the ceiling, as if there was something of great importance there. 'People hold me in awe. They respect my knowledge. They respect what I have achieved. And this man... he was trying to stamp out my name.' Karan's eyes opened wide, flaming red through his glasses.

'Where is Anya?'

Karan ignored the question. 'So, I had to get at him, you see. Get at him with everything I had. It was difficult to do professionally; he was, after all, a genius. But his smartness stopped the moment he stepped outside the lab.'

'I asked you a question. Where is Anya?' Samar's heart was galloping fast. 'Please... I am trying to provide you an explanation for what you just saw.'

'I don't care. Where is she?'

Karan's voice still had not lost its good-naturedness. 'You might want to reconsider the tone of your voice. I am sure you will agree your situation is somewhat precarious.'

'Fuck you.'

'Yes, yes, I understand. But to use your own rather colourful invective, it is you who is fucked here. For the past few minutes, you have been trying to move your legs and they are not cooperating. Am I right?'

Samar did not reply. It was difficult to get anything past the old man.

'Oh, I am sure you can still feel them. Your legs, that is. A tingling maybe. Soon, that too will be gone. And then the neurotoxin will start moving up, up your body, shutting down one system after another.' Karan tapped his chest to show where the effect would stop. 'So, Mr Bose, you are not in control here. I am. For that matter, throughout our journey, not once have you been in control. I have been.'

'Please. Just tell me that Anya is safe.' Samar spoke slowly, articulating every word, trying to keep the tone as polite as he could.

Karan leaned into one of the seats, settling down comfortably. 'You are talking to me now as if I am a madman. Aren't you? A word of advice. You, sir, are a smart person. Yet you have made several mistakes these last few hours – missing traps, looking upon me as being slightly cuckoo, the kindly old gentleman who deserves sympathy. Which is why you have allowed me to manipulate you. Don't make another one by thinking me to be a lunatic. Believe me, I am more sane than you could ever be.'

He leaned forward and tapped Samar's hands reassuringly. 'Sit tight and listen to what I have to say. It's not as if, with those legs freezing up, you are going to be catching a train any time soon.

'So where was I? Ah, yes. Nikhil being an absolute klutz in the real world. He got married to this lady, Anjali. Oh, Mr Bose, I have had many... let me make this sound not dirty... mmm...

intimate interactions with women. But this one was the best. A little volatile. Actually, a lot. But from experience, I can assure you, that the crazier they are, the more they crackle and pop.'

He smiled at his own joke. 'It was easy – the kind uncle routine, the compliments, the "Nikhil needs to take care of you more", the patting her on her back, letting her cry on my chest... I will spare you the lurid details, but I broke her in, like I did the horses back on my dad's stud farm. But you look like a city kid, wouldn't know anything about breaking fillies in, would you?'

Samar tried to speak but Karan pointed his finger at him. 'Don't disturb me, if you want to know where Anya is. Sshhhhh...

'There was a beast inside Anjali, and I let it loose. She wanted men. She wanted women. She wanted them every which way. I encouraged her, worked on her as a matter of fact. There was a reason of course. I wanted to record her while she ooh-ed and aah-ed, then build a nice highlights package of Anjali Menon's best moments and leave it carelessly on the lab's shared server. Wouldn't I love to see Nikhil's expression once everyone laughed in his face, the husband of the porn queen? That explains the spy-cam, in case you are wondering how that came to be.

'Of course, Anjali was not the only rod that I had in my fire. I had been sabotaging Nikhil's research, tampering with his data, fooling around with the simulation results, all from his home machine which he kept unprotected, the silly fool. For me, you see, it was not just enough to destroy all he had worked for, but to destroy him, personally and professionally. Only in that way could I regain my control.

'Everything was going just perfectly. But then, one evening Anjali calls me and says "Dr Rathore, I killed Nikhil." Just like that!'

Karan stopped, his eyes closed, rubbing his forehead. 'The stupid bitch. Just one moment of insanity. And my revenge, the revenge I had plotted for so long... Gone... gone in a flash.

'When I saw Nikhil with that knife in him, lying like that, something just gave inside me. Bam. I threw Anjali on the table, ripped off her clothes and started... I don't know why I did what I did. I guess I wanted that at least his dead body should see me violating everything he held dear. He had to know. You would not believe how utterly powerful I felt, the wife bawling, me inside her, all hot, the husband, dead, a foot away, all cold – one of those moments in life you wish you could rewind to, again and again. That's why I kept the tape... A foolish decision, I will once again accept.'

'Story finished. Explanation given? Now, where is Anya?' A pain shot up Samar's spine. He grimaced.

Suddenly Karan stood up, moving the seat back. He laughed loud. 'Come on now. Confess. You admire my deviousness.'

'Admire?' Samar spat out. 'Admire a sick fuck? No thank you.'

Karan Rathore pounced forward and, reaching across the table, grabbed Samar by the neck of his shirt. 'Don't fool yourself, Mr Bose. I am as sick as you are, as sick as those that died before, as sick as anyone else out there in the world. The only difference is that you find comfort in the delusion that you are good. While I... I find comfort in the knowledge that I am evil.'

Karan slurped back his own spit like a wolf gloating over a kill. 'There is a line, a thin line we walk every day, the line between good and evil. People like you and Anjali and Preeti and Akshay, when you cross that line over to the dark side, you do so without realizing, like a baby crapping in its diapers. Me – when I cross the line, I know exactly what I am doing and why I am doing it. Always.'

Karan started smoothing Samar's collar gently with almost fatherly affection. 'And that is why sick fucks like me have always had power over sad fucks like you. And that is why I am standing now, and you are sitting, like a vegetable, just watching me.'

Karan picked up the Agent Astra cylinder from the ground, weighing it in his hands. He no longer seemed agitated. 'Dr More, I am pretty sure, was planning to steal some of the stuff from here. Well, this actually does look like something I can make some money from, the technology seems rather valuable. This wretched place owes me for all the trouble.'

'So, you think you can just walk out of here. Have you forgotten the carvings downstairs?'

'The carvings downstairs? Don't tell me you have actually started believing Anjali's garbage?' He laughed heartily, amused at his cleverness. 'I know I played along with it. That was, of course, for your consumption. It made me sound...' Karan seemed to search for the exact word, pensively holding his chin. 'Pious. A good word that. The world always likes the believer. The believer is humble... not as arrogant as the sceptic. I like to be liked. You liked me too, didn't you? The man who gives up the cylinder, the first onto the cable car, the uncomplaining granddad who carries the wheelchair. You are so easy. Way too easy.'

'Now that you have had your gloating little speech, where is Anya?'

Karan clapped his hand smugly, like a child who had stumbled on a treasure. 'Strange isn't it how the hope of justice becomes a comfort for the weak? When you were strong and in control, you held onto the rational "military experiment" explanation. Now that you are just a breathing blob of jelly, you turn to the comforting irrationality of "You bad man, you may get away from me, but you will be punished by God."' Karan wagged his finger mockingly in Samar's face.

'I wouldn't pretend to understand everything that has happened here, like why the gas has not affected me at all.' Karan laughed yet again. 'Maybe it is because I am from a generation that ate right. Maybe because I can still punch a sandbag pretty hard. Maybe as Dr More had said, its effects are unpredictable, and I have just been lucky. Whatever be the reason, I am pretty sure that the Mine, like the world, isn't interested in dispensing justice.'

Karan slapped Samar chummily on his shoulder. 'I know I should not be this rude after all you have done for me. I will accept, had it not been for your knowledge of security systems, I would not have made it this far. And now that you have sent your transmission, I am sure your military friends will be standing outside to receive me. Too bad you won't be there to swap war stories.

'And so, because I am grateful to you, I am going to tell you where Anya is. She is a few yards up the passage. I had left her wheelchair there when I heard the sounds from the video. Surely you would not expect me to bring a child into this room when you are watching such a vulgar thing. Even I would not have come in if I had a choice; watching myself perform is intensely embarrassing.' Karan winked.

'I don't believe a word of what you say. I want to see that Anya is alive and well.'

Karan rolled his eyes. 'You don't understand me at all. Why would I harm Anya? She is the ticket that makes sure that your military friends actually rescue me. An old man, all alone, they might think it's not worth the price of jet fuel to fly him back. But a little cripple? Which human being could leave her to die in the desert? Also, when I go outside and put Anya in a home and bear her costs, people will say, once again "Dr Rathore is a God." You cannot buy that joy, no you just cannot.'

Samar kept breathing heavily. The pain down his spine had intensified.

'I see you are hurting. So come on, put your arms around my shoulder. See with your own eyes that she is safe and sound.'

Samar looked up, not moving, trying to understand the reason for Karan's kindness. The beacon had been transmitting, the elevator was working, the gate would be open. There was no further use for him. Then why?

'It's just a few minutes to the main door. Won't you see us off?'

The sparkle in Karan's eyes said everything. *The bastard wants to enjoy his final moment of victory.*

They were approaching the gate now. One elbow bend on the right and it would be a straight line to the top. Freedom. Life.

But not for Samar. One of his legs hung limp like a withered twig. The other barely moved but still sent waves of pain up his body, like an army of ants feasting on his skin. He had his right arm around Karan's shoulder, being dragged along like a felled deer.

One hand pushing Anya's wheelchair, with the Agent Astra grasped tightly in his armpit, Karan was beaming in triumph. 'Mr Bose, there is this thing I just have to tell you. I know I shouldn't. I have never ever told anyone. But I just… I just have to... God, I sound like a teenager! Seeing, though, that you won't be leaving this place, I think I can safely confide in you. And Anya here, the dumb vegetable she is, I don't mind her hearing this. Actually, I rather prefer that she does.'

Karan's eyes gleamed, red and black. He was sure of it. The light of the temple, in its absolute evil, burned there. 'The thing about revenge is that, like popcorn, you take a bit, close the packet, munch a little and then find your hand moving to grab more. You just cannot stop. After Nikhil died, I still felt the need to leave that final blow... that last haymaker the prize boxer throws even as the referee comes in to stop the fight. So, I did something poetic. I took the two things he loved the most, his daughter and his work, and put them together. I took the vaccine material that he was working on, added a bit of my love and care – after all, true revenge has to have something of you in it, that personal touch. One day, when Anjali was away, I injected it into...'

Samar kept looking at Karan, his mouth open in amazement. It took some time for what he was saying to sink in.

'Waist down paralysis, permanent loss of voice, limited upper-body movement, every day for this bitch is a day in Hell. That, my friend, is vengeance, the kind that can shake even the dead.'

A tidal wave of rage washed over Samar. Asgar had murdered his little Reshmi. And this... this monster had murdered this little girl, without killing her. He had not been able to personally wring Asgar's neck. But Karan...

Channelling every ounce of strength to his shoulders, Samar used his forearm to lock around Karan's neck. 'You motherfucking...' Samar's face twisted in frothy anguish as he tried to use his entire bodyweight to bring Karan down.

But Karan Rathore had anticipated the attack. In a blur of movement, he dropped the cylinder and turned around, twisting Samar's arm, turning him around. In the middle of the passage and with no way to prop himself up, Samar stretched out both his hands, swinging them in a vain attempt to remain standing.

Karan's punch smashed into Samar's right jaw with the force of a sledgehammer. Blood swirled in his mouth, overpowering him with its metallic fullness. He careened back, tottering on the edge of his heel for a moment before crashing to the ground.

'Didn't I tell you to not think of me as a weak old man? Did I or did I not?' Karan roared, kicking Samar in his ribs with savage ferocity, again and again.

Samar curled into a ball, rolling away from the flying kicks, trying to lessen their impact. Karan followed him, the shoe crashing indiscriminately into his chest and back. He towered over the fallen Samar, trying to gather his breath. 'Funny. I thought you were the kind who refuses to get involved, the kind that brushes away things that don't directly concern him with a conscience comforting "It's not my business." What changed? Why all this love for Anya?'

Samar spat out a tooth. He did not try to get up, just stayed sitting, propped up against the wall.

'Aaah, I remember. She reminds you of your daughter. Second chance and all that. Well, sir, here is my last word of advice. Life never gives you a second chance. It hardly gives you one, and that too if you are lucky.'

Karan patted Samar on his shoulder softly. 'Well, Mr Bose, this is where we part ways. Thank you, once again, for all the help.'

The blood from his broken tooth dribbled down the side of his mouth. 'No, that's where you are wrong.'

'What?'

'You are going nowhere.'

They had just made it around the bend when the fight started. In all the excitement, none of them had looked at what lay ahead. Samar pointed. Karan turned around, following the direction in which Samar was pointing.

The elevator lights were on. But the door at the end of the passage, the access to the elevator, the final gateway, was sealed shut.

The mechanical voice confirmed Karan's rising panic. 'Main access door relay failure. Override failed. Please contact vendor.'

An Agent Astra cylinder without a password. The final exit irretrievably sealed.

There was no getting around it now. They had been buried alive.

'Where is your control... now?'

The pain in Samar's mouth was pleasantly sweet. Given the numbness advancing slowly upwards, it was comforting to know that at least for the moment he could feel. Which meant he was still alive.

Karan had stood silently still, looking straight down the passage at the sealed door. Every mask that he had worn – of dignified nobleness, of confident arrogance – had been ripped away by the inevitability of fate. In its place, stood an animal – red, enraged, fists clenched, the vestiges of control melting away with every heaving breath.

Wrath. Lust. Revenge. All the panels of the shrine. For Samar, they all had come together in the face of Karan Rathore.

'Main access door relay failure. Override failed. Please contact vendor.'

Samar laughed out loud. 'I told you... I told you... this place won't let...' A wave of pain hit him from the spine, making him lose his words. The world swam before his eyes. Doubling up in agony, he still had the strength to whisper out. 'Welcome to Tartarus, you sick fuck.'

Karan turned around, his face drawn back into a feral snarl. 'Hell? You have no idea what that means. But you are going to find out, soon enough.' He moved to the side where Anya sat, caught hold of the wheelchair handle and pushed it sideways with a violent thrust. The wheelchair tilted to the side throwing the crying Anya face down onto the floor.

Samar instinctively tried to stand up but stumbled back. Anya fell on the ground, lying on her stomach. She looked at Samar, her hands stretched outwards, screaming silently, like a fish thrown out of her bowl.

Anya was too far away. Too far away for him to reach. Samar started crawling forward using his elbows. 'Let her go, you bastard...'

Karan circled menacingly, like a vulture around the dead. 'Let her go and do what? Pick on someone my own size? But what to do? I see in front of me two cripples... which animal should I have sympathy for? Or more important, who do I have my fun with first?'

He rested his right knee on the ground, bending down near Samar. 'Dying isn't that bad a thing, as long as you go doing what you enjoy most. And the thing I love most of all, if you haven't realized already, is pain... giving pain...'

Karan wiped his hands on his trousers, his eyes now shimmering with insanity. 'Oh, all the ideas I have in mind, all the games I can play. And time... time is my friend. It always has been.'

Samar still pushed forward, dragging his limp body along, despite the futility of it all. *Abebe. Take me. Make me suffer. Me. Please don't take your revenge on her.* The tears burst from him like a cloudburst. Samar cried out, like a father had cried out to him, years ago in the death-field of Sierra Leone. 'Help me, help me, please.'

Karan sidled up to Anya, his face a riot of hatred. He raised his foot, straight over Anya's back, poised it there for a second, preparing to bring it down with full force.

'Main access door relay failure. Override failed. Please contact vendor.'

'Mr Bose, I just remembered. Your little darling here, she can still feel above her waist.'

Samar screamed even louder as he realized what Karan was going to do.

His voice cracked. 'Help, help... have mercy... God.'

Karan stood with his leg raised and said, 'One whole lifetime. One whole sorry lifetime. And yet you still don't get it, do you? God... He has no mercy.'

The foot descended on Anya with the full force of his hate.

But it never reached her. In a blur of motion, Anya had turned on her back, looking straight back at Karan.

'What the...' Karan spluttered.

A hand thrust out, catching his boot in mid-descent. Anya's hand. Samar could barely believe what he was seeing. *Anya could move*. Not just that. Anya could fight. And how.

With one twitch of her elbow, she shoved Karan's foot straight back up. Almost a hundred kilos of Karan Rathore flew through the air and crashed onto the ground with a resounding crash.

Anya had sprung up, her shadow thrown on the back wall, looming like a giant.

It could not be. It just could not be. Samar's thoughts tripped over themselves. How? What?

Then he remembered. Akshay More. What he had said about GX. His student was trying to use it to stimulate neural pathways to enable humans perform super-human feats to be used in the battlefield – make them move faster, lift heavier weights.

Crank up the power of the signals, in essence turning on the cells in the dormant parts of your brain. Wasn't that what he said?

With the GX they had inhaled, Preeti's hidden memories had been brought out. So had his. Now the gas had made him lose sensation below the waist. But for Anya, it had... had it cured her? And even more?

'It can't be...' Karan lay on the ground, looking at the little girl. She stood there, silently still, her eyes far away, in a trance. Then she spoke. It was not the voice of a child, but that of an adult, firm and steady. It echoed through the Mine.

'Karan Rathore, you will pay for what you have done.' Samar recognized the voice. So did Karan.

The temple and that *memento mori*. '*We were in your past. Your futures will be with us.*' The living had answered to the dead.

Preeti. Akshay. Anjali, all of them. Now it was Karan Rathore's turn.

Karan's eyes glowed with undiluted, pure terror. 'Anjali? How can it be? But... you are... dead.' he quavered.

Suddenly, he pounced forward, a cornered animal flying through the gate of its cage. Using the full momentum of his body, he swung his fist straight at her face. Anya's hand shot out at the last moment and intercepted his punch as easily as if it was a falling feather. 'No more...' said Anya calmly, betraying not even the slightest effort at restraining Karan's full-body lunge. He tried to say something, but before it came out from his throat, Anya had grasped him by the neck. Then he was airborne, flying backwards towards the door, as if a hundred-wagon express train had crashed full tilt into him.

Samar's mouth remained open in amazement. An eleven-year-old girl, who had been a paraplegic a few moments ago, had just sent a man flying back twelve feet.

Was it the gas? Was it the Mine? He did not know. Nor did he care to.

Karan's back hit the main hatch with a sickening crunch. He slid down onto the ground howling loud and long in excruciating pain. But, like an injured jackal, there was still fight left in him. Pushing himself up from the ground, he prepared to make another rush.

And then he froze. 'What the Hell? I... I am stuck... I am stuck to the ground... Glue... who put glue here...'

A high-tech glue-trap. Samar had seen an experimental prototype once. Triggered by pressure, like that exerted for instance by a man stepping on the ground, the material on the floor would secrete a special industrial adhesive, pasting the target to the surface. It hadn't always worked in the lab tests. Now it did.

But wait, hadn't all the traps been deactivated? Or is there always one left for he who deserves it?

Like a fly stuck in a spiderweb Karan struggled. But to no avail. His forearm and his legs sealed to the ground, he hollered in incoherent rage.

It was then that Samar realized that Anya was no longer looking down the room at Karan, but had turned her head towards him, a universe of grief in her eyes.

No, not grief.

This was something else, something else he understood perhaps more than anyone.

Regret.

Samar now knew. He knew what he had to do. The Agent Astra cylinder was lying next to him. He used every last bit of his strength to push it forward. It rolled noisily over to where Anya stood.

'No, no, no...' Karan screamed. Anya bent down to pick the cylinder up. Then her fingers started punching in the password. There could be no more doubt. Only one person knew that password.

Anjali.

Her spirit, just like that of the others, had come back to make the living answer to the dead.

Samar now understood. The temple. It had always been the temple driving everything. His mind went back, back to that mysterious image of the white figure surrounded by the dark shadows, the last carving, the one that had nothing written below it.

Anya was that white spirit of purity, untarnished by the evil of the world, against whom the powers of darkness were helpless. She was the fulfilment of the temple's prophecy, the final vindication of its message.

If the Mine could kill, it could also save.

The cylinder was now active. The liquids had started flowing in, making it glow blue. Anya held it over her head for a split second, her pale face also glowing unearthly in the light of the acid. Then she threw it forward as easily as if it was a small paper lantern. Making a deadly arc, the cylinder hurtled towards the door, right where Karan still struggled against the trap.

He looked up as the acid screamed towards him. He made a final attempt to break free, putting forth every last bit of strength to rip the adhesive bonds that tethered him to the ground. But even though the skin stretched away from the bones like rotten parchment paper, and his body shook with excruciating pain, he could not budge. Karan closed his eyes. It was then he saw it again. That rat, stuck to the ground, its legs burnt through, vomiting burning petrol.

He was no better now.

The cylinder hit Karan perfectly on the mouth, knocking his head back so that it hit the door. The momentum of the blow broke his jaw, sending a sharp crack echoing through the passage.

The cylinder exploded. In the light of the glowing acid, Samar saw Karan, an expression of uncomprehending fear stretched across his face, the final mask for the man who had worn many of them in his life.

The toxic liquid ploughed instantly through to the bone, melting away his flesh. But he was not dead. Not so easily. His head and neck kept moving in a final frenzy, trying in vain to shake off the acid, as it pierced through his pores like a million burning needles. Then he started turning to noxious sludge, first the body, then the face and then finally his last scream dissolving away into bubbles of blue and red.

Samar closed his eyes, trying to shut out the scene. It had taken only a few moments. But he was sure that for Karan, inside the acid bath, it had been an eternity. The most horrible death of them all had come to the most horrible monster among them.

Maybe God did not have mercy. But at least he had a sense of justice.

The words of the panel echoed in Samar's mind. '*Those that poison shall be poisoned*'.

The vapour swirled around for a while. Then, when it cleared, he saw, to his relief, the door had been burnt away, enough for them to make through. The blinking lights of the elevator could now be seen. They would be free. Nothing could stop them.

It was then that Samar became aware of two things. Anya had collapsed in a heap on the ground.

And the mechanical voice now said, 'Unrecoverable critical security breach. Self-destruction procedures initiated.'

A large explosion shook the floor, sending fragments of metal raining on them from the ceiling. The lights sizzled and blinked. Cracks spontaneously appeared on the walls. There was not much time.

Samar struggled on his elbows, the weight of his body pressing hard against the ground, reaching for Anya as fast as he could. She remained still, fallen to the side, her eyes closed.

He had to take her across. But how? How would he do it, with half of his body shut down dead? Breathing hard, he tried to push back the rising panic. *I will. I must. As Lilith had said, this is my journey of salvation.*

Using every bit of power he could muster, he lifted Anya's limp body onto his back, manipulating her arms so that they stretched out above her head. Then, with Anya's face at his shoulder, he gripped those arms to hold her in place. This meant he could no longer use his elbows to move. Like a snake, using just the motion of his chest and his stomach, he propelled himself forward. Progress was slow and painful.

A second explosion ripped through the place, much closer this time, sending debris flying about.

The train of destruction was coming up. He needed to move faster. Samar tried to speed up, but each inch seemed a mile. The metal floor was now a dirt road, strewn with rocks, debris, broken dreams and ripped-away lives. Samar was back in Sierra Leone. Only this time it was him on the ground, helpless and in pain.

Abebe's ghost was here. He could feel his presence. *Abebe, please. You lost your son. I lost my daughter. Has that not been enough?*

The place shook violently again. A metal pipe fell inches from where he was, bouncing and rolling away. Steam bellowed through the cracks, filling the room with hot smoke.

Samar kept going, tears of pain and penance streaming down his cheeks. *Those that watch shall be made to watch. I have been made to watch the death of Reshmi. Please. Have I not suffered enough?*

There was no response, except for the increasingly ominous rumblings from deep inside.

Samar was now at the last stretch, the final door in reach. On the floor there were still traces of adhesive, the liquefied remains of Karan Rathore and drops of fuming acid. He tried to avoid them as best as he could. Yet, droplets of active acid soaked through his shirt, sloughing the skin, frying his flesh. At one stage, a part of his arm got stuck to the floor. He paused not a moment, lunging forward as the adhesive pulled his skin back, feeling the skin ripping from his muscle like rotting cloth. He was beyond physical pain now, his eyes soaked clean by the brine of tears. His life had simply one meaning. *The Mine has given me a chance at redemption. I am not going to fuck it up. Not again.*

He was inside the elevator. With a heroic effort, he reached for the lever. The doors slid shut just as an explosion ripped through the top level, sending tongues of flame reaching out for them. Please. Please. Not when we are so close.

It started ascending rapidly with Samar still in the same position, face down on the ground, streams of blood flowing out in different directions from him, Anya's limp body on his back. All he could feel was her breath. That was all that kept him alive.

Then the elevator door opened – sounds of helicopters, of heavy boots pounding the ground and of barked orders.

Samar tried to say something, but he felt consciousness seeping out of him, like water through a hole. Large men in military fatigues and black gas masks seized him by the arms, bringing him out through the door into the blazing sun.

Samar breathed in the light.

Epilogue

Where was he?

A blue-white light cast shadows down from the ceiling. Blinking lights on panels, transparent tubing running from his arms, a white bed and blue sheets. He was in a hospital, this much he could make out.

Anya? Where is Anya?

He tried to reach out for his blanket. But he could not. His right shoulder would not respond. He tried using his left shoulder. It seemed to belong to someone else. His legs? Dead as logs.

Samar screamed. No sound came out. The hum of the air conditioning seemed louder than a roaring ocean. He emptied his lungs yet again. Dead silence.

Panic gripped him. He could see and hear but could neither speak nor move. He fluttered his eyelids. That was all that lay in his power.

A strange face looked down at him. Then another. They all wore white coats. 'The patient is regaining consciousness.'

One spoke brusquely. 'Mr Bose, if you can hear me, blink once. Please do not try to make any another movement.'

Samar did what he was told. The doctor nodded his head with clinical detachment. 'Patient responds to external stimulus.'

Samar shouted once again. From the expression of the doctor, he realized that his lips had not moved. Even his throat had not clenched from the effort. They would surely have reacted if they had seen him agitated. But they did not, looking at him serenely like he was a specimen under a microscope.

His body felt heavy, as if he weighed five hundred pounds. Yet he knew there was no body left for him to feel. Phantom sensations. Samar knew what this was. He had once met an amputee in Paris who had told him how sometimes he still felt his legs running. False memories, he had called them, false memories interpreted by the brain.

He thought of Reshmi. He had sensed her all these years, a phantom throbbing pain in the raw stump that had become his heart. Now he realized how false that had been, how every moment of hope, and every dream had all been a pack of cruel lies.

Anya... he groaned. *Anya...* Then the darkness took him.

For hours, or was it days, he flitted in and out of consciousness. Scraps of conversations from the doctors. Images of Reshmi shouting for help. Images of Anya being thrown to the ground. Asgar's leering face and his shining knives on the leather cloth. The triumphant smile of Karan Rathore. The squishing sound of the boulder crushing Preeti Singh. Akshay More's scars. Anjali Menon impaled on the ceiling.

He was awake. As he focused his vision, he saw on the right side, a familiar face. Dr Gafoor. Their family friend, his brother Sambit's long time doctor.

Their eyes met. Dr Gafoor's face lit up. He clasped his hands onto Samar's. 'How did this happen? Oh, how did this...?' Dr Gafoor blinked back the tears. Samar fluttered his eyelids fast. That was all he could do.

'Relax, now. Relax. Your body has been through a lot. A hell of a lot.' Dr Gafoor paused. 'You want to know what happened... of course you do... let's see... it seems to be years now... but yes, last week someone came to my chambers saying they had found you in the desert. I didn't know who "they" were and I felt it was not my business to ask, knowing the kind of work you do. Then I was brought to the hospital and...'

Anya... Anya... please where is she?

Dr Gafoor looked into his eyes and guessed correctly. 'There was a little girl with you. She was in as bad a shape as you were. A bad case of amnesia, remembers neither her name nor how she got there. The doctors, though, are confident she will recover. There's something really strange about her though... her legs seem atrophied, like someone who has not walked much. Yet she can move just fine. The doctors were quite... surprised.'

Dr Gafoor seemed to hesitate for a while, as if deliberating whether to continue or not. 'She looks a lot like... a lot like Reshmi. I was glad... you know... I know...' He struggled to frame the words. 'I have made arrangements for her to stay at your place, hired a nurse and... It was either that or a government-run house. We know how those are. I know, maybe I should have asked you, but you know... Well... I put her up in Reshmi's old room. There were already toys and everything there, so I thought...'

Samar closed his eyelid gently, hoping Dr Gafoor would take it as his heartfelt approval.

'One more thing. Ever since you came back sick, your brother has not slept much. I tried to tell him many times that so much excitement was not good for his health, but you know him... refused to listen. He can be very obstinate at times.'

Dr Gafoor looked at the door. 'He is standing there outside. Just, you know, spend some time with him. Once he sees you, I think he will go back to sleep.'

There he was, the gigantic Sambit, standing half-inside and half-outside in a white buttoned-up shirt, his hair combed neatly like a small boy's, an expression of eager anticipation on his face.

Samar was glad to see him. He knew that he would never live like a normal man again. But at least he would be surrounded by people he loved. He wanted to go home. He wanted to start life anew.

Dr Gafoor gestured to Sambit. He entered and stood hesitantly in a corner, shifting his balance from one foot to another, in the way that he always did. Patting Samar on his shoulder, the doctor said, 'Just a few more weeks here... Then we will go back. I have talked to some of the best therapy specialists – trust me, things are going to get better.'

Samar sighed inside. *I wish he would stop giving me fake reassurances. I've lived too long with my own lies.*

Dr Gafoor moved slowly away. 'I will be outside...'

Samar very slowly opened and closed his eyes, hoping Sambit would understand that as an indication to come and sit next to him. Sambit did, lumbering up slowly and sitting down. It was then that Samar noticed what was in his right hand. A mouth organ.

Sambit had stopped playing since that brain seizure, the one that had left him mentally crippled. They had tried to convince him many times to resume playing. The doctors had felt it would be good therapy. Not just that, Sambit had genuine talent; his teacher used to call him a prodigy before the accident. But he had steadfastly refused, throwing violent tantrums every time the question came up. So, seeing him today with that very instrument was surprising, very surprising.

He kept it on the side table gently. There was a minute of silence. The brothers just sat there. Samar wanted to reach out and hold Sambit close. He looked miserable, like a poodle caught in a shower.

Then Sambit spoke. 'The flowers have been very good this season. The last supplier was cheating us with the fertilizer – it took me some time to realize that. But the new guy, he is very good. He understands exactly what I want. An honest man, so difficult to get one nowadays. The flower stems are healthier; you do know that the stems are the most important thing...'

Samar wished he could tell him to stop. One of Sambit's problems was that he could go on and on about trivialities no one really cared for. It was then that a firm 'Sambit I have work to do' would get him to shut up. Now, of course, there was no way to even say that.

'Oh, I am sorry, here I go again.' Sambit said, with a frightened look. He sounded hurt, like a child refused an ice-cream. 'I know you don't really care for the flowers. You never open your window and see them growing. They are right below your window, you know. I have asked you so many times, haven't I? But you don't care much for my garden... and why would you? It's just a thing the doctors make me do – to keep me occupied, to get some exercise. It means nothing, nothing at all.

'But you should have... you should have... cared.'

Sambit again fell silent, having lost his train of thought. He did that often. 'There was this man who came to our house a long time ago, one of the contractors who was remodelling the east wing. Baba had gone to London; you were on one of your trips and Anita was also out. God knows where she went sometimes.'

Sambit started biting away at the nail on his thumb. 'Yes, this man... I was outside doing some garden work when I saw him. He was... well... doing something he shouldn't have been doing. I didn't say anything. After all, no one takes anything I say seriously. I am not well. I know that.'

He kept chewing at the nail, which he had now torn away from his finger. 'Then, one day, when I was coming out of Dr Gafoor's crazy clinic, I ran into him again. He was attending some group meeting... they don't talk about those group meetings to me.' Sambit locked his fingers together and stretched out his hands, giggling. 'But I knew what happens there... sex addicts talk among themselves about the filth in their heads... Dr Gafoor thinks that they can help themselves by talking. "Sharing makes it better," he tells me. But he knows nothing.' Sambit said with a strange finality.

'Well, I followed that man to his car and told him straight off: "I have seen you going through Reshmi's inner secret clothes in our house." He told me his name was Asgar.'

Samar's heart pounded against his ribs. Trapped inside the blackness of immobility, he struggled inside to break free and pounce.

'The fool was so eager, he actually came to our house early, a good ten minutes before I had told him to come. Here you are, the man who catches all these bad men, with all those medals, and there is this bad man, in love with little Reshmi, at your door for a date. You walked by him, you know... you didn't even turn around once. So much for your smarty-ness. And I am the one who is crazy.'

Sambit's smile glowed in the bluish-white light. The gentle lost-puppy cluelessness was gone. 'He took her to this place he had outside the city. I, of course, went with him – would not keep my niece alone with such a man. I sat behind with Reshmi in the car. She was unconscious from the thing in the handkerchief he had held on her nose. So, I kept her head on my lap. Her eyes were still wet. She had been crying for you.'

Sambit was now looking intently at his finger as if the teardrop was still there. 'Asgar had this dungeon – now, what did he call it? Yes... his hobby den. He had... like, two hundred different types of knives. A museum that place, I tell you.'

Tears were now streaming down the side of Samar's face, past his ears.

Sambit rolled his head around, as if relieving a crick in his neck. 'He really carved her up. Took his time, did it slow. Reshmi cried a lot, took your name again and again. In the beginning, she didn't see me since I was in the next room. But then Asgar called me. He wanted me to hold the camera. That was when she saw me.'

Daddy, Daddy danger. Poor, poor Reshmi. She was not crying out for her life. She was trying to warn me about the danger I was in, not from the man with the knife but from the man behind the camera. She thought her uncle was going to kill us all.

Even in her last moments, all she thought about was me and her mother. His eyes fluttered in impotent rage. Sambit was not even looking at him.

'Such a lot of blood. Who knew a little girl could have so much life?'

Sambit's hands reached out around Samar's neck, gently massaging it around his blue hospital jacket. 'I know you want to know why. Why? Isn't that the loneliest question in the world? Why?'

He moved his hand back to his lap. 'I have wondered "why" myself. Why did you and dad leave me in the room when I was sick? Why didn't you stay back? Why was seeing the blue mountains so important to you? Why did I, the smart one, become the half-wit? Why was it you who had a wife and a child and not me? Why did you go around the world while I was asked to tend to the garden? And why, why does it hurt so much inside, in my head and in my heart?'

Sambit sucked in his breath. 'But I know you do not care for my "Why"-s. I am the crazy one, why should you? But there is a "Why" for you too, Dada. Why did you never open your window to look at the flower bed? Why? You should have. That is where

I buried Reshmi, each and every little piece of her. She never left the house. Yet, you spent all these years looking for her, all over the world. All you needed to do was to open the curtains and see the flowers. And she was there, as beautiful as ever.'

Lilith Adams's voice echoed in Samar's mind. '*The Mine isn't just a place underground. It's with you, inside you, everywhere you go, your own little personal Hell below Hell, created from the shadows of your own actions. What I just said might not make much sense right now, but I know it will.*'

It did make sense to Samar now. He had been in the Mine all his life.

'*Of course, my idea of Tartarus has never been of a place buried deep inside the earth, but one perched right on top, in plain air, under the sun, the ultimate testament to God's hatred of mankind.*'

That was what Karan Rathore had said. More tears streamed down his cheeks as pain etched into him with a carving knife.

Sambit took a handkerchief from his pocket and started wiping Samar's tears away. 'One of the doctors told Dr Gafoor that you will remain a vegetable all your life. No talking, no walking, no writing. So, I can tell you all this, you won't be able to tell on me to Daddy, you tattletale.' Sambit swung his index finger accusingly and poked Samar in the nose playfully.

'We are both freaks now. Two mad brothers, who love flowers. That day in the mountains took you away. Now, I have you back after so many years. You don't know how much I have loved you, Dada, how the only thing I ever wanted was you. Not your pity. But your love.'

Sambit patted Samar's jaw tenderly. Then he picked up the mouth organ from the table. 'You know I never played this after that day. Well, I have started music again. Dr Gafoor allowed me to bring this on the condition that I don't play it in the hospital. But when you get home, you will hear how good I am. But you always knew that, didn't you?'

A pause for a few seconds as Sambit's eyes looked all around the room, vacantly. 'Remember that poem Reshmi would recite while playing in the garden? Whenever I think of her, it comes to me... again and again... You know, she always used to tell me "I will make you remember the poem." I would tell her, "I cannot remember." But I could. I could. I could.'

He leant forward, moving his back to and fro, reciting by rote:

'One for sorrow,
Two for mirth,
Three for a wedding,
Four for birth,
Five for silver,
Six for gold,
Seven for a secret, never to be told...'

A secret never to be told.

Sambit rose up from the chair, suddenly impatient, his eyebrows knitted close. 'I should get going.' Then he stopped. 'There is a girl who is staying with us nowadays. Dr Gafoor let her sleep in Reshmi's room. She does look a lot like her, slightly thinner though.' Sambit's pupils seemed solid black, swirling with hatred. 'I don't like her. Just like those weeds in my flower garden.'

Then his face loosened, and he smiled. 'But I still have a few of Asgar's knives in the tool shed. I think I remember what all he did.' He paced around the room. 'The silly fool had two hundred knives. Whereas all you need is one. Okay... perhaps two... cause when you start using them, they do lose their sharpness pretty quick.'

Samar's eyes opened as wide as he could. Terror of a kind he had yet to experience filled him, flowing through every vein with a cold dark chill.

He remembered the panel on the shrine. A woman wrapped from head to toe in a cocoon and tied to a pole, with her eyes and her lips exposed, her lips sewn together, and her eyes kept open with needles through her lids. '*Those that watch shall be made to watch.*'

'The worst punishment of all is reserved for those who, by staying silent, let all other forms of evil flourish unimpeded.'

Samar had been wrong. His ordeal was not over. It had just begun.

Anjali's voice floated from afar. '*There are fates worse than death, like being trapped in a state of perpetual pain – neither alive nor dead.*'

Samar realized he had made another mistake. In interpreting the panel, the one with the white image of innocence surrounded by dark monsters, he had thought of it as a depiction of the power of good, a vision of the pure triumphing over evil.

But the black shadows were not being kept at bay by the figure in the white. No. It was they who were closing in for the kill.

In this hellish world, not only do sinners have their curses, so do the innocents. And theirs are the worst of all, so horrible it may not be written down.

Embrace the darkness or be consumed by it.

Sambit was watching him, a victorious smile still stuck on his lips, shaking his head to the side. All his life, Samar had looked for danger in the dark, little realizing that true evil stands in the light, right next to you.

Dr Gafoor had come into the room. 'Let's go, Sambit. Your brother needs rest. And you, my man, need to take your medicines.' Holding Sambit by the back, he prodded him to the door. Suddenly, Dr Gafoor stopped. 'By the way, one thing I forgot to mention. That person who came to tell me about you being found, I just remembered the name – not that important, of course, but a rather odd name. Lilith Adams. Funny... it had slipped my mind totally.'

As they walked out through the door, Sambit turned his head back one last time. His brother lay there still and unmoving, eyes not even blinking.

Very slowly, taking care to pronounce every word clearly, he said softly: 'Remember... remember to forget.'

Acknowledgements

Thanking everyone who helped me write *The Mine* would have added fifty more pages to the book. So, I will keep it short. I would like to thank the original publishers, Westland, for trusting the story, and now Hachette, for relaunching, in a new avatar, my first novel. I would like to thank my parents, my grandmother, my teachers from school, and that person without whom no word would ever be written – my wife. And for this edition, one person I couldn't thank twelve years ago only because she had not been born then – my daughter.